Waiting for Fitz

Waiting for Fitz

SPENCER HYDE

SHADOW
MOUNTAIN

For those still waiting.

Visit us at shadowmountain.com

Library of Congress Cataloging-in-Publication Data

Names: Hyde, Spencer, author.

Title: Waiting for Fitz / Spencer Hyde.

Description: Salt Lake City, Utah : Shadow Mountain, [2019] | Summary: Hospitalized for her OCD, Addie Foster and her new schizophrenic friend, seventeen-year-old Fitzgerald Whitman IV, escape the psychiatric ward and undertake a journey to find the elusive—and endangered—bird, the Kirtland's warbler.

Identifiers: LCCN 2018029416 | ISBN 9781629725277 (hardbound : alk. paper)

Subjects: | CYAC: Friendship—Fiction. | Love—Fiction. | Obsessive-compulsive disorder—Fiction. | Schizophrenia—Fiction. | Mental illness—Fiction. | Kirtland's warbler—Fiction. | Hospitals—Fiction. | CGFT: Fiction.

Classification: LCC PZ7.1.H917 Wai 2019 | DDC [Fic]—dc23

LC record available at https://lccn.loc.gov/2018029416

Printed in the United States of America

Publishers Printing

10 9 8 7 6 5 4 3 2 1

I don't think writers are sacred, but words are.

They deserve respect.

If you get the right ones in the right order,

you can nudge the world a little.

—TOM STOPPARD

Author's Note

Mental illness is so idiosyncratic that it is impossible to nail down. "Like trying to pin a medal on a shadow," as they say. The very act of categorizing different mental illnesses seems to deny a sense of individuality in some way. When people say they know what my OCD is like, I often balk, certain that they have no idea—even if they grew up with OCD! And yet, they must in some way be able to empathize, right?

I currently work in a youth group with two boys who are living with autism, and their experiences could not be more different from one another, or from the autism my nephew knows and lives with, yet they are all labeled *autistic*. What I'm saying is, my experience with mental illness is certainly not anybody else's experience. My OCD ticks, rituals, and washings are my own. We are labeled one way, and we live a life that fits our own definitions. I also have personal experience with individuals who have been diagnosed with schizophrenia and Tourette's. However, even those experiences are individualized and likewise distinctive and personal.

Now, this fictive world may not necessarily jibe with your experience of a psych ward (be that from popular media or firsthand living). Some illnesses are intense but the person can stay in a local hospital instead of a state hospital; some rooms are private, others shared; some wards are coed, others are not. The list goes on. These issues vary from place to place, doctor to doctor, era to era, and from person to person. For example, I was in a hospital where twelve-year-olds ate breakfast (runny applesauce) and watched movies (almost always rom-coms) and played games (without batteries) with seventeen-year-olds. But that may no longer be the case. And that is okay. The world in this novel is made up in order to portray a specific experience, for numerous effects.

Addie's OCD is a reflection of my experience translated through a fictional character. Some might think she doesn't act impaired enough or show enough moments of frustration or exhaustion. That's just it—I worked hard to keep those emotions at bay. That is how I coped, and that is how Addie copes as well. And that's okay. Likewise, Fitz, Wolf, Leah, Junior, and Didi all fit with personal experiences I have had with each illness, or with each exceptional, unique, remarkable, wonderful human I know who dealt with a similar issue. If the way I portray OCD (or anything else) is different from your experience, mediated through your mind and your life and your struggle, well, you are totally right. Even better—we are both right.

In *Waiting for Fitz*, I have taken my personal experiences and fictionalized them. I have created this made-up world and tried to fill it with real-world significance, with meaning, with truth. I believe that is the aim of all fiction: we strive to put words into a rhythm and order that will reveal something redemptive about what it means to be human. It is a lesson in empathy; it is practice in how to live.

Discussing, talking about, writing about, and experiencing mental illness in all its permutations is tricky, delicate work. But that doesn't mean we should avoid the conversation. Frankly, we're all a little crazy. And that's fantastic. So let's learn how to be okay with discussing what it means to live (I mean, really *live*) with mental illness in this world, *and* in the worlds we imagine.

One

My life took off the comedy mask and put on the tragedy mask at the end of my seventeenth year. I won't get all sentimental about it, but you need to hear the whole story to make sense of that mask swap or whatever.

So my mom thought I needed more help than I was getting from my regular psychologist, Dr. Wall. I remember him getting upset once when I jokingly told him I felt like I had my back up against him at times. I started seeing him after my rituals got real bad. Like, really messy. He was less than motivational, to put it kindly. But I'd started showering about four times a day and washing my hands over a hundred times a day because my mind was telling me the people I loved would die if I didn't. That sounds absurd, right? Don't I know it. But in the moment it was life or death. Seriously.

If you look up "obsessive compulsive disorder" you'll probably run into some really obnoxious stuff that isn't all that accurate. Or, if it is accurate, it's made to sound like it's something that just takes care of itself or that gets resolved by some loving therapists, followed by some block party thrown in your honor. It's not all Hallmark-channel type stuff. Trust me.

Let's be honest: We all have issues. Let's be even more honest: Sometimes we need help but don't want to face it. I understand now why my mother was looking for more help, for better help, but at the time I thought she was just overreacting. I mean, don't most teenagers have a three-hour morning ritual before they can walk out the door? Don't most teenagers wash their hands to keep their families alive? Just kidding. A little. But that's how it went with OCD. I guess if we get super technical, it's not all that untrue. But I did need help, and Mom took action.

She took me to see this nationally renowned doctor the summer before my senior year of high school. Apparently it was the only time in the last decade that this particular doctor had worked the floor of the psychiatric ward at Seattle Regional Hospital. But it also meant that I was to be an inpatient.

So, before you get all excited about this kind of added support, know that it meant I had to postpone my senior year of high school and stay in a psychiatric ward—the nuthouse, the puzzle box, the cuckoo's nest. Whatever. Look, Seattle is far from being a bad place to live, but if you are only able to see the world from six stories up it's just like any other place.

Here's how my first day went: I started the day by talking with Dr. Riddle—yes, that was his name, get over it—about the severity of my OCD. I wasn't hiding the fact that I needed help, but I also wasn't going to admit that staying in a hospital was the best thing for me. I mean, I was trying to focus on important things like *The Great British Baking Show*. Have you ever wondered what it would be like to sample that stuff? What do they do with it all after they bake it? What a waste.

I made a killer baklava, and I was going to miss, like, an entire season at the very least. I made Mom record every episode and promise she wouldn't watch them without me. The last time we watched had been a few weeks before I entered the hospital. I remember Mom walking over to the couch and crowding my space a little. She sat on my feet and warmed them up.

"Richard forgot the bread portion of the presentation this time, and he forgot to preheat the oven," she said, spoiling it. I wasn't there yet. Two minutes later, Richard indeed made both those mistakes.

My mom was a bit of an amateur baker herself, though she never let her bread dough prove for long enough; she was too impatient. I had proof.

"Look at that," I said. "Richard lacks toast, and he's still tolerant. More than I can say for you."

"What? I'm tolerant. Except for lactose."

"You don't lack toast. You had some for breakfast. I saw it. But sometimes you're still intolerant," I said. "Maybe you're also gluten intolerant. Maybe you're also flour intolerant."

"This is why nobody can watch shows with you, Addie," she said.

"You're a flour-ist!"

"A florist?"

"No, but I'd love to see a florist who only sold flours. Tapioca. Potato. Spelt. Buckwheat," I said.

"You're obnoxious," Mom said, smiling.

"Also, you can't preheat an oven. It's not possible. Anything is technically preheated. What you do is heat the oven," I said. "It's like how we say an alarm goes off. Well, that would mean it was

on to begin with. We'd be relieved to have an alarm go off, so it
would stop sounding, you know?"

"Like I said—obnoxious," she said.

I was so sick of Richard being named Star Baker over Martha
just because he had better presentations. It only matters how it
tastes! Martha was the baker with the right flavors, and I thought
that should win out over looks. Frankly, that should win out over
anything.

I was there in the ward after Mom had explained why I
needed the extra time in the hospital or whatever, so I wasn't too
shocked by her leaving, though the fact that I was alone really hit
me later on.

"This is about you, Addie," she said.

I alternately blinked each eye because I was counting to the
number seven each time I heard my name. I'd been starting to
think of the disorder as a paradox. Zeno, the School of Names—
they both had the same idea, which was this: "A one-foot stick,
every day take away half of it, in myriad ages it will not be exhausted." That's how I felt. Like I could walk halfway to the end
of the room but never make it to the wall. Not really. Because
I'd only ever be able to go halfway. I felt that even with all of my
rituals, I'd never really make it to the end. It'd be impossible. At
times, *I* felt impossible. Zeno had it right—an infinite number of
rituals, and I'd still never arrive.

"I'm just winking at you, Mom. You know that."

She smiled and hugged me and started crying. Like, big and
wet and messy kind of crying. I won't lie and say I didn't feel it,
but with all the doctors milling around, I tried to be strong, and
I thought not crying was mature. Looking back, I know I was
wrong and I should've just let it happen.

I know a lot of things now, but at the time I was so consumed by my own disorder. It might look like my stay at the hospital was just a stopover for some new meds, or for added doctoral support. But it wasn't. I needed serious help, and I didn't want to admit it.

Each morning before school, I'd walk to the bathroom, careful not to brush the wrong carpet thread when I reached the threshold. I'd stand up and sit down three times before entering the bathroom. I'd sniff two times with each step while also counting the tiles beneath each foot. I'd make sure I blinked with my left eye before entering the shower. Counting each time I tapped on the shower wall, each tap on the faucet, and each throat-clearing, I'd net two hundred and seven. I'd do this seven times before exiting the shower. Then I'd wash my hands forty-three times. Those two numbers added together made two hundred and fifty, and the two and the five made seven, of course—my favorite number. Finally, I'd dry off, sit on the bed, and count to eleven. What a great number, eleven: it's first place two times, or seven and four, which is nice.

If anything went wrong at all during the ritual, I'd have to leave the bathroom and start over with a new towel, the carpet fibers back in the right place, the right amount of blinks per step, the right motion for each scrub, the right thoughts for the entirety of my time in the shower. If I pictured Mom's face and thought of the words *death* or *cancer* or *tragedy*, I would have to turn the water off and start over.

Again. Again. Again. The dichotomy paradox in action. I was a living paradox.

My downward spiral was similar to that water, getting sucked down and down until the rabbit hole was no longer a myth, and I was stuck in some alternate reality wishing there was a potion I could drink to get me out of there.

But I had to hope. That's all I had left between my bleeding hands and crushing thoughts.

My rituals weren't just confined to the bathroom. They followed me everywhere. I'd have to flip the lights on and off seventeen times before stepping on the stairs. I'd count each step, blinking three times with each left-foot step, four with each right-foot step—all the while, thoughts of death circling in my head. If I didn't tap the stair banister in the right increments, three times each, I was convinced that cancer would eat my mother from the inside out, turning her bones to dust.

She'd watch me with large, sad, hopeless eyes as I'd back up the stairs and start over. Each number I counted was tied to the safety of my mother, of my dog, of anybody or anything close to me. One misstep, one ritual imperfectly observed, and I had to start over so my mom wouldn't get in a car wreck on her way to work, so the dog wouldn't get tumors in her legs and slowly crumple to the floor. Stupid, I know. But try telling my mind that it wasn't as real as the thumping machine in my chest, pulsing behind my rib cage.

I felt embarrassed and ashamed in equal parts every morning. I hated taking so long, making my mother late for work, even as I knew that what I was doing was saving her, was keeping her alive.

I know it sounds ridiculous. But if you had to face three hours of that kind of thinking every day just to shower, you'd know there had to be something more, some other kind of recourse, some other kind of help. And while the compulsions didn't stop after the shower, at least I was able to go to school and lose myself in class lectures and books. In words. My only savior sometimes.

We'd drive to school, and she'd tell me I might need to start getting up earlier, or she'd gently ask me if I'd like some lotion, while not mentioning the cracks in my hands where the cold was eating its way in, splitting my skin like veins rising to the surface, or the dried blood caked on my knuckles.

She was always careful with her words, and she never talked about how hard it was for her to sit and listen to the light ticking on and off, to the shower handles getting tapped, to the water purling through the drain for hours. But I knew.

Desperation skulked in the corners of my mind, in the shadows, snaking through my body and squeezing my heart.

I counted each beat. I had to.

Mom tried her best to keep me focused on other things. She was good at that. She even got a purple streak in her hair one day at the salon to remind me that things we do on the outside don't always determine the inside. But I still washed my hands that night. Whatever. She was trying.

"Make friends. Be nice to the doctors. Don't mock them. Don't be a smart aleck."

"But he's the best Baldwin brother."

"Stop it," she said.

"C'mon, Mom. Give it a rest. I only joke with people I like."

"Making fun is not the same as joking," she said.

"Semantics."

"Addie, I want you to be able to go to school without worrying about your hands bleeding because you wash them too often, or worrying about your family, or never feeling clean."

She started crying again. I looked down at my cracked hands and rubbed them together, then folded them under the sleeves of my sweater.

"I want that, too," I said.

I told you I wasn't going to get all sentimental, so don't think this was a regular interaction. I was the queen of avoiding emotions by putting on my comedy mask and acting like everything was fine. I made up stories about my life, about who I would be later, about who I was then, about who I was friends with, and about what I was destined for. Whatever. You would too if you had to live with the aching parasite of relentless obsessions.

"Comedy or tragedy, Addie?" Mom said. It was a game we always played, but I wasn't in the mood, so I hugged her closer and cried on her shirt. Don't judge me. It was real.

So Dr. Riddle threw me into Group Talk the first day. I quickly learned that Group Talk was just an overly generalized name for spending an overly emotional, overly dramatic, and overly annoying hour and a half with seven other people. We'd eat lunch after group, then I'd meet with the Doc one more time before heading off to Therapeutic Activities and Cognitive Behavioral Therapy. In the evening, the other patients and I usually sat around and watched a film together before separating to our small whitewashed rooms with small white beds and a ridiculous excuse of a pillow. That's about how most days went.

But I want to start with that first day for two reasons. One, obviously, it was the beginning of my journey. But it was also the day I met Fitzgerald Whitman IV. Totally pretentious name, I know. And don't worry, he knew it too.

So, Group Talk. The seven of us sitting there on cheap metal chairs with one of the main therapists in the ward who ran the whole thing. Sometimes Dr. Riddle sat in and listened, but more often than not it was one of his lackeys. That's what I called them, anyway.

Dr. Tabor was the leader of the group that first day, and most days thereafter. He wore these oversized glasses and was balding and looked to be in his late-twenties or early-thirties. He had this corny smile that reminded me of the guy on the Quaker Oats logo. Dr. Tabor started every freaking meeting by asking us to explain our most recent encounter with our "Core Issues."

We met in this lousy room with a bunch of over-the-top clichés printed on the walls. Things like "Stop Wishing, Start Doing" and "Your Only Limit Is You" and my least favorite, "What You Are Looking for Is Not Out There, It's in You." You know, overly trite quotes that made me want to throw up all over the walls. I was pretty sure I was allergic to banal platitudes. Whatever.

But that first time I really didn't notice the quotes. I just walked in and sat down and blinked at the floor and tapped my leg six times on each foot and rubbed my hands together and waited for something to start.

After Tabor talked about our core issues, he related a story—as he would do every day, I'd come to learn—that we could discuss. We had to introduce ourselves before making our first comment: first name, age, what you were in for (like I was in prison or something, no joke), and how you would cope with the issue presented that day or that week.

"Addie. Seventeen. OCD. And I came in late so I didn't hear the prompt or whatever," I said.

I looked at my feet and then back up and noticed that, while most of the group were staring at the floor or at Tabor, one boy across the room was looking right at me and smiling with this ridiculous, smug grin. He had curly, dark brown hair and these really cool gray eyes and these broad shoulders. He looked to be about my age. He slouched in his chair and had his feet crossed and his arms folded over his sweats. He was wearing a tie-dyed bandana and a hoodie that said *Om Is Where the Heart Is*.

"It's a real crumby situation," he said.

"Thanks, Fitz. I'll fill her in," said Dr. Tabor. "But first I'd like you all to say hello to our newest member of the group, Addie."

They all gave me halfhearted waves. Except Fitz, who just nodded his head like he was hip or something—or too cool to raise his hand.

"I often start with current events, Addie. Then we gauge our reactions and discuss the emotions inherent in those reactions," he said, smiling and leaning forward and putting his hands on his knees. His massive, white doctor coat fell over the chair and made it look like he was floating. I hated that coat.

"In the news this morning, there was a story about a man found dead in a giant dough mixer at a bakery on Beacon Hill. He left behind two dogs. His neighbors loved him. His family is seeking millions of dollars from the bakery for this accident. Now, I want you to consider what you'd do, as a family member. How might you react? What would be the best way to deal with the situation? How would you cope?"

Dr. Tabor opened up one of those stupid manila folders and prepared to write down my comments, I assumed.

"Sounds like he really loafed on the job," I said.

Look, it's not like I was trying to get a laugh. In fact, it was way too easy. I like challenges for my comedic outbursts, but this one was meant to deflect, which is why I passed over all the great proving jokes available. I hated being put on the spot, and I hated talking about my emotions, so I pushed them away by being deadpan or whatever.

Fitz sniggered, and Dr. Tabor ignored my comment, maybe hoping my comment was accidental in nature. Hint: nothing I say is accidental in nature, or in any other way. I'm kind of always acting, if you will. And you will.

"What's that?" said Tabor.

"I take it his family is suing because he just couldn't rise to the occasion?" I said, raising my eyebrows and feigning seriousness.

Dr. Tabor didn't know me yet, so he was unsure how to respond. "I doubt his family is worried about how hard he worked, though I'm sure they are saddened by his passing. What would you do, if you were his sister?"

"I'd tell my parents that at yeast they still had me," I said, hurrying over the pun so Tabor would think I was actually being honest.

"That's good, Addie. Remind them that they still have things to look forward to, people to care for, and other fires of love to stoke."

"Guess that's what happens when you stand a scone's throw from a mixer," said Fitz, smiling at me.

"That'll be all, Fitz," Dr. Tabor said. "This is a real person."

"A real person working on a recipe"—I paused—"for disaster."

I smiled. That one had been for Fitz, if I'm being honest. And I am. But then I was immediately aware of how inadequate I felt in the presence of so many people. I was talking like I was at home in a familiar setting. Maybe it was because that's how Fitz made me feel, because he kept the joke going.

He smiled back, and I noticed he had this huge Julia Roberts-type smile, but with a big gap between his two front teeth.

My look: I was in jeans and a sweatshirt, balling the sleeves up in my palms because that's what I did when I got nervous. My long brown hair was always twisted into a bun on my head with a pen in it to keep it stable. I had dark brown eyes that I hid behind numbered blinks, and a chest that was smaller than I'd hoped and legs shorter than I'd like. I was entirely average.

But at that moment I realized my sweatshirt was, like, incredibly bland, and I felt super self-aware. Whatever. We were all in the same adolescent psych ward, and clothing options were limited.

Dr. Tabor was explaining how our jokes were a typical avoidance tactic, but I was ignoring the doctor because I was watching Fitz. I thought the gap in his teeth was kind of handsome, especially when his gray eyes lit up his large features. I'm not trying to fixate on the fact that he was attractive—he *was* attractive—I just wasn't sure of anything else about him at that point. Well, I knew he was clever, but that was also partly based on basic assumptions.

I decided I'd keep looking at him throughout the meeting to show him that I wasn't going anywhere. Maybe that's not a good way to put it. I mean, I wanted to be going somewhere—read: home. Anyway, he seemed very confident—not just based on posture, but the way he ignored Dr. Tabor and kept whispering to the people on either side of him. I'm surprised the doctor didn't ask him to stop talking.

Next to me was Doug. He was fourteen, had Tourette's, and was a pathological liar. Like, something beyond what you're thinking. Something serious. He was wearing this massive fur hat with the earflaps poking out from either side of his head. I learned to really like Doug because he was totally arrogant but had no idea that's how he was coming across. And he was kind.

Across the room, next to Fitz, was Junior. That's the only name I ever heard him mention, anyway. He was a big seventeen-year-old who looked like an all-star athlete, but he had this crazy-bad acne all over his face and it made me feel sorry for him. I hate that sometimes we don't get to choose what our masks look like. At the same time, I guess that's what makes us turn on other parts of our personalities that otherwise would stay hidden. You know, like working a muscle that would otherwise atrophy or something. Fitz looked like an athlete too, but a little smaller, I guess.

Anyway, Junior was in for anger issues and seizures—I know, a super weird combo. He often said, "It's just funny, that's all," and that's how we knew he was starting to get really angry and on the verge of completely exploding. He said when the seizures were on their way he heard something like birds' wings rapidly beating in his ears, or the sound of cards shuffling.

I liked Junior because he was the most honest of anybody in the group—meaning he didn't cover up his emotions by putting on a comic (or even a tragic) mask, or anything in between. What would that be, anyway? A rom-com mask? A tragicomic mask? C'mon. Semantics.

Dr. Tabor finally got around to Fitz for real and had him introduce himself.

"Fitzgerald Whitman IV. Seventeen. Hold on, I'm getting some new information," he said, leaning sideways. He wasn't leaning into Junior next to him, but acting like he was listening to someone just behind Junior, some imaginary person.

"You sure?" Fitz said, then waited as if for a response. "Okay, I'll just roll with it. Thanks." He turned his attention back to the group. "Apparently I'm in for schizophrenia, according to my friends over there." He pointed to an empty corner of the room near Dr. Tabor.

Dr. Tabor immediately settled his face in a *Let's be serious* look, lowering his eyebrows and looking at Fitz in that annoyingly doctor-ish way—a mix of disappointment and encouragement.

Fitz looked at me and saw that I was smiling, I think, because he smiled pretty big himself before turning back to Tabor. The hour and a half flew by, and I started looking forward to spending my mornings perpetually disappointing Tabor by not ever allowing true emotions to enter the room.

True emotions would mean that I was facing my OCD, and that would mean I was ready to do some actual work. I didn't want to do either. I hated the fact that I needed serious help, but more importantly I hated that I *knew* I needed serious help. I couldn't deny it anymore. But I wasn't just going to let it happen. I was too defiant for that.

My junior year had been a mess. I spent pretty much all of my time at school, or visiting the psychologist, or at home reading or just hanging with Mom.

Mom taught history at the high school near Puget Sound where we lived. Dad was out of the picture pretty early in my life; he'd died of heart failure. It always made me angry. Everything was now post-death. Post-Dad. And it's genetic, so I'm constantly listening to my heart and counting the beats and wondering how big my heart is. That's another thing I do in the shower—I have to count seventeen beats before I can wash my hair, and if I miscount, I have to start over. Like, the whole process has to begin again. The paradox of Addie. That's me. Sometimes I wonder how big my heart is not because of Dad or death, but because I tend to push others away. I wonder if my heart is abnormally small in that way.

Mom was fun to talk with, and she kept me living outside of my disorder at the worst times, but I spent most of my time reading short stories or plays or screenplays of movies I really liked. Sometimes, if Mom wouldn't let me see a movie in the theater, I'd order the screenplay and read it anyway. Sounds nerdy, but nerds are cool. Get used to it.

I wanted to be a playwright someday, so I was working on reading all the classics and studying story arcs and how they created emotions in the audience, and how they built characters and all that. Everything from Shakespeare—I called him Mr. Shakes, but that might be inappropriate with Junior's seizure issue and all, right?—to August Wilson.

I wasn't a shy person or anything, but I also wasn't one to show off my, like, performative disorder. I didn't want to go to a friend's house and alternate eye-blinking and hand-washing and throat-clearing in specific, numbered intervals and have everyone be all uncomfortable and afraid of how to respond or how to avoid mentioning something that I was struggling with. It made me a selfish person, but I had no other options.

My mind didn't allow me much time between washes. The hospital was different because they didn't allow me to wash, so I just got angry. Junior understood that world better than I did.

"How would you deal with this incident, Fitz?" said Tabor, drawing my attention back to the story of the man who died at the bakery.

"Well," he said, looking at me, then at Tabor, "I'd make sure to check with my friends first." Fitz looked at the empty corner just behind Tabor. "But then I'd approach any extended family and see if there was anything I could do to help."

"Very good," said Tabor.

"But that wouldn't work," I said, surprised at my own boldness and eagerness to engage in the conversation.

"Why not?" said Tabor.

"Because people don't do that. Nobody asks the family if they need anything, if they can help, and really means it."

"That's a pretty bleak perspective, Addie," said Tabor.

"But it's the truth. Nobody in this room is going to say anything that's true and completely unmediated. We all have masks we wear and games we play to try to portray the least vulnerable version of ourselves. We want to be looked at but not really seen. It's all a performance. We might ask that family how we could help, sure, but we're doing it while wearing the mask of 'the helpful neighbor.' We're doing what society expects of us, not something we truly want to do."

"Okay," said Tabor. I could see he was formulating a response, but he was too caught up in writing down notes in his stupid folder.

"In the end, we're all pretty selfish. We like the stage and we like the lights on us and we like hearing the crowd roar, but we don't really want anybody to know just how long we studied those lines or worked on those facial expressions or sweated and prayed to find some understanding of what it all means to be given a role in life and how we are supposed to play it. We're all just comic figures hiding the tragedy beneath. Or we've given up and accepted that our play ends in death, so why bother getting the makeup on or even performing to begin with? We don't really want to help that family. Especially when it's a family in knead. Get it, Tabor? K-N-E-A-D?"

I couldn't help myself. I felt myself getting too serious, so I turned back to humor. I didn't like facing the serious side of myself.

"I get the first part, Addie," he said. "And I think we should discuss the idea of vulnerability at our next Group Talk."

I saw Fitz roll his eyes when the V-word was mentioned.

"We should also discuss what she said about acting and masks," said Fitz. "That was interesting. I hadn't thought of it like that. Shoot, maybe it's all just an act, Tabor. Maybe you feel like you're under the lights right now, and all you're doing is playing a part. Do you really want to help us, or do you just want to study us so you can write a paper for one of those pretentious journals? What are you after?"

Dr. Tabor brushed the comment aside and told us we'd come back to my comments the next morning. Then he instructed us to all say something positive to the person next to us. As group ended, orderlies waited at the door to direct us to our next therapy sessions.

"Don't worry," said Fitz, walking my way as we all stood. "The orderlies only help you for the first couple of days. Then you get some freedom."

"Freedom?" I said, pointing to the barred windows on the far side of the room. Not all the windows had bars, but our room did for some reason.

"Don't worry. One day Junior is going to rip those out of the wall and we'll all be able to jump. Also, be careful saying that word around here. We're all a little *jumpy*."

He shouted the last part and smiled at Dr. Tabor, who just shook his head disapprovingly.

"Quite the mask," Fitz said to me.

"What?"

"The one you're wearing. It's gorgeous. And if it is really all an act, I want to see you take the stage, Addie. Front-row seats, please."

"I'm jealous of you," I said.

"Oh, yeah, why's that? Can't do a one-woman show? Or do you just like the handsome gap in my teeth?" He smiled bigger and pointed at his mouth.

I laughed. "It's just that if I had you on the stage, I'd have a full cast. Do you have names for your invisible friends?"

I was worried I may have overstepped, but I tried to act confident in my comment.

Fitz sidled up to me, leaning in and almost whispering. "That's not a good way to introduce yourself, Addie. I mean, I can call them imaginary because we're so close, but when you say it like that, it makes them feel like you don't believe in them. It's okay, Toby. Don't cry," he said, acting like he was putting an arm around someone's shoulder to console them. "Big, crocodile tears," he mouthed to me, as if shielding Toby from his words. I'd learn later that Fitz kept up this cheery façade so he didn't have to confront the shame of those insistent voices and their ever-present squeeze. But like I said, that came later.

I coughed three times because two made me feel uncomfortable and four was a number I equated with death. Sometimes. Sometimes four was nice. Whatever. Then I blinked, alternating eyes, seven times. Being this close to someone I found attractive made me nervous, and when I got nervous I got anxious, and when I got anxious my compulsions tended to skyrocket. Like, to an obnoxious level.

"Morse code isn't going to work either," he said, pointing at my blinking, "but it does make those big brown eyes even prettier. If you want to get to know the whole gang, we should meet up for lunch. I know this great place. They have these awesome orange trays and this incredibly runny applesauce. It's so runny you could swim in it. Just imagine it—it's kind of beautiful, isn't it?"

I was kind of turned on by the way he stared at me with so much confidence. He had zero apprehension, or so it seemed.

"You should sit next to me at lunch. First, I have to go find out which one of my imaginary friends tried to steal some meds from the pharmacy and a keycard from an orderly. Probably Lyle. He's wily."

"I would love to meet Lyle."

"I'll see if he can make it," he said.

We walked to the door and out into the hallway, sunlight pooling from windows that overlooked the Seattle skyline. The fiery leaves of September caught in branches like small embers tipping on to the ground. Threadbare clouds scudded past, and a small smudge of orange hovered in a corner of the sky.

That's when Martha stepped into the hallway. Martha had worked as an orderly at the hospital for years. She wore those ridiculous shape-up shoes that claimed to improve your calf muscles. She was a little on the heavier side, and had this amazing grin and this awesome black hair that always looked like she just rolled out of bed. Like, always. She also wore a fanny pack. I wasn't sure what it held, but I was glad fanny packs were still going strong. Best of all, she was always genuine. I never had a bad thing to say about her, though sometimes I tried.

"She's here, right? You see her too?" said Fitz, motioning to Martha.

Martha and I exchanged a look.

"Can never be too sure in my condition," he said. "Meeting new people is always a test."

"Sure, act like you don't know me, Mr. Fitz," said Martha before moving on.

"Okay, I guess it's time to go, Addie . . . ?" he said. He hung on to my name as if asking for the rest.

"Addie Foster."

"Okay, Addie Foster. See you at lunch. I'll be wearing the

slip-resistant booties and these killer sweats. If I'm late, don't wait for me—it just means I've been detained because I have a serious, tragic condition eating away at me constantly."

"And a morbid sense of humor," I said.

"I also love fast food and B-grade movies and Ultimate Fighting, so I'm probably up there with the elite thinkers you seem to like. You know, the ones who write those plays you seem to enjoy, based on your comments in group. You like to talk about acting, at any rate. But didn't Chekhov say you can't put a truffle on stage if you're not going to eat it in the next scene? Something about not breaking your promise to the audience?"

"A rifle," I said.

"A trifle?"

"Rifle," I repeated.

"Semantics," he said, as he began walking in the opposite direction. "See you at lunch, Addie Foster. Don't stand me up, unless you find me on the floor."

The orderlies nudged me and nodded in the direction of Dr. Riddle's office. I started to walk down the hall with my two new friends. When I looked out the window on my left and saw the clouds splitting and gathering weight, I smiled. I watched the white clouds set against the darkening sky and I could only see it all as nature's handsome gap.

I wanted to know more about Fitz. I needed to know more. He was the only thing keeping me from getting lost in the whitewashed walls and medical halls of the hospital where I was supposed to be confronting my core issues. Whatever.

It's not like I was ready to eat that truffle anyway.

Two

Hours piled atop one another, two on three on four on five. After the first day, I felt a bit closer with the rest of the patients in the ward—except for Doug because I couldn't believe anything he said—but I wasn't any closer to understanding the new scheduling or the purposes behind those specific sessions.

Now the rules: bathrooms were locked and only allowed use upon request. Parents visited once a week for two hours on Sundays during Parent Visit time, though sometimes Dr. Riddle approved an extra "bonus" visit. And, I know, clever name— Parent Visit. No other contact or meetings with parents unless Dr. Riddle called them in for something specific—hint: usually not a good thing. Booties on feet at all times. Bedtime at ten, breakfast at seven.

No books except those approved by the therapists. No movies except those approved by the Treatment Team. Another clever title. And yes, I needed an entire team of doctors to help figure out why my OCD would not lay off my taxed mind.

Dr. Wall had been giving me new medications every few months, and I was certain Dr. Riddle was already trying the same thing but only with more resilience and speed. I hoped he'd have more luck.

You're probably wondering about Fitz, too, like I was.

That first night, Fitz wrote me a note and slid it under my door, probably when he was on his way to use the bathroom.

Will you go to lunch with me tomorrow? Y/N.

Lame, I know. But it was also old-school and kind of fun. Childish, but charming. I mean, we had to make up for the lack of a freaking cell phone somehow, right?

I circled the "Y" and held on to the note so I could return it the next time we saw one another.

I didn't see Fitz for a few days, though, because of all the annoying introductory stuff I had to wade through—a "welcome to the psych ward" talk from Tabor, and then I had to watch a series of training videos so that I'd be "qualified" to make lunch in the ward's cafeteria. After a meeting with Dr. Riddle, of course. Yes, bussing tables had been my first job. No, those videos could never make cleaning up vomit and smashed kung pao chicken look like some dream job filled with endless happiness.

Dr. Riddle was a kind man. He had small, blue eyes and giant glasses and features too small for his large face. He had a massive white beard and wore that stupid doctor coat with pens in the breast pocket and his name stenciled in blue. My third day in the ward was our first real talk. He wanted me to "Get a feel for things," as he put it, before having our first official meeting. Whatever. I was geared up for just about anything after meeting the cast of characters staying in the ward with me.

"How did you sleep, Addie?" said Dr. Riddle.

"Like a mental patient without a key to the bathroom," I said, giving him a sarcastic, thin grin. I picked up the stress ball on his desk and sat back in my chair. I looked into the happy face of the stress ball and poked at the eyes with my thumbs.

"Any obsessive thoughts lately?"

"Tons. You know that."

"And is being here making it better or worse?" he said, writing something down in that ridiculous manila folder that doctors—plural—seemed to carry everywhere. I'm sure he had more than one folder, but it was all the same to me.

"I can't tell. Probably worse," I said. "Actually, definitely worse. I don't have as many distractions available to me. At home I could watch a show or read a book whenever I wanted. Or I could go on a walk with our dog or something. Here, I have too many meetings. I hate schedules."

"I understand, Addie," he said. "But lines have to be drawn if you want to get healthy."

"I'm no artist, Doc. Besides, I feel like I'm way more together than most the people in here, right?"

"You're smart, Addie. In fact, you are incredibly high-functioning for such constant obsessive thoughts. But you still can't get out the door in the morning in under an hour, can you? And what about bedtime rituals? I'm very selective about who I choose for inpatient treatment. I hope you know that I'm looking at your case from a far different medical and psychological perspective. I hope you'll learn to trust me," he said, nodding.

Dr. Riddle cleaned his glasses on his white coat, and I thought of how cliché that move was—but then, clichés have to come from somewhere, right? Whatever. I stared at his bookshelf and saw so many boring titles about gardening and architecture that I wanted to tell him to get a grip on what's worth reading, but he filled the silence before I could.

"Your mother tells me you are interested in hearts," said Doc.

"Yeah."

"Why is that?"

"Not sure," I said. "I mean, Dad died because he had a big heart. I guess I've always been interested in hearts because of him. I don't know. It's not like he was around when I was growing up, so I guess I feel angry about it. But it's not his fault, right?"

Cardiomyopathy. That's the technical term. And yes, I was way into hearts, but I didn't feel like talking about it with Dr. Riddle. Not yet, anyway. My dad's heart had literally been too large and couldn't maintain a normal rhythm. I wasn't going to dive into that well with Doc.

"No, it's not his fault. But it's not yours, either," he said.

Doc didn't need to know that I counted my heartbeats all the time. He probably had that somewhere in his notes from my old doctor anyway. Some nights, at home, I would stay awake and read about hearts to try to distract myself from counting the beats. Other nights, the act of counting just made things worse. Those nights, I would make lists of things I wanted to know more about or research random facts about stuff I found interesting—astronomy, hearts, horse racing, you name it. And yes, that kept me up well beyond midnight most nights, which made my morning rituals even harder to push through.

I once ordered a book from the library about the whole horse-racing thing and found out that you really can't get involved with that racket on the upper levels unless you are literally created from a pile of money. Seriously. Like, the money had to conceive you or you could not join that club. I knew I'd never have the fajillion dollars I needed to be in that world. Not like I cared too much.

But those hearts. After reading that book, I kept wondering about how much blood was pumped through those giant horses every second. I wondered what it would be like to press my head up against Secretariat's chest after the Preakness stakes, to hold my hand against the heaving withers and just listen. Listen to that heart pound away, vibrating the very dirt from the tip of the crest down to the muddy hooves.

Have you ever thought about the size of your own heart? I have. I wonder if mine is big—not because cardiomyopathy is a genetic thing but because I wonder if I could ever be as loving as Mom or as caring as Doc. I wonder if my heart is big enough to house someone else or whatever. I wonder how many of the four billion heartbeats in my life will be used on other people, for other people.

I think Doc could tell I didn't feel like engaging in a long conversation, so he handed me a sheet of paper. "Here's the schedule for today. You need to start thinking about drawing lines and making decisions. I will be continuing the new medications and adding another today so we can try to beat this thing. And please give behavioral therapy an earnest effort. Please. Dr. Ramirez said last week you just made jokes about his mustache."

"Have you seen that thing? Freaking caterpillar eating away at his lip, Doc. It's like, number two on the definitive list of world's greatest 'staches, right behind Tom Selleck. It's so authoritative. Makes me nervous."

"Seriously?"

"I don't joke, Doc. You know that."

He sighed and looked at the clock. I knew I could wear him down.

"Please give him your best effort, Addie."

"I'd rather just act like Jackson Pollack and throw some paint on a canvas with no ostensible pattern in mind," I said.

"And I'd rather not see you wreck your car, Jackson Pollock. So get to class and promise me we can continue this talk tomorrow morning. Sorry to keep you till lunch, but I had to run those tests to make sure we were getting started on the right medications."

I was pretty surprised by Doc's art knowledge. And I liked that he was willing to take me on—most people either walked away from me or ignored my comments or changed the subject. I rarely found someone willing to engage in conversation on the level I aimed for. He couldn't maintain it, but maybe he was just in a hurry. At any rate, it helped me forget about my OCD for a brief moment, like a vista opening up on an otherwise foggy lifetime at sea.

The hallways were pretty empty. I saw one or two orderlies on their way to who-knew-where. Light was cutting through the windows in big, buttery slabs, and the white walls were tinted yellow in the warm afternoon sun. I heard the ding of elevators in the hall beyond the ward and imagined all the people moving through the building. The elevator made me think of the blue whale's heart, the valves opening and closing like giant doors, the bodies in the hospital just blood cells on their way in or out.

I saw Fitz at the lunch table next to Doug. He hit Doug's hat off his head and gave this real goofy smile. He was still wearing that stupid bandana.

I sat down next to him and pointed at his shirt that said *Namaste in Tonight.* "I like it. I'm gonna stay in tonight, too."

"I got nowhere else to go!" he said in an excited tone. "Good to see you, Addie Foster. I was just telling Didi here that he didn't actually invent a fifth corner of the earth. That's not how maps work. Right, Didi?"

"I thought his name was Doug," I said.

"It *is*," said Doug. "But Fitz calls me Didi because it's short for Did-it-all-Doug. I really have done a lot of cool stuff. My mom doesn't believe a lot of it, but it's true. *Backstreet Boys!*" He covered his mouth and got red in the face. "Sorry," he said.

"Good job, Didi. That was one of your better ones," said Fitz. He turned to me. "Didi shouts things he's embarrassed about liking."

"My doctor says it'll train me to shout things that are acceptable instead of all the swears I used to scream. I hate it, but it is cleaner and all," said Doug.

"It's okay," I said. "I get it. If the Backstreet Boys come on the radio, I don't change the station. And those outfits they wear in front of that private jet? And those shades? C'mon. Have mercy!"

Didi smiled and ate some of the super bland chicken and rice on his tray. The food was always blah. Didi had this long blond hair that fell over his forehead, and these really bright blue eyes that reminded me of Duck, my Alaskan husky waiting for me at home. Yes, I named him Duck. I like the name. Don't worry about it.

I felt like I was in elementary school, what with the colored trays and cardboard milk cartons and all. I half-expected to see the "Have You Seen Me?" on the back with a picture of a missing person—that person being me. I was gone. Lost in the world of the mind. I finished eating pretty quickly because I was eager to do something—anything. There was far too much sitting around. I stood to dump my tray in the trash and bumped into Junior.

"Sorry," I said.

"Don't apologize. Makes people think you're weak."

"Oh," I said.

"Don't worry. I got it," said Junior, bending to pick up the cartons I'd spilled.

"Nice to meet you," I said.

"You too," he said. "Nice to have a new face here." Then he nodded and walked off to clean his tray. He seemed nice enough, if a little unsure of his responses at times.

"So, Addie," said Fitz, drawing my attention. "Want to visit the game room so I can school you in Boggle? We have a free hour before behavioral work. I'm done in the lunchroom and done being a juice-box hero."

"It's *juke.*"

"I've heard it both ways," he said. "Just thought I'd give you the chance to lose to me."

He smiled in a way that told me he was hopeful, then sighed in a way that told me he was also weary of the psych ward. I was aware he'd been there a few weeks longer than I had. At least that's what I took from it.

Of course I agreed. I wasn't a coward, and I had never lost in Boggle. *Never.*

The "game room" was more of a small reading nook with some giant beanbag chairs and a few small tables. There were cupboards filled with games and a pathetic row of books to read, if you were desperate. I worried I might become desperate, so made a mental note to let Mom know I needed her to get some books approved for me. Like, pronto.

Fitz and I sat across from each other at one of the smaller tables and got out the game. He shook the cube, and the letters fell into place, clinking into their individual boxes. I looked in the box, then around the table, then under the table.

"What in the dickens," I said. "No timer?"

"Dickens?" said Fitz.

"Something my mom says every now and then. Get over it."

"Some kid broke the timer and ate the insides," he said, matter-of-fact-like.

"What?"

"I'd say it's depressing that he was trying to harm himself, but it kind of makes me laugh. The stuff in a timer? Really? That's why we don't have anything around with batteries in it."

"I have to ask," I said.

"No, you don't," said Fitz. "But I'd like you to. Go ahead."

"You're an obnoxious mansplainer! I can figure things out on my own, thank you."

He laughed and put his piece of paper over the letters. He raised his eyebrows and gave me a look to let me know he was doing it so I wouldn't cheat.

I realized I hadn't been blinking as much since I bumped into him, and then I immediately felt self-conscious. The second I realized that my obsessive thoughts had quieted, I started in on them again. I started tapping my leg in sets of three and thinking about finding a bathroom to wash my hands and count my heartbeats. It made me angry.

"Why are you still here?" I said. "I mean, you seem incredibly alert and normal and functioning well. Except for your name. But otherwise. How long have you been here?"

"If this is your attempt at flirting, Addie, please go on. Tell me how well I'm functioning. Nothing gets me going like that."

I punched him in the arm, and he laughed. I was wearing

the same sweater as the day before but now with sweats and, of course, those stupid slip-resistant booties with the little grippy circles on the bottom. My hair was in a bun held together with a pen, as usual.

"I guess I'm just good at acting. Like you said yesterday." He let out a heavier sigh than I was expecting. "And my name was given to me. I can't change that I'm the fourth in line of a very abnormal and convict-laden Fitzgerald Whitman lineage." He paused and leaned back in his seat. "I've been here for two years. My auditory hallucinations—a fancy way of saying the voices in my head, mind you—have been less frequent. Dr. Riddle has me on this cocktail of meds, and it's the first time anything has remotely worked in . . . forever."

"Two years? Wow," I said.

"Yeah. Well. It's not like I'm cured or anything. I still hear things all the time. Some things are funny. Willy can make me laugh, and Lyle is often spot-on with his observations. Toby is usually nonsensical. Others are cruel. Some scare me. Most are stupid. But it's not like they show in the movies, with fun characters who follow around the brilliant, beleaguered hero. Sure, I'm brilliant, but those movies tend to leave out the shame, the conflict, the doubt. Like that OCD detective on TV—they never show him crying over his obsessions. He's just fun and quirky. And that's not the truth."

I started scribbling on my piece of paper, afraid of looking him in the eyes. I wasn't sure how to handle the seriousness of his tone or the intricate nature of his condition and all the pieces I didn't understand. I didn't really have time to process that kind of disorder, but I gave it a shot by trying to connect on some level.

"I know what it's like to be afraid of your next thought," I said.

"Sometimes, I hum real loud or sing or even shout because I know the next thought is going to be one I obsess over for hours. Just one word, and I'll drop everything to obsess. That means lots of washing and ticks and rituals and repetition." I fiddled with my pen and then folded the paper in front of me. "But I shouldn't compare mine to yours." I wasn't sure if I'd upset Fitz because he didn't speak for a beat.

"Part of my behavioral work has been to respond to the voices and make a joke of it. I think it's helping. It definitely suits me better than ignoring the voices entirely. But the episodes have been much less frequent since I started on the new medications," he said, pausing for a minute. "I also think I should stop being afraid of what could go wrong and start thinking of what could go right."

He looked past me to the wall on the far side of the little nook.

I turned to follow his gaze. Afternoon light bathed the far wall, and I saw the lame quote exactly as he'd stated it, word for word, in bold, glossy letters framed in this flowery décor. It looked like, way too kitschy.

"Ugh. I knew that last line wasn't real. I hate that phony, cotton candy crap," I said.

He started laughing. "Go!"

He removed his paper from atop the letters on the Boggle board, knocked my pen onto the floor, and began writing down words. I laughed, too, and grabbed my pen. I knew he was avoiding talking about his disorder. I didn't blame him. In fact, I did the exact same thing.

But seeing him do it made me realize how many walls I'd put up in my own life, and how those walls might be keeping me away from any real improvement in my therapy. Whatever. I had to hurry and catch up to his word count.

"Cheater," I said, looking down at the board. It did actually contain those letters, but I was mostly saying it to goad Fitz.

"Marsupial," he said. "Acrobatic, quantity, humidity. And I haven't even looked at the board for that long."

"You're so arrogant," I said. "But it would be impressive to see all those words on one Boggle board. Not likely, but whatever."

We wrote down words as fast as we could. I bit my lower lip—something I did when concentrating or nervous or anxious.

"How are we timing this?" I said, realizing again that we had no clock.

"I'll tell you when I can't find any more words, then we'll both stop."

He laughed, deep in his throat, and it made me smile. You know the kind of laugh that makes *you* want to laugh? It was one of those.

We both set our pens down a few minutes later, recognizing that we'd run out of words.

"So, Addie Foster," said Fitz, pushing his paper away, "tell me about yourself. A little more, I mean. Something you don't usually tell people. C'mon. We're wearing booties. Can it get worse?"

I looked at Fitz and back at my paper and started doodling because I wasn't sure if I was ready to open up just yet.

"You know Group Talk will bring it all out anyway," he said.

He had a point. And I was hoping we'd get to know each other better, so I decided to tell him part of my story.

When I was much younger, I found myself counting things, concerned with proportions, worried about cleanliness and germs at school, and constantly sniffling. I don't know why certain ticks stopped, but it was one tick that started me off on an endless journey. I knew that my mind raced all day, every day, but I was so young, I figured every kid was dealing with the same thing. Who knows enough to ask if something's wrong with them at such a young age?

Anyway, I grew into the obsessions and started spacing the hangers in my closet, and counting all the steps in the house each time I walked to a different floor, and the sniffling got worse. Throat clearing was added as a new cast member around that time. Hey! Come join the play, everybody! I hired new cast members by the day, it seemed.

I started taking on so many ticks that I started losing friends. Like, my obsessive cast was growing, but my cast of real-life friends was dwindling because of my selfishness. It wasn't because they disliked me or judged me, but because I was afraid to be with them. I left them; I didn't lose them. I replaced them with obsessions, compulsions, thoughts, ticks, rituals, worries. I had to turn inward, to face the thoughts and bend to their will. My will. Whatever. I was too in my head. I was holding on to ghosts meant to save me from the hauntings in my mind. It was embarrassing.

Truly though, things were like, abysmal. My routines began taking me three hours to complete every morning. I couldn't sleep at nights either, because I kept getting up to wash my hands after a new obsessive thought entered my head the moment I set it on the pillow.

That's also when I started worrying more about the safety of the people around me. My mind was telling me that if I didn't complete the rituals, Mom or someone in my extended family, or even a close friend, might die. Absurd, right? But I felt that washing was an act of saving, of love. It made perfect sense.

Mom took note of my odd behaviors early on, but she didn't know it was serious until I started crying about not finishing my rituals. If she tried to rush me out the door, I'd totally lose it and start saying someone would get hurt or she might die and I couldn't live without her. What a joke of cosmic proportions, right?

She was able to afford a psychologist visit for me twice a month, so I lucked out in getting some basic medication. However, that medication only slightly lessened the obsessions and made me incredibly tired. I hated it. I started cutting the pills in half or not taking them at all because they changed me so much. It was like my brain had to act as some traffic controller, and the pills slowed down the flow of the planes or cars or whatever.

Then the real godsend came. Dr. Wall, though he wasn't all that great, took the initiative and contacted an old med school friend of his about an OCD case that he couldn't figure out—hint: me. I'm the conundrum wrapped in a mystery and deep-fried in an enigma. Dr. Wall's friend happened to be Dr. Riddle, the leading adolescent psychiatrist in the entire country. What a friend to have, right? I know. I know.

Telling Fitz all this made me like him a bit more. I mean, he was a great listener, and I could tell his walls were not as high or as impenetrable as I first believed them to be. But maybe I was wrong. It was just a facial and body-language read anyway.

I left out all the depressing nights and long talks with Mom where I could hear the hopelessness and the worry and the sadness in her voice like gravel, the rocks turning and her voice losing the soft edge, the vowels elongating and wandering, but c'mon, I was talking to a guy I was kind of digging—he didn't need all the facts at that point.

Fitz nodded as I spoke, smiling in a wistful way. "It's pretty amazing what our brains can do to us, you know? Like, here's this thing sitting in this dark room that is just lighting up our world and making us do things we find absolutely off the wall. But we do them. We listen— Shut up, Willy!" he yelled, interrupting himself, his eyebrows lowering. I was surprised at his anger, but he quickly softened.

"Willy?"

"Just another voice. Sorry about that. He kept making jokes while I was trying to listen."

I patted Fitz on the arm. "So far I know of Lyle and Willy and Toby. You got something you need to tell me, cowboy?"

Fitz tilted his head back and laughed, a real sardonic grin on his face. I couldn't get past those amazing gray eyes. Maybe it's weird that I notice eyes first and last and in-between whenever I meet someone. Maybe that's how I get such a good read on people.

"I gave them all names of country singers so I wouldn't feel so bad about yelling at them. I hate country music. Willy Nelson is always telling dirty jokes."

I laughed and watched as he shifted in his beanbag chair, showing me that handsome gap.

"That sounds like Willy," I said. "What you really should go for are his pigtails. Braided pigtails. Super studly."

The sunlight was spangling the wall where there was a bunch of artwork hanging—mostly stuffy quotes and overly decorated garbage, but there were also some paintings of boats that I didn't mind too much. One in particular was called *The Boat Graveyard* and showed these two washed-up boats totally falling apart on the shores of a Scottish isle. The colors had faded to the point where they blended almost perfectly with the landscape. Maybe that's what I wanted—to lose the extremes of my disorder and blend in, to be normal, to change my colors.

Fitz looked at his list of words. I could tell he wasn't all that interested in discussing those voices, but he was also pretty open with me, emotionally. He was incredibly hard to figure out, but those kind are the most fun, in my opinion.

"Did you get 'chartreuse'?" he asked.

"Get real, guy. What do you really have?"

He started listing his words off: *Berry. Err. Yarn. Brawn.* The list went on. I crossed off some of mine, having doubled up on a few. Then I read my list until I got to the seven-letter words I was most proud of.

"'Warbler,'" I said. "That's a good one, eh?"

I looked at Fitz and alternated my blinks because I was excited. I waited for his smile to mimic mine, for him to make some joke about warbling in the shower and maybe mock country music again. But he didn't.

He threw his pen down on the table and said, "See you later, Addie."

Then he stood and walked away.

Just like that.

I saw his silhouette bathe the opposing hallway wall as he faded from my view. I heard the wind push against the windows, the breeze a living thing that beat like a heart against the glass.

Was he really that competitive? Did I offend him in the way I said it or something? Was he just a sore loser, or did he think of something that upset him at that exact moment?

I didn't see him for a week.

Warbler. Seven-letter word. A type of perching bird.

Maybe I was finally sniffing around the right place if I was going to eat that truffle in the second act.

Three

I was sitting in the Study Room one morning when Martha came in. She walked over to Leah Garza, a young Mexican-American girl with short brown hair, like almost a buzz cut, and beautiful brown eyes, a shade darker than her tan skin.

"You owe me. We made a bet, and you lost," Martha said with a smile.

"Don't worry. I'll put my money in the horse's mouth," Leah said, smiling back.

Martha raised an eyebrow.

"Just kidding," Leah said. "I know it's really 'Put your money where your china shop is.'"

Martha started laughing, then, and patted the girl on the arm.

I moved over to sit next to Leah Garza. I didn't really know her all that well, but she looked nice. Besides, it's not like I had a crazy amount of options when it came to conversational partners. And I needed that. I mean, I could easily get lost in a movie or book, but I needed conversation to remind me why I was fighting to get out of my own head.

Leah and I did the usual war-story-let's-hear-why-you're-here talk, and she told me she was recovering from glioblastoma. She said it super loud and slow, like I was a foreigner and didn't speak English. She said it was basically like having a constellation of tumors in her brain, and I could think of it like "*Glee,* maybe this thing isn't so bad," then "*Oh Blast,* it really is that bad," then an "*Oh man*" at the end.

"I have to add the *n* to make it work," she said.

I liked her sense of humor and the way she was able to laugh, but I figured it was another case of doing so in order not to cry.

It was weird having a twelve-year-old in the psych ward because she seemed so young, but I guess I was only five years her senior. Whatever.

I told her I didn't know the psychiatric ward was for that kind of sickness, but she said it was for the depression she couldn't kick.

I moved closer to her and put my arm around her. She was a quiet girl. Small yet so strong—I could see it in the way she carried herself. She often talked about her mother at home and how she lit multiple candles each day for Leah's recovery. I thought of Mr. Shakes and *A Midsummer Night's Dream.* Leah was little, sure, but she was fierce.

The Study Room held two tables and a few chairs and some posters that were trying to sound inspirational but just ended up sounding corny. You know the drill. Same as every other room there. But these posters were more focused on hard work and learning and determination. The one hanging closest to where we were sitting was of this massive bald eagle and below the picture it said, "Your attitude, not your aptitude, determines your altitude." What a cheeseball of a poster. I hated that crap.

"What are you working on, Addie?" said Leah, closing the

book she'd been reading. It looked like a fun sci-fi series for children and had a spaceship on the cover with a warrior holding some sort of weird, neon weapon.

"Trying to ignore the beautiful alliteration of that poster," I said, pointing at the eagle.

I realized Leah maybe wasn't old enough to get the joke, so I quickly adjusted my mannerisms and my delivery, as well as my tone.

"Sorry. I'm working on some English homework. I'm trying to get at least *some* credits so I'm not too far behind for graduation. I want to go to college when I get out of here."

"That's cool," she said, looking back at her book. "I hope I can go to college."

I kept reading because I didn't know what to say. I mean, how do you deal with a head full of tumors when you're so small and just getting a grasp on things? I felt awful. But the doctors said they'd gotten all her tumors, so she would definitely be okay, right?

"You'll definitely go," I said, giving her a half-baked smile that I could tell was overly showy. Stupid. I felt stupid.

I could tell that she wasn't done asking questions because she kept glancing over at me and then at my book like kids do, waiting for you to notice them.

Yes, I was still taking classes, mostly AP English Lit from my favorite teacher, Dr. Morris, but Mom brought me packets of work each week so I could finish up some credits while I was still in the psych ward.

Yes, Dr. Morris was nice about it all. He knew me, and understood that I couldn't attend class but still wanted to be involved. He knew that words were the thing that saved me from getting lost in my obsessive thinking. Words were my savior. Sounds weird, but it's true.

Think about it. All that matters in life are the right words in the right order. We make meaning with words, and we base everything on meaning and understanding. Words—that's all we've got. We're tied to them, inexorably. And I wasn't about to lose a full year of school. I knew I'd end up a little behind, but a little was better than a lot.

Dr. Morris had sent three books that first month, along with a syllabus. We would be reading a couple plays every week, so clearly senior year AP English Lit was going to be all about dramatic texts. Maybe that's why I was so interested in becoming a playwright at the time. I mean, my trajectory or goals or whatever tended to change because of the impulsiveness I lived with. I think it was some ridiculous OCD side effect.

Dr. Morris sent the complete works of a specific author along with these really awesome introductions he wrote about the author's history and everything. It was especially cool because everything he sent got automatically approved. I mean, he was an English teacher, so they didn't question his recommendations. Also, Mom had already talked with Dr. Riddle about Morris and my homework and got some special hookup or something. Whatever. I loved it, is all I'm saying. I was really digging the work.

"You looking at my book?" I said to Leah. It was *Waiting for Godot* by Samuel Beckett.

"Yeah. Looks weird," she said.

"It is. So far. It's a play about a couple of dudes waiting around for something and making elliptical jokes. Nothing's happening," I said. I remembered I was talking to Leah and changed my words. "They're just talking and sitting. Seriously. I bet yours is way cooler."

Leah nodded and went back to her sci-fi book.

I wish I had more of a talent for that kind of interaction. Kids are so awesome when it comes to doing what they want, when they want. They'll ask a question, get their answer, and then move on to the next thing without bothering to reply.

She was a cute little girl—look, twelve isn't that young, but I felt like two decades older for some reason. I felt this like, motherly instinct to protect her from the world. But I couldn't even do that for myself, so what did that say about my situation?

Leah glanced at me again. I could see her in my peripheral vision, this eager blur of energy waiting to come materialize before me, uncomfortable and fidgety and rubbing her hand back and forth over her incredibly short hair.

"What's up?" I said.

"You said your teacher was a doctor, so why isn't he here? My mom is a doctor. She does family practice." Leah shifted in her chair. I guess I took too long to respond because she spoke again while she tapped her book in a rhythmic pattern with her fingers. "We moved from Uvalde, Texas, when she got the job. I miss my family. I miss Texas. Last memory I have is of our visit to Corpus Christi for Dia de Los Muertos, right before we moved here. We went to the beach every year to celebrate. Tamales. Silly jokes. Lots of laughter. But that was the day I started seizing and they found the first tumors. Now everybody in the family has started calling it 'Dia de Leah.' My mom thinks it's hilarious. I get it—she's a real barrel of split sides."

"Nice. That's a good one," I said, appreciating her word game.

"Thanks," she said with a grin.

"Anyway, she said the best doctors are here, so that's why I came. But why isn't your friend here if he's a doctor?"

I set the book down. In that moment I imagined some dude collapsing in a restaurant and a waiter yelling, "Is there a doctor in the room?" and Dr. Morris running over all eager and being like, "I'm a doctor—what can I do?" and the waiter saying, "He's not breathing. I don't know!" and Morris replying, "I'm a doctor of philosophy, man! We're all trying to understand the things that take our breath away!"

It was dumb, but I had those moments in my mind and they always made me laugh.

I think Leah thought I was laughing at her because she got all timid and kind of hunched her shoulders, like she was curling into herself, and I didn't know how to pry her back open. I touched her shoulder.

"I was laughing about something else, not you. Split sides of barrels and all. My teacher is a doctor of school stuff only. He studied books. He doesn't do medical stuff like the doctors here or like your mom."

"Oh. K. Thanks," she said. She turned back to her book.

I turned back to my own homework and looked through Morris's lesson plan. Apparently the play was, like, Samuel Beckett's big breakthrough. Beckett was trying to say less with more, so there are these long procedurals where nothing much happens, but it all happens with the sense of *something*. Kind of cool, really. Maybe that's all I was doing in the hospital. I read on. I had to. Morris had given me more of Beckett's works to read, and I found myself going back to the last line from one of his books: "You must go on, I can't go on, I'll go on." I felt like everyone was shouting the first phrase at me, but I was living in the middle phrase, and I was afraid I'd never reach the last.

I was halfway through Morris's notes when I realized I was late for my cognitive behavioral therapy session with Dr. Ramirez. Cognitive behavioral therapy is like personal training for brain muscles—only imagine that your personal trainer has a gorgeous face and a huge ego. Not a great combination. You can't say he needs to be more humble because his face is so perfect. Anyway, that afternoon Dr. Ramirez told me I should try to expose myself to more uncomfortable situations. He told me to try not blinking for two minutes at a time, or to not wash for a day, even after I used the bathroom. Ugh. Gross. Even without OCD I felt that would be nasty.

He also told me to try doing things I'd never do. Like becoming a different person just for short bursts. His last challenge was about thinking more about someone else than about myself.

"Just for one day, Addie," he said, his face bright with those dimples dipping as he smiled. He sent me on my way to dinner. It was Monday night, so we'd also get to watch a movie before heading off to what the hospital apparently called "beds." I thought about Ramirez and his beautiful mug as I wandered the halls, wondering if Fitz was going to show for the movie.

He was there and wearing another ridiculous yoga T-shirt—*Highly Meditated*. I was glad he was there, and his shirt made me laugh because it was so fitting for the psych ward. All of his shirts were lame, but the kind of lame that made them almost hip. Like, a meta way of saying that he was cooler than the popular phrases because he could wear them and make them cool even though everyone knew they were only popular because obnoxious people liked to wear them to show off that they worked out. Whatever. I was thinking too hard about it, probably.

I almost sat next to Leah because she had her head bent over her food and looked sad, but she was already sitting by Junior, so I took one of the awful, cold metal chairs next to Fitz. Martha was up front giving us the usual reminders about movie rules: no touching other patients, whisper if you need to communicate something, ask Jenkins at the door if you need to leave to the restroom.

I wasn't sure if Fitz would talk to me or what he'd say if he did because I was still confused about how he'd left me after playing Boggle. I had been replaying that scene for days, wondering if I'd offended him in some way. I wanted to let him know I was sorry for whatever had happened, but I didn't have the chance.

"I'm sorry," he said first, bumping me with his shoulder. He stared intently at me and gave me a half-smile.

"Why do you have such ridiculous shirts? Did you buy all your shirts at the same yoga store or something?" The orderlies were in the room so I whispered, but they usually ignored things until it got to a low roar. They were just as lazy as everybody else.

"That's exactly what I did," he said.

"Such a guy thing to do."

"Are you stereotyping based on gender, Addie Foster?"

"Mostly. Thanks for noticing."

"I try," he said. "No, I just do yoga to relax. And because the first shirt I bought at this place was comfortable, I returned to get more. That's that. Stick with what works. Path of least resistance. Now move your *asana* a little closer. See what I did there?"

He smiled and slouched. I had seen him doing yoga in the exercise room a couple times during the week, but I was still apprehensive about approaching him. I figured he'd come see me when he was ready.

"Is that why you ran off on me after Boggle? Path of least resistance?"

He sighed heavily and sat up again, then put his hands on his knees. "I have to make it quick. This is one of my favorite movies."

"By all means," I said.

"I can't use all means, Addie. I can use words, though."

"Smart aleck."

He smiled and took off his bandana, winding it around his hands.

I could tell he didn't feel like talking about it, and I tried not to be angry about his silence. I mean, we were in a psych ward, so I should not have expected any straightforward answers, or relationships for that matter. Still, it was frustrating and kind of annoying.

"It's about San Juan Island," he said quietly. "I made a promise to someone, and the anniversary is this fall and I'm in here and the island is out there. I have to be there. I have to." He clenched his fists around his stupid bandana. "And yes, to answer your question—path of least resistance."

"That's lazy," I said.

"This place makes me tired."

"I'm not this place. I'm in this place, but it's not me," I said.

"You're right. I'm just not in the right place to be talking about it, is all."

He seemed sincere, and I didn't want him to get into something too heavy if it wasn't a good time. I looked up to see two orderlies sitting on either side of the TV.

Martha was my favorite orderly. She wore scrubs every day and a smile that always said that life was hitting her just as hard as the rest of us, if not harder, so why not look for the good stuff, the *real thing*? She often talked with us about our treatment, and it seemed like she used those moments to try to improve her own situation, whatever that was. She was sincere and kind, and I appreciated her candor. I could tell she didn't love the job, but her sarcastic commentary made it enjoyable to be around her.

The lights dimmed, and the pale walls of the entertainment room spilled into one another, creating a deep gray.

"Fine. But you better tell me more during free time this week," I said, whispering again because Martha gave me a glance as the lights went out, and I realized I'd been talking a little loud.

He gave me a goofy grin.

Just then, I heard Didi yell "Britney Spears' earlier work!" right as the movie title appeared. I figured Didi either hated the movie or his Tourette's was getting to him. When he yelled it again moments later, Fitz responded with, "'Hit Me Baby, One More Time'!"

Martha, sitting at the front of the room, looked our way with raised eyebrows.

I hit Fitz on the arm. "What are you doing?" I said in a half whisper.

"I'm trying to make it so Didi doesn't feel so bad about his outbursts. Imagine if everyone yelled things they're not supposed to be proud about knowing and liking—it could really help, right?"

I was beginning to really like Fitz. I mean, like, I really, really liked him. Whatever. It's not like anybody needed to know, but I was definitely falling for him. How often do you find someone who is willing to embarrass themselves to make someone else feel better? Not very often. That's the answer.

"So what's this movie about?" I said. "Why are you geeking out about it?"

"It's incredible," he said, rubbing his bandana into a ball and smiling, looking at the screen at the front of the room.

"Let me guess," I said. "There's a single girl in the big city who is clumsy but beautiful and really into cooking and she meets a guy in an accident—like, she drops something on him in the bakery or something—and they smile at each other over the cream from the pastel macarons that fell all over his new suit or something.

"Then they meet up a couple more times and end up having spats over insignificant minutiae, but gradually they become attracted to one another. Oh, and one of them was lying to the other one about something. Gotta have that hidden thing about how they actually knew the person and the accident was not all that accidental, if you catch my drift. Hilarity ensues because of the lie, but then the one finds out about the lie and is sad. Then they chase each other down after they realize they are really in love and the lies were only meant to help fate with the rocky process of love. They kiss in the middle of the street. Credits roll. Am I close?"

Fitz leaned forward in his chair with his face in his hands, mocking my plot outline, shaking his head back and forth. "Not all movies follow the same plot. Plot doesn't matter as much as the ideas."

"Agreed," I said.

"It's called *Aguirre, the Wrath of God*. It's a German film about conquistadors looking for El Dorado in the 1560s."

"A foreign film?"

"Hey, I like B-grade movies and fast food, but that doesn't mean I don't have a passion for the really good stuff as well, Addie," he said.

I guess I had been a little shallow in assuming he liked the simple stuff because that's how he acted, and most of his comments were jokes. Then I realized I did the exact same thing and felt like a jerk for not noticing that he was probably a lot deeper than he let on, just as I hoped I was. Whatever. I was not going to let him in that easily. Maybe he was playing the same game.

"So they look for El Dorado the whole time? Maybe they get lost and think they're doomed, then reluctantly give up, but on their way back to the trail, they find some sign that leads them to the city, and they end up rich, with palm fronds and grapes for ages—gold to last eons. Am I close this time?"

"Not even a little," he said. "They travel in a large part at the order of Pizarro. Just a little aside, Addie—Pizarro is not a pizza or calzone brand."

I punched him in the arm pretty hard, and he smiled and rubbed where I'd hit. Just then, Wolf shushed us. I'd met him right after Mom dropped me off that first afternoon. He had been standing against the wall by the fake plants and staring out the hospital entrance saying "I want my horse" on repeat. Wolf was so earnest and calm; I liked him. Apparently, though, he was enjoying the movie. We quieted down again. It was tough regulating the volume.

"So things aren't looking too hot for our conquistadors, but they forge ahead rather than count their losses. One of the leaders is shot by a dissenting officer named Aguirre, who is dead set on continuing. Aguirre declares one of the nobleman in their party the new emperor," said Fitz. "Shut up, Lyle! That's not how it goes." He looked to his right where nobody was sitting. "Sorry," he said to me. "So they carry on into the jungle and everybody dies, either by disease or unseen natives or drowning or a number of other things, until only Aguirre remains on their raft, which is now covered by monkeys. He declares himself the wrath of God. It's pretty epic."

I sat for a minute and thought about the plot. I looked around the room and realized Leah had left, which made me happy in a way—I didn't want her watching such a depressing film after the day's therapy session. Martha often took Leah out of movies when they had grown-up themes. That usually meant any type of violence. I often forgot how young she was.

Earlier that day, after Tabor had finished talking to her, I noticed her curled up in the reading nook with these books her mother had dropped off for her about dinosaurs and what they ate and stuff. She looked the happiest I'd ever seen her.

Fitz started laughing, and then told Willy to shut up. I asked what the joke was about, and he said it wasn't funny and he shouldn't have laughed.

"This movie sounds so uplifting," I said, lathering on the sarcasm.

"Not everything has to be uplifting to have meaning," he said.

He was right. But I wasn't about to give him that kind of validation, so I shrugged my shoulders. "We'll see."

"Harsh critic, eh?"

I didn't respond, but instead looked forward and let my leg drift closer to his. I hoped Fitz would notice and let his leg drift closer too. It felt childish, but then I noticed that he set his hand close to mine. The warmth of our hands was exciting. So stupid, I know, but it got my heart racing. I felt like I was in elementary school or something, but with all the rules surrounding us there was this weird kind of excitement that came with breaking them.

That was the problem though—as soon as my heart started racing, I had to put my hand up to it and check my watch. The heart of a great blue whale can weigh over a thousand pounds, and the aorta is big enough for a human to crawl through. Its heart beats only eight or nine times a minute, but the sound can be heard for like, forever. That's the part I always think about when I set my hand on my chest. I wondered who could hear my heart, how far that sound traveled.

The movie was actually pretty good. It felt like found footage, very surreal at times. At one point Fitz nudged me.

"Watch this," he said. "Junior is a know-it-all. I like to tease him about stuff just to get him going."

I looked at Junior sitting two rows ahead. It was kind of dumb they had so many chairs set up. I mean, there were only like five or six of us in the ward, so we didn't need that much space. Then again, maybe it was pretty packed at other times. That was depressing to think about.

"Pretty cool that Pizarro was born in Portugal. I wish I could go to Portugal," Fitz said, obviously too loud for a conversation between the two of us. "I've always wanted to visit South America."

Junior's head twitched, and he sat up. He didn't turn around, but spoke with his eyes still on the screen. "He was from Spain. And Portugal is in Europe."

"Pretty sure it was Portugal," said Fitz. "And Brazil speaks Portuguese, so it must be in South America."

Junior breathed heavily. He had these really large features and broad shoulders, and he always looked like he was on his way to some important meeting. He walked a little rigidly and carried himself with a lot of confidence, like an overeager soldier. He seemed so certain of everything. I wondered if that may have been what led to some of his anger problems.

"Spain," said Junior. "Europe."

Fitz left it at that.

"I don't want to make him too mad," he said, whispering my way. "I think he'll find the ending of the movie frustrating as is."

Seeing Junior upset made me anxious for some reason, so I started tapping my feet, then my hands on my knees, then I alternated my blinking and cleared my throat seven times. I liked that Fitz didn't ask me questions when I was in the middle of a ritual. He knew I counted my heartbeats and had other ticks, but he didn't bring it up or bother me about it. He just watched the movie and ignored my fidgeting. I guess he also had his own demons—all those voices constantly in his head.

I got lost in the movie after that, consumed by the story, glad that movies and books had the power to almost completely remove me from my obsessions and my hummingbird-heart-paced thinking.

Hummingbird hearts. I placed my hand on my heart again and counted. Hummingbird hearts can beat over twelve hundred times a minute. I guess that's kind of how Fitz made me feel. Not like I was going to tell him that, though. He already had a big enough head. Seriously, it was pretty big, but fit his muscular body. Whatever, don't get me started on his body.

"Shut up, Toby. I don't want to hear about it. Yes. No. I'll tell you later if you just shut up for a minute!" Fitz said, standing and shouting at the wall behind us. He kicked his chair over and then crouched and buried his face in his hands. He wasn't crying, but he looked sad as well as furious. "I'm sorry, Quentin," he said, whispering to nobody.

I hadn't seen this side of him, really, so I didn't know how to react.

Martha walked back and knelt next to Fitz. "You gonna be okay, sweetie?"

"Fine. Sorry, Martha," he said. He stood and picked up the chair he'd kicked.

"Don't say sorry to me. I don't understand this movie either. Sometimes hearing those Germans talk makes me want to kick a chair too," she said. "Just want to make sure you're okay."

"I'm good. I'm good. Sorry for the outburst."

"Quit apologizing," she said. "Just sit down and enjoy the movie, if you can. Maybe I'll sneak you guys some candy next time. Shame we can't eat more here. Stupid rules," she said, turning to go back to her chair at the front of the room.

Fitz sat down, and I could tell he was uncomfortable.

"It's whatever," he said. "I mean . . ." He sighed and blew out a long breath in a way that seemed to calm him. "I mean, Toby tries to tell me lies about my past or lies about myself and who I am. And I don't like it. Sorry about that."

"It's fine. I thought you were supposed to joke with them," I said, worried I was overstepping a bit too soon.

"Toby's a jerk. He likes to tell lies, and some of them are kind of funny, but ultimately they tick me off because I don't want to think like that. You didn't hear anybody make a joke, did you?"

"Nope. I've never met a Toby I liked," I said.

Fitz's smile told me he didn't want to talk about Toby.

"Who's Quentin?" I said.

"What?"

"You apologized to Quentin after you got mad at Toby."

Fitz looked uneasy. "He's just another voice."

I didn't feel like he was telling the truth. I didn't know of any country singers with the first or last name of Quentin.

I turned back to the movie but pulled my hand back to my lap because I was feeling a bit uneasy. We let the movie fill the space between us. I was able to allow myself time away from my mind, time I could devote to getting lost in the movie. That rarely happened.

As the movie neared its end, I rubbed my stomach and leaned forward. Doc had me on these new pills that were already making me sick, and only a few weeks in. Oh, and hungry. I'd already gained three pounds, at least. Doc wouldn't weigh me or let me weigh myself, but I felt heavier, plumper, more bloated and large.

Just because I had a good reason for my plumpness didn't mean I was excited about it. Whatever. I wasn't getting all that big, but I didn't like that my body was hanging on to everything I ate.

When the movie ended, Fitz leaned into me and whispered, "Not your typical movie, huh?"

"Not even close," I said.

He waited a beat before speaking again. "So what masks are we wearing, Addie? Are we tragic characters or comic characters? What does our journey look like? Maybe you're the protagonist, and I'm the anti-guy?"

"You mean antagonist?"

"Whatever," he said. "What does our story look like? We're all just acting, right?"

"I don't know where the line is anymore," I said.

"What line?"

"Between the authentic me and the acting me. Maybe it doesn't exist. Maybe it's all acting. Maybe it's just a successive line of masks that we put on and take off as we enter or exit the various stages of life—pun intended."

"Where do I fit in your story arc? Maybe you should just let me write it. I'm kind of an expert at anything I set my mind to," said Fitz.

"I'm not sure yet," I said. "But based on your arrogance, I'd say you're exhibiting classic signs of the tragic character. It will be your downfall, you know? Aristotle made that pretty clear."

The credits rolled. Fitz looked like he had something else to say to me, but just then Martha ushered us out the door, each of us to our own room for the evening.

I was overjoyed with the early bedtime because the pills I was on made me sleepy. I was gaining weight and needed more sleep. What a wonderful journey! Who doesn't love gaining weight, and on hospital food to boot! Whatever. *Laugh so you don't cry*—that was probably some stupid quote hanging somewhere in those halls, although it wasn't all that inspirational.

I stared up at the ceiling after turning out my light. Moonlight hit the wall by my bed with laddered light. I was lucky enough to have a small window in the corner of my room overlooking the city. Most rooms didn't have any windows at all. But I wasn't a risk for breaking it, I guess.

I thought about Fitz and asked myself why I found him so intriguing, and why I'd even imagine that a relationship with him was possible. We were in a psychiatric ward of all places. And even *if* and *when* we did get out, how stable would that relationship be? I'd be dating numerous people at once. I liked a challenge, but that seemed a bit much. And who was I to claim stability? I could barely keep both eyes open or my thoughts focused on one thing for any extended period of time.

My heart sped up, and I looked at my watch and spent the next hour counting the beats in sets of seven.

I heard something scratch at the floor near my door and turned to see a small square of paper, folded into a tight block. I leapt from the bed and picked it up and opened it. I turned on my light, but immediately heard Martha shout "Lights out!" from down the hall and turned it back off, grimacing. What a stickler. Maybe she wasn't my favorite.

I knew it had to be from Fitz because, well, who else would write me a note and slide it under my door? I was friends with Didi, but not like that. Junior would've just punched a hole in my door and yelled whatever he was thinking. Leah was too shy for that kind of thing.

Thinking about Leah made me sad. She was so little. Not like I was some retired sixty-year-old reminiscing about my many years of life, but there was something tender about having to deal with heavy stuff at Leah's age. I mean, at what age do we really understand death? Does anybody? She had come so close to it that she probably knew more about it than I did, like her life was touching the truth because the exterior had been rubbed off by her closeness to whatever comes next. I couldn't imagine diving that low and coming back to tell the story—like spelunking in a massive, sinuous cave only to return to the top with the news that things go much deeper than originally thought.

I heard Martha in the hallway shuffling around on her rolling chair. Probably reading one of her romance novels, I thought.

SPENCER HYDE

I stepped into the moonlight thrown from the small window and opened the note.

> *All the world's a stage, and all the men and women*
> *merely players. Will you help me break out of this place,*
> *fellow player? Y/N*
> —*The Tragic Character*

I knew Fitz was joking about breaking out. I hoped he was. But quoting Mr. Shakes to me—that was a smart move. That was speaking my language.

But the more I thought about it, the more it sounded kind of nice—maybe Fitz and I could walk to the Cinerama on Fourth Street and watch some old Kurosawa film or something and get sushi with my friends from high school, Emily and Paige, though I was sure they'd both already forgotten about me at that point.

Friends are like that—out of sight, out of mind. Well, I still thought about them, but I was certain they weren't worried about me. I mean, Mom hadn't mentioned them asking about me or anything. I didn't even have a freaking cell phone so I couldn't keep up with anyone or anything. That first month, I found it super annoying, being phoneless and all. Maybe I would bring that up during Parent Visit weekend. I was without a mobile. I had no mobility.

But I really had no reason to leave. I mean, Mom visited every week, and the doctors were trying to help me. Why would I want to leave? Maybe Fitz was tired of being confined in such a hopeless place for two years. I wasn't sure. I guess if it came down to happiness then it made sense. I mean, if he wasn't happy, there would be no point to anything. Life is about finding and keeping happiness. Or it should be. For some reason, that made me think of Ulysses and his bag of winds and how, like, Fitz was maybe waiting on Aeolus, and the only wind not in the bag was the one that would carry him home.

Anyway, it took me two more hours to fall asleep. I kept thinking what two years in this place would do to my mind, to my hope, to my own bag of winds. Maybe I'd be totally cured. Maybe I'd get worse. Maybe I'd end up questioning myself to the point I no longer recognized the stage or who my fellow actors were or what act we were performing or if the director was actually directing or quietly backing away to work on another, more important, project. Maybe I'd do anything to get out.

I used the bathroom three more times, and then Martha wouldn't allow me out anymore so I had to count my heartbeats for an entire hour. I also counted the number of times I cleared my throat and tapped my fingers on the cold rail of the bed frame. Despite the niggling urge to get more sevens and fewer threes, I eventually stopped.

I imagined myself a great blue whale, but not because I was gaining weight—c'mon, that's messed up. But as I counted and listened, I wondered if anybody could hear my heartbeat outside of my room, the valves opening and closing inside my chest like little doors of possibility.

Four

I saw the stack of new plays on Riddle's desk and broke into a big smile. I think Doc thought it was for him. I didn't mind though because Doc was a good guy, far as I could tell. I was excited at the prospect of new reading material, so I began blinking rapidly. I hated when the ticks manifested in Doc's presence. But I couldn't help it. And it's not like I needed another reason for ticks. My mind had been racing since I woke because of Fitz's note. I had it in the pocket of my sweatpants, and I kept turning it over in my palm. It was all sweaty and gross, and the edges were bending in on themselves, but I kept turning it and counting the turns.

Was Doc aware I had the note? No. Nobody knew.

"Seems like we're having a good morning," he said. "And it seems like our ticks are still present."

Doctors have this really annoying way of using the first-person plural, the royal *we*, making it sound like they are a part of the journey in the same way as every patient. It's so bogus. They say things like, "How are we doing this week?" I hoped that annoying habit carried over into Doc's life. Like, I hope he talked to his dog and was like, "We really do need a bath, don't we?" or "Boy, we really made a mess on the lawn, didn't we, little guy?"

"That's well put, Doc," I said. "How *are* we doing with our ticks? We seem to be working on them, but we also seem to be gaining some weight because of our pills, don't we?" I said, grabbing my stomach and slouching into the chair.

I flashed Doc a sardonic half grin and then saw the smiley-faced stress ball on the desk near my knees. It was a good break from turning the note in my pocket. I wiped my sweaty palm on my sweatshirt before grabbing the stress ball. I started gouging the eyes, as usual, the squishy material molding around my fingers and slowly indenting and refilling as my fingers moved. I really wanted to wash my hands because of the note, but I convinced myself that I was transferring that bad energy to the stress ball, and it worked, at least for a while.

Doc just looked at me over his horn-rimmed glasses. They must issue those at med school graduation to every person picking up a certificate. It was such a doctorish look. He even opened my file at the same time, not even needing to look down anymore. It's like the papers were attached to his hands. He probably slept with his files near his bed, under his pillow, stacked and used as a bedside table. The files had become an extension of his body. Like, completely.

In that moment, I imagined myself some kind of hero breaking out from the now-somewhat-familiar world of the hospital, grabbing a sword or something on the way out, and fighting the evil in my life that towered over me like some monster. I'd be a total badass and do it all on my own. Every good story needs adventure, right? And there has to be some sort of goal, something the main character wants. That's what Dr. Morris's lessons were saying, anyway. But what did I want? Maybe my dilemma was the fact that I had no idea what I wanted. I wasn't sure how to resolve that kind of paradox.

Anyway, I had finished *Waiting for Godot*, so getting new reading material was perfect timing. Parent Visit was also later that week, and I was pretty excited to see Mom. I had to have things to look forward to or else I got totally lost in the monotony of the psych ward. I thought of hurrying Doc along by ignoring his questions, but that never worked.

So I relaxed into my chair and got ready for his annoying questions. He had good intentions, of course, but they were still annoying.

"How would you say your obsessions have been this past week, Addie?"

Doc awaited my answer with bated breath, pen in hand. I wondered again if he knew about the note. Maybe it was just a regular question that he honestly wanted to know the answer to, but that morning it felt directed at something specific. Whatever. I was paranoid.

"Average," I said. "But worse when I'm nervous or excited. So, pretty much the same, I guess. Well, I don't have to wash my hands as often. Or maybe it's because I have to ask permission to do it now. I don't know, but I think it's better. My morning rituals are significantly less, at least. I'm just playing it by air."

"By air?"

"Just making sure you're still listening, Doc," I said, motioning at his files. "It's like Pascal's Wager."

"Go on."

"So this Pascal guy, this philosopher, says that if you believe in God and God exists, the result is goodness or heaven or whatever.

If you believe and He doesn't exist, no harm done. If you disbelieve and He doesn't exist, again, it doesn't matter. But if you don't believe and God *does* exist, that's bad news for you. We're all just wagering on what to believe."

Doc was writing away, scribbling down everything I said. "And what does this wager have to do with you? What does it have to do with today?"

"It has everything to do with me, Doc," I said. "If it turns out that my rituals indeed *do* save my mother or Duck or even you from death, then it's worth the time and pain and grueling slog, right? That's how I wager. I'm a betting girl. I have to be."

Doc continued to write. I wondered how often he went back and read his notes, or if it was just to prove he was doing something in his office each day when his boss asked for proof he hadn't just been playing Covert Warfare all day or something, the gaming console hidden under his desk and a headset stashed in a desk drawer next to the Cheetos and Mountain Dew.

I bet Doc loved video games. I figured he was a deadeye with a steady hand. He certainly had the beard for it.

I imagined him staying up late and playing online with Dr. Tabor and yelling into his headset stuff like, "Dang it, Tabor! I ran right over that stupid land mine you put down. Tell me where you place them so I don't blow myself up every freaking time I respawn!" while brushing leftover Cheetos dust from his beard and Tabor responding, "Riddle, our lives are filled with those mines. You must always be looking for them. In the end, didn't you do that to yourself? Was it really my fault? Or is it easier for you to pass the blame? Are you not just projecting onto me? And didn't you *want* to respawn so you could try again, so you could start over and imagine the past never happened?" and then Riddle just losing it and throwing his controller into the screen. Tabor was such a snob.

But back to reality.

"Pascal was speaking of God, yes?"

"Yes, but how can I know OCD from God if my mind is only aware of one set of rules?"

"Exactly. Let's change the terms you've set for yourself."

The rest of the visit went as I expected. Doc brought up the side effects of the medication I was taking, and then asked how I was feeling using one of those stupid charts with the smiley faces. I hate that crap. Can you really sum up your feelings using a cartoon image? Not a chance. What a joke.

"And you've been getting along well with the others in the ward, it seems," he said.

"What do you mean?"

He looked up from the folder. I was worried he was asking about Fitz, and I put my hand back in my pocket and turned the evidence in my palm.

"Just that. You haven't complained about your fellow inpatients, so I'm assuming things are going well in that regard."

I nodded yes, and he looked back at the folder. I felt nervous, like, maybe I was giving something away I shouldn't. Like, maybe I was letting on that I was liking them too much or whatever. I didn't want to be the reason the plan fell apart, even though it wasn't like there was even a plan yet and even if there was, I hadn't agreed to help. I just had the note.

That always happens in movies when the amateur tries to join the crew and show them what she's made of, right? The rookie always outs the whole crew at the worst possible time because she can't keep her emotions in check. Whatever. That wouldn't be me. I was sure of it.

Doc glanced at the clock on the wall behind me. "Well, I don't want to keep you any longer. You have Group Talk with Dr. Tabor right after breakfast. Don't be late—or at least don't be too late. Make sure you get enough food. Remember, your mother will be visiting right after lunch. Have a great day, Addie. And keep betting on yourself. We'll get this."

"Thanks, Doc. Are those books for me?"

"Almost forgot. Sorry about that," he said, spinning around in his ergonomically correct chair and snagging the stack. "Here's the work from Dr. Morris," he said, smiling in a doctorly way that felt fake even if he didn't mean it that way.

All for show. Just wearing the doctor mask.

I was aware of Fitz's note in my sweatpants as I stood to leave Doc's office with my books in hand.

I shuffled to another bland breakfast of oatmeal and yogurt and bran muffins. I ate it all because my appetite was monstrous. I was a monster.

I still felt hungry, though. My new medication was really working on my appetite. I looked over at Didi's plate, and he kind of pulled it away like, *Hey, this is my food.*

Fitz must have already eaten because I didn't see him anywhere. At one point, Didi yelled the name of a soap opera I'd never heard of and Junior threw his tray into the wall. Good times.

I looked at the time and realized I was pushing lateness for the morning Group Talk. I wasn't all that worried about holding up Tabor, but I wanted to see Fitz. Still, I lingered over breakfast, taking my time before heading to group.

When I walked in, I overheard Didi talking to Junior. Didi was looking up into Junior's face like he was super eager about whatever it was.

"I was Tolstoy's editor. *War and Peace*, before my help, was entitled *Gruesome Battles Followed by Living in Ostensible Serenity*. Yes, long-winded is what I thought as well, Junior. Glad you asked! The Tolster never stopped thanking me for my help. I even wrote a dissertation on 'thanking.' You're welcome," said Didi. "Copernicus stole my worldview!"

"That's enough, Didi," said Junior, putting his massive hands on Didi's face and turning it to face Tabor at the front of the room. "And I didn't ask," he said.

Didi still—always—had on that ridiculous fur hat with the catawampus earflaps.

Tabor started the meeting with only a few of the chairs filled. Leah gave me a small wave and shy smile, so I returned the wave and sat next to her.

"Feeling okay?" I asked her, unsure of what else to say.

"I guess," she said, rubbing her hand over her buzzed hair.

"I dig the haircut," I said. "It's, like, way more in fashion than mine. And you totally pull it off."

"Really? I guess a bird in the hand is worth greener grass on the other side."

"You can't see the wood for the bees. I get it. Seriously, Leah, you look like a total rock star," I said.

Tabor cleared his throat in an obnoxious let's-get-started type of way.

Leah mumbled a "Thanks" under her breath, and I saw, for the briefest moment, a genuine smile creep on to her face as she kept brushing her hand over her buzz. That made all of those moments worth it for me—all the moments I questioned what I would say to her and how I should act around her. Turns out, most people just want to feel loved and like they belong somewhere, like they have friends and a place to go and someone waiting for them. I don't know why I was always thinking it had to be something grand.

Cancel that—love *is* grand.

Fitz walked in late, and I felt a tightness in my chest, a kind of excitement at seeing him again at the start of a new day, but also a worry about agreeing to his escape plan. I turned the note in my pocket and wiped the sweat off right after.

Did he really mean it?

Tabor was talking about some headline he'd read that morning—apparently, two siblings had been reunited after years of not knowing the other one even existed. It was like one of those boring stories you see on *60 Minutes* where identical twins meet up after forever and realize they both used the same brand of toothpaste their entire lives without realizing they shared that intense, personal detail. Like, they also enjoyed drinking water after a long workout session because that's so incredibly unique. Whatever. Tabor wanted us to talk about how those two would get along, and why that reunion might be difficult.

Fitz plopped down next to me. He was wearing another ridiculous yoga shirt. It said, *I Have Nothing to Wear, All My Yoga Pants Are Dirty.* He seriously didn't run out of those things. I imagined his closet as something sponsored by a yoga store in Seattle. He still had on that ridiculous tie-dyed bandana as well.

"Were you waiting for me?" he said, smiling.

"Only existentially," I said.

"Addie Foster, taking on existentialism before lunch. That might be more than I can stomach."

"Can you tell us what you'd feel, perhaps, Addie?" said Tabor, obviously upset that we were talking instead of listening to him.

I hated that move, where the teacher calls on the person talking. I bet my conversation with Fitz was more interesting than Tabor going on about a lost sibling or whatever.

"I don't think they'd get very far," I said.

"Care to elaborate?"

"Not really," I said. "But I will."

I cleared my throat and slouched in my chair. The door to the Group Talk room was open, so there were these awesome rays of sun cutting through the dusty air, and I could see all the little particles swirling in the beams. I felt the warmth of one of those large beams on my leg; it felt nice.

"I don't think we're all that open with anybody, in the end. I mean, imagine meeting up at lunch with your parents, let alone some person you've never really known. Just because they share your DNA doesn't mean they're going to be all open and understanding all of the sudden. If you told me I had some sister I never met and you set us up, it would be incredibly awkward and not much would happen. What were they expecting?"

Tabor wrinkled his brow and adjusted his glasses—a gesture I found incredibly doctorish. I bet he met up with Dr. Riddle to discuss what doctor moves they'd incorporate into their repertoire for the day or something.

"Okay," Riddle would say, "I'm gonna adjust my lab coat at one point while looking over my glasses," and Tabor would be like, "Shoot, I was gonna adjust my glasses! We can't both do that move today, Mark!"

Tabor's white coat swept past his knees and cascaded over the cushioned chair. He glanced around at the others before turning back to me. "What do you mean by 'in the end'?"

I adjusted my position in my seat. Fitz, in my periphery, held his hand next to his face so Tabor couldn't see his expression, and he was giving me this annoyingly large smile, mocking me, while I was trying to stay serious. I smiled but controlled the laughter.

"I like to think of it as the walls of the heart, Tabor. I don't care to get all sentimental though. Every day we talk about being vulnerable, and I'm kind of exhausted."

I saw Fitz cringe when I said the V-word.

"That's okay," said Tabor. "That's okay. I understand that dealing with these emotions at this level can be difficult. In fact, I'm impressed you all are so gracious about it all," he said, opening his hands and motioning to the entire circle. That's right, all six of us: Me. Fitz. Junior. Leah. Didi. Wolf.

I hadn't talked to Wolf much. His real name was Ralph, but Fitz said every time he tried to say his name, it came out sounding like "Wolf," so that's what everybody called him. He was fifteen, maybe, and was short with these really dark eyes and long hair and a big stomach.

Nobody knew what Wolf was in for, or how long he'd been there. But every morning Wolf would go to the doors of the ward where the orderlies buzzed people in and he would just repeat, "I want my horse. Give me my horse," just like he was saying the day I was admitted.

Fitz said he'd asked Riddle and Tabor about it, but the only thing they ever said was that Wolf had a promise to him broken years ago coupled with a lot of other mental issues and trauma. That's all we ever heard about it, anyway. But Wolf said that phrase at the door every day until the orderlies took him back to therapy or group meetings or whatever. Then he'd keep repeating that phrase to anybody who would listen. Or not listen. He just talked. Like, always.

Anyway, I couldn't just leave what I'd said on that note, though. I knew I could be a know-it-all. I tended to think my opinion was the correct one. All the time. Just a thing I did. You know the type, I'm sure. Me. That's right. You know me.

"We build up these big walls around our heart," I said. "Brick by brick. Layer by layer. We churn our own mortar and slap on giant chunks of it between bricks, and we reinforce those walls every chance we get because we're all afraid someone might see through one of those cracks. So we remodel every day, and we add layers and retreat into ourselves.

"Nobody can penetrate walls that thick, layers that deep. It's a lost cause. I wonder what groups like this are really achieving because nobody here is letting their walls down. They might tell you they are," I said. I could tell Tabor was about to step in because he leaned forward in his chair, so I finished quickly.

"Shoot, they might even knock down an outer support to prove they're trying, but you're not really glimpsing the heart— just a sculpture in the form of the heart. A facsimile. The real thing is never on display. If it is, it's dressed up to look like something else. It's wearing a mask, just like we all do. The real thing is hidden deep behind those walls, boxed up tight in some impenetrable case and tucked away, buried beneath hundreds of layers of rock, the tectonic plates always in motion, the most intimate knowledge being removed to a place even deeper, even harder to get to."

Tabor crossed his legs and started writing in a folder.

That ticked me off, and I was angry I'd said what I did. That was a way of chipping away at the mortar, and I realized I'd knocked at one of my own walls unintentionally, pieces of brick chipping and falling at my feet. I needed to put the comedy mask back on and stop being so serious.

"I don't know if I agree," said Fitz, leaning on his knees after nudging me in a way that told me he got it, or at least that he appreciated what I was after in my comment. "I like what Addie said, and I agree that we build up those walls, but I also think those walls can crumble in an instant." Fitz looked at me and held my gaze. "Because it's happened to me."

I waited. We all waited.

"You just have to hear someone say they have something important to say, something like, 'It's about your brother'—or even just hearing the sound of screeching tires or an ambulance siren—and I think those walls disappear. The moment someone says the right thing, or you get a second glance from that girl, or someone calls early one morning with news, those masks come off, those walls come down. I think those walls are softer and more fragile than any of us let on.

"Dang it, Willy, not now! Yes, I think that's pretty funny, but I don't think I can share it. No. I can't," Fitz said, catching himself at the end and turning back to the group.

He looked upset when he finished. He gave a half smile, but his heart wasn't in it—I could tell. He slouched back in his chair and didn't talk for the rest of the meeting. He kept whispering in my direction, but I could tell it wasn't meant for me.

He was in his own world, the world of the mind, and he wasn't accepting visitors. I recognized myself in his defeated slouch, looking totally lost to everyone and everything around him. I recognized myself in that hopeless moment, that moment when my ticks and rituals won out over my own thinking, over my own desires and comments and attempts at meaning.

I wanted to talk to Fitz after the meeting, but he hurried away before I could get past Tabor and his incessant questions. I mean, Tabor was going to meet with me later that day anyway, so I wasn't sure why he was so eager to discuss my comments right at that moment.

I headed to the Study Room to work on my homework because I didn't have a therapist meeting for another few hours. Junior was walking the same way. I saw his giant head bob as he walked, his large body almost filling the hallway. He had a buzz cut and constantly rubbed at his head when he was thinking or bored. I wondered if Leah rubbed her head because she saw Junior do it. Maybe it was some impulse of short-haired people that just couldn't be helped. I wasn't sure. Junior didn't smile much, but I could tell he was softer on the inside. Just my intuition.

Anyway, I had only been reading maybe thirty minutes before Fitz dropped in. I was happy to see him sidle up next to me and flip open a book.

"What are you reading?" he said.

"A play. You?"

"*Ninja Assassin Protocol 4*," he said. "It just came out last month, and it's way better than *Ninja Assassin Protocol 3* because the characters finally figure out what the rebellion in *Ninja Assassin Protocol 2* was all about. I've been waiting forever to figure that out. What play are you reading?"

Junior sat in a cushioned chair just behind the bar where Fitz and I sat on tall stools. I could tell Junior was bothered by our conversation because he breathed heavily through his nose as if to remind us we were in the Study Room.

"It's called *Waiting for Godot*. It's about two guys who sit around and wait for a couple days. Nothing really happens."

"Sounds incredibly boring," said Fitz.

"Nothing happens, but they discuss important things," I said. "I'm reading it again."

"I like more action."

"I thought you said it doesn't have to be uplifting to have meaning."

"It doesn't. But it does need action. Two very different things, Addie. The characters have to move. They have to want something. They have to accomplish something."

"Dr. Morris would never assign something that didn't have value. I mean, he's the best teacher I've ever had. Although, he does always catch me mixing my metaphors in my essays."

"I always pegged you as a mixing-the-metaphors type," said Fitz.

Junior stood up and left the room with his book in hand, frowning at us. I felt bad that he was frustrated, but it's not like I was too worried. I laughed at Fitz and set my book down.

"You're a snob," I said.

"I'm a blessing in the skies," said Fitz, extending his arms like wings and moving like he was soaring. "So why are you so interested in this stuff? Why not pick up an easy read and relax? It's not like you're getting out soon, right?"

"Well, I have to write essays to get the grade, and I don't want my grades to slip while I'm here. I'm struggling with the final question though, so I'm reading through the thing again. It's really bothering me. I even asked Doc about it, but he didn't have an answer. I don't know, when I run into something that I can't answer, I get super frustrated and my ticks and rituals kind of take off into some other realm of annoying and I obsess over it until I find the right answer."

Fitz took his bandana off and started rolling it in his hands. "What's the question?"

"Seems simple enough," I said. "Morris just wants to know what the play is about. That's the last question: 'What are the characters waiting for, and why is it significant that it/he/she never shows up?' I can't just say it's about two guys sitting around and waiting for something to show up that never shows up. Or like, detail their conversations or something. That isn't the answer—that's just what happens, not what it's about."

He rolled his bandana back and forth and then rested his head on his *Ninja Assassin Protocol 4* book that looked quite well-worn after only a month's use.

"I read about this guy in Vermont who deals with the same thing I do. He called the police about domestic violence. The cops showed up, but it was just him, sitting in an old recliner, shouting. Apparently two nonexistent people in his head had married without telling him, and they started fighting. That's what happened, but it's not what that guy's life was really about. I get it."

"What I really like is that this author wrote about damaged individuals. He wrote of the travails of these characters who were trying to make sense of a world that would not accommodate them. I love that," I said.

He lifted his head to look from his book to me. He was listening to me, for sure, so I went on.

"I mean, look at us—we're not really being accommodated,

are we? But that's not the answer for the final essay question, either. Just something I found pretty awesome about the writer. His stuff really seems to emphasize repetition as the engine of silliness."

"So the play is about damaged people being silly? Still doesn't sound very interesting. And they just sit around the whole time?"

"They're waiting for Godot to show up," I said, realizing that my answer didn't offer any new evidence.

"I'm sick of waiting!" said Fitz.

"And yet, we wait."

He dropped his head back onto his book and hit his fists on the wood table a couple times before sitting up and sighing. He looked at me closely, fully, and I could tell he was sincere because there was this softness I'd never seen before in his gray eyes. Or at least I'd never noticed it before.

"I can't wait any longer, Addie. I need to take action. I need to go out and find that thing—Godot, whatever it is, whoever it is—and I need to do it soon. I'm gonna lose it if I stay here any longer. I have to keep my promise."

"A promise? Like, you want your horse?"

I could tell Fitz was trying not to laugh. But even mentioning Wolf's dilemma made me feel sad for him, though I respected that he wasn't going to give up until he got that horse. Then I got sidetracked by thinking of the characters in the play as if they were in the present day: Godot texting them and saying he's on his way, but never actually showing, and the two guys waiting, sending him multiple pins from the maps app and wondering why he was taking so long.

"I need to go to San Juan Island," Fitz said. "It means a lot to me. And I'm running out of time." He balled up the bandana and moved to the cushioned seat where Junior had been sitting. "We need money. I've already got the plan pretty much figured out. I mean, there are a few wrinkles I still need to iron out or whatever, but I need your help. I can't do this without you."

"You're being serious?"

"I gave you that note, didn't I?"

"This isn't Toby's idea or something? He's not setting us up with a lie?"

"It's the real thing, Addie," he said.

I didn't know what to say. I mean, I wanted to help him because I felt like he was really yearning for that thing, whatever it was. Whoever it was, as he said. But I also was aware that things were going well for me. Sure, I was gaining a little weight, and I didn't feel awesome all the time, but my ticks and rituals and the intensity behind my obsessions had decreased little by little, and only after a few weeks. It was some kind of miracle, and I didn't want to mess with that.

But I also didn't want to let Fitz down. I mean, he was right. My dilemma was that I didn't know what I wanted to do or who I wanted to be. I'd been coasting up until that point—in choppy waters, mind you, but it was still just a type of coasting.

Also, I wondered if maybe he was just asking me because he needed more bodies—like, maybe Junior and Didi could play a role, but he needed someone else kind of put together and able. Why was *this* year so important? Why was *this* anniversary such a big deal?

I didn't like the idea that he needed me for no other reason than to help him get out, but it did cross my mind. Maybe I was just filling a role, and he'd go after the next girl thrown in to the ward with just as much gusto. I hated that thought, but I couldn't help but entertain it momentarily.

"Let me think about it," I said.

"What's to think about?"

"Why haven't you tried before now?" I said.

"I have," he said, slouching. "We almost made it too."

"What happened?"

"Three weeks before you showed up, Junior had a seizure in his room a half hour before we planned to run. They locked down the ward. I can't blame Junior. Just luck. Just a moment away from success."

"I don't know, Fitz. Things are going okay here."

"For you," he said, standing. He looked at the papers spread out in front of me. They were Dr. Morris's notes for the first part of the semester. Fitz stared at me.

"What?" I said.

"What is this?"

I grabbed the paper he was pointing at. It was the most noticeable page because it had a giant circle on it, cut into zones of a journey. The bottom half of the circle was labeled "The Special World" with a ninja jumping in the air. Probably why Fitz noticed it.

"Notes from my teacher about Joseph Campbell's book. It's all about the different types of heroes and the journeys they take and how they fit into a bigger narrative. All cultures have stories like that. Even your ninja dudes experience this journey in some form."

"I know what it is. Maybe you need to read through it again," he said. "Or look at that special world again. You need to make sure you properly understand the hero's journey, Addie." He leaned on the table and got closer to me than he'd ever been. "I'm not mad. But I'm also not playing around. I need this."

"Okay," I said, unsure of how to respond.

"I have to meet with Riddle. See you at dinner, Addie." He grabbed his book and left.

The fluorescent lights above me flickered, and one tube went out completely, leaving me in a state of half-dark. Sorry—maybe I'm being too pessimistic. I was in a state of half-light. I kept reading my book, but I had to put it down after a few minutes. Why was Fitz so eager to leave? Why did this trip mean so much to him? I didn't like being pressured, but maybe he was right. I started rereading Morris's notes just as Junior spoke up. I wondered how long he'd been standing in the doorway, looking weary, holding his book.

"Is it gonna be quiet in here for a bit?" he said.

"Yeah. Sorry about all that, Junior."

"It's fine. I get it. Fitz is a talker," he said, slumping back into his chair and holding up a paperback that looked like it was about motorcycle maintenance or something. "Like you," he said, smiling at me. "I'm used to it."

"How long have you known Fitz?"

"Long as I've been here. Four months now, I think," said Junior.

"Does he ever talk about getting out?"

"All the time. We tried it once."

"Yeah, he mentioned that."

"Something to do with Quentin," he said.

I think Junior immediately regretted what he'd said, because he took his feet off the coffee table where he'd propped them up and closed his book and looked my way. Then he stood up again and started to leave.

"Not my place to talk about his personal stuff," he said. "See ya, Addie."

I didn't know what to do with that information. Was Quentin a real person, or just another voice telling Fitz he had to leave the psych ward? If that were true, then it would be risky to follow that kind of lead.

My thoughts swirled around Quentin and Fitz for the rest of the afternoon.

Lunch and the physical fitness hour were ho-hum as usual. I basically sat on a stationary bike for an hour staring at the wall and thinking about Morris's notes about the hero's journey.

When I walked into the cafeteria for dinner, I saw that it was just Didi and Junior, no Fitz or Leah or Wolf. Martha was sitting next to Didi, so I joined them because Junior was still reading his motorcycle book.

"Don't you ever sweat in that fur hat?" I said to Didi.

"I sweat just peeling an orange," said Martha, holding her arms up for me to see the pit stains.

"That's disgusting, Martha," I said, laughing.

"At home, people come visit and ask if I've been on a treadmill or something, but I tell them the truth—just rolling out of bed makes me sweat."

"Gross," I said.

She just smiled. She had no shame. I loved that about her.

"Didi was telling me about his life before the hospital," she said. "I figure, if my shift leader asks me to be in the kitchen for dinner, I might as well get to know this guy a little better," she said, patting his fur hat.

"It's all pretty basic stuff," said Didi.

I never saw much of Didi's hair because he always had that weird hat on. But then I wondered why I always noticed the hair and the eyes first. Why did those stand out so much to me? Why not just describe the shape of the body? The ears and the eyebrows?

Then I thought about being in a detective show, like where I'm constantly asked to vet the perps in the room with that two-way mirror and after I spend hours grilling a suspect, the captain says, "So, Foster, is this our man?" and I respond with "Hair and eyes. They give it away every time," and then there's the sound of a gavel and loud music like in *Law and Order* and they cut to the title of the detective show as the camera zooms in on my eyes and a small gust of wind blows my hair from my face and then the screen lights up with *Fostering Justice*. So stupid.

But that's how my mind was working before Didi's hat grabbed my attention and pulled me back to the present.

"All news to me," I said.

I smiled at Martha and set my tray of food down next to her—sweet potatoes and bland chicken fingers. I wasn't nervous, and I didn't notice any ticks, but Martha still had to walk me to the restroom so I could do a small pre-dinner ritual washing of my hands and face. I noticed the cracks in my hands were gone, leaving just smooth skin, and it made me smile.

When we returned to the cafeteria, we resumed our places next to Didi.

"What are you thinking about, Didi?" said Martha. "Why do you have that big grin like you're hiding something under your hat?"

"Tomorrow we have Parent Visit, Martha," he said. "I'm just

excited to tell my mom about some of my newest exploits. *Wolf Blitzer!*"

Martha looked at me, and I looked at her. Junior didn't even blink or put down his book, but just kept reading.

"That's how I feel about the chicken fingers, Didi," I said. "They've been around a long time, but they know how to manage a room. We all want that."

Martha laughed and rested her giant chest on the table.

"Sorry," he said.

"Don't apologize," said Martha. "No shame there. Just tell Addie what you were telling me."

Didi sighed, acting like he was above recounting his grand adventures again, but I could tell he was excited to talk. I'd never really given Didi the time to just relax and talk because I'd been too caught up in my own therapy those first few weeks.

Dr. Ramirez kept telling me to worry about others more, but to also focus on my own treatment. I didn't know how to live within that paradox.

But maybe Dr. Ramirez was wrong, maybe I needed to get lost in others and do the opposite of what he said in order to leave my mind. Maybe not focusing on my treatment at all would help. Whatever. As for my own therapy, I was starting to relax into the routine a little, and my blinking was a little less obnoxious—as were the washing and the rituals.

"It's all pretty boring, really," Didi said. "I mean, I did most of it before I got in this place. I think people were scared I was doing too much too fast."

"Then bore me," I said.

"Well, I've written dissertations on pretty much everything you can imagine. I wrote a dissertation on imagination, actually. I came up with the term 'no-holds-barred entertainment' that critics so often use."

"Wow," I said.

"Oh, he ain't done, honey," said Martha.

"I am the embodiment of success, Addie. In fact, I invented the word 'success' because I needed a new word to define my lifestyle. If you want an 'in' in life, talk to me. I know it all because I've done it all. I've been to every popular tourist site, and by so doing, made it even more 'must see!' I don't sleep or take naps because I don't need them."

"But you have to be in your room at night, so what do you do?" I said.

"I remind myself how I let old Benny-boy-Franklin discover electricity because he needed more street cred. I already had more than enough. I wrote the first draft of the Declaration of Independence when I was taking a break from creating a de facto US national government and forming the Continental Army. I helped end the Safavid dynasty by siding with the Afghans. Why? I was bored. I founded the New York Stock and Exchange Board at the same time I was involved in convincing Upper Canada to end slavery. I invented the Spinning Sally but realized my friend Hargreaves needed an income boost, so I let him name it the Spinning Jenny and take all the credit. I wrote a dissertation on 'taking the credit.' I carved the Rosetta Stone. I wrote a song called 'Incredible Grace,' though, obviously, someone stole my idea. I blackmailed Russia so the US could have Alaska—what can I say? I'm a sucker for salmon. I'm also clearly a sucker for astronomy because I gave Tycho Brahe his golden nose. Detachable? Yes. Why? Because I care."

"How old are you, Didi?" I said, but Martha shushed me, and Didi kept talking.

"Before I came along, Einstein only had a theory of relativity; I made it 'special.' I gave Orion a belt because, hey, even hunters are fashion conscious."

"That's cute," said Martha. "Hadn't heard that bit."

"Agreed," I said. "Quite an impressive past."

"I also found out where the wild things were and gave the idea to an unknown writer. I wrote a dissertation on 'giving' and gave the resultant money away. No surprise. I showed Monet the pond with the lilies. Please. You can't expect a guy like that to find water lilies by himself."

I rolled my eyes at Martha but was actually too impressed by the sheer range of lies to stop listening. I saw Junior put his book down and lean on the table to get a better ear on the conversation. Well, more of a diatribe or monologue or whatever Didi wanted to call it, who apparently was much older than I'd originally suspected.

"I came up with surfing because I knew the participants would provide numerous slang terms for eternal use. I wrote a dissertation on 'slang,' and it was *epically rad.*"

Junior laughed and walked over to our table to sit next to Didi.

Didi didn't flinch. He just kept talking. "The Constitution of the United States of America was my idea, but I wanted our 'fathers' to have some feeling of 'founding.' They say history is written by the winners, but please don't make that word plural," he said, putting his hand on mine. "I wrote history. *Miley Cyrus!* Sorry. Michelangelo painted the Sistine Chapel using a paint-by-numbers scheme that I created, and Raphael was a witness if you need proof. I wrote a dissertation on 'proof.'"

By this point, Martha was grabbing at her stomach and totally losing it.

I thought it was all pretty funny, but I was more intrigued by the fact that Didi could lie to himself in such grand ways. It was mesmerizing.

"Did Newton get hit in the head with an apple? Yes. Did that apple fall from a tree above him? No. *Hall and Oates!* Sorry."

"Don't be ashamed of Hall and Oates, sweetie," said Martha, but Didi just kept going.

"I threw the apple at him because he fell asleep during my lecture on something I had recently discovered: gravity. Deductive logic was my idea. That reminds me—Doyle owes me for Holmes," he said, pointing to the heavens. "The only reason Cooper had a popular book is me. I found the last Mohican while I was hiking Everest barefoot, and I shared the story with Jim. I told Frost to take the road less traveled. C'mon, Frosty, be original. I wrote a dissertation on 'originality' for all the boring people. Hey, boring people, read it!"

He yelled that last bit. I laughed, and I saw that Junior was too.

Martha leaned close to me and said, "Most of this is new. I just heard the first piece, I guess."

"I can speak English, Arabic, German, French, Finnish, Russian, and Urdu all in sign language, using only one hand. I am extremely important. I created the 'high five' and the 'thumbs-up,'" he said.

Didi took a big breath and grabbed his water and slurped it down. None of us responded. Junior stared at him with his mouth open and his eyebrows creased. Martha was doubled over and patting Didi on the back between laughs. Didi looked serious, like he wasn't lying at all.

I gave him a calm smile. "Sounds like you've got it all figured out."

"Had it figured out ages ago," he said. "That's probably why Mom makes me stay in this place. I'm too dangerous to be out there roaming around. *'She's my cherry pie'!* Sorry," he said.

He always covered his mouth after he shouted a guilty pleasure band or song or show or newscaster or channel, and I could tell it made him feel bad because his face always went beet red. But it didn't make anybody upset, so I didn't know why he was so embarrassed.

"You got five minutes till the movie," said Martha, wiping tears from her eyes. "I'm gonna swap with Jenkins and get it started for you. It's the one you requested a week ago, Addie. That Hamlet comedy, something or other. Hey, Didi, you mind if I record you saying all that stuff some time for me?"

"Wouldn't be the first time," he said, confident.

"Son, you've got a mind on you like nothing I've seen," she said.

Martha disappeared around the corner, and we all stood to empty our trays and head to the movie room. I figured Martha probably shouldn't tease Didi like that, but he didn't seem to mind. It made me wonder what kind of training the orderlies got before joining the ward.

I was ecstatic when I heard that the movie I requested was going to be the film that night. There was so much to look forward to, what with the movie and then a Parent Visit the next morning.

I walked next to Didi with a big smile on my face. "You're going to tell your mother all of that? Won't she feel overwhelmed?"

Didi looked down at his feet with a smug, little, side-smile. "She'll be proud."

"Who wouldn't be?"

"Thanks, Addie," he said.

At that moment, I realized he was at least partially aware of the grandiose nature of his comments. Therapy must have been hard for him initially, maybe even consistently.

"I'm excited to see everybody's parents—or parent. It's always fun to see what features people get from their parents, or how they have similar mannerisms or whatever. Kind of fun."

"Parent Visits are nice, but they also make me feel bad for Fitz," said Didi.

"Why?" I said.

Junior hit his book against the palm of his hand and sighed. "Fitz's mom has never visited."

"Never?"

"Not once," said Didi.

Five

was almost late to the movie because I stopped to look out the big bay windows in the hallway leading to the entertainment area. Birds dotted the sky like some type of Morse code. Small specks in the fading blue. Short. Short. Short. Long. Long. Long. Long. Long.

Seattle had these gorgeous clouds chattering to one another all over the darkening sky. The trees looked like little spikes dotting the landscape, the mountains rising out of distant waters, the landscape beginning to blur. I was caught up in the view and thinking about the essay question on Morris's exam. Why did Beckett write in such an absurd manner? Why have two characters sitting around, waiting for something to come along? I couldn't figure it out. Why all the rituals? Why not leave instead of sitting there and waiting for days? Why trade hats instead of skipping town?

"Did you reread those notes like I told you to?" said Fitz, when I saw him in the movie room. He gave me that goofy smile with his handsome gap.

He looked calm and casual—at least he was consistent about

that. But maybe that was his way of hiding all the inconsistencies inside. His hair was curlier than usual, some strands falling over his eyes.

I was aware I didn't look all that presentable—red T-shirt with sweats and my hair in a bun. How exciting, I know.

Martha waved at me, and I returned her kindness. She had this semi-smile that was more than I was used to getting from an orderly, or even a doctor. I liked it because her smile seemed genuine. I liked Martha—a lot more than any of the other orderlies.

Martha dimmed the lights, and I sat next to Fitz. Didi and Junior and Leah were in the first row. I hated front-row seats at movies, but I was glad Leah had people next to her. Wolf was sitting two seats away. He had this massive head of curly hair that was never combed, and big bushy eyebrows. I think his eyes were brown, but I never really saw them closely through all that hair.

"My notes were a mess," I said to Fitz. "What did you want me to read?"

"That thing about the hero's journey. Looked like you needed to give it some more thought," he said with a mocking smile.

I knew he was half teasing, but I also knew the other half was seriousness and an eagerness to hear my thoughts. Like, when people are sarcastic only it's funny because there's some truth in it, right?

"That journey is not realistic, Fitz," I said. "Real life is right here in the psych ward. Real life is therapy. Real life is the truth: most drives don't end up on the fairway. Most meat is tough. Most people grow up to be just people and nothing more. Most people leave here and only recover some small portion of their identity. Most people struggle to find real love. Most people struggle to find real happiness."

Fitz didn't respond for a minute. Then he said, "Wow. That's super depressing."

"It's true," I said, feeling bad that I'd mentioned anything. But it's how I felt sometimes, and I thought he should know.

The introduction to the movie was playing. I was excited to see the movie I'd picked, but I was also interested in my discussion with Fitz.

"What if you could try, though? Just once. What if you tried the journey just once, Addie Foster?" he said, taking off his bandana and rolling it in his hands. "What if you tried for real happiness? Wouldn't that help answer your essay question?"

"I don't know," I said.

"You're too good for this world, Addie. You won't break the rules, even if it's to answer an essay question for a grade in school?"

"It's not about the grade," I said.

"Then what is it about?

"It's about figuring out what Beckett was trying to say by telling such absurd stories filled with ridiculous rituals. I have rituals. We all have rituals. But there's something more because the thing doesn't have an answer. It's funny, sure, but I'm after what's behind that humor."

"Okay. So take off the mask," Fitz said.

"Whatever. Let's just watch the movie. I love this film."

It's true that the essay question was starting to consume my thoughts—my obsessive tendencies were taking over in a big way, compounded by the fact I was forced to stay in my room. I was only allowed a certain number of bathroom visits per day because of my washing. It seemed like my obsessions wound back to the same starting point the more I thought about that question on

Morris's exam. Reading more about the time period and other writers and other works wasn't helping me as much as I thought and hoped it would. I needed to change the rules.

Maybe I needed to see the world from a different perspective, like one filled with country singers' voices or something like that. Maybe Fitz was right. Maybe I needed to leave a safe place and go against everything I thought I needed in order to find out what I wanted to know.

It was all so confusing.

"Wait. Is this some rom-com or something?" said Fitz.

"I want my horse!" shouted Wolf.

"Somebody get this man his horse!" shouted Fitz, pointing to Wolf.

Martha told us to be quiet, and Jenkins came back to check on Wolf.

"You're so obnoxious," I said.

"He should have his horse," said Fitz.

"I agree."

Jenkins helped Wolf calm back down, though he continued to mutter about his horse under his breath as the movie rolled on.

"I like those movies sometimes. But, no. This movie is not a rom-com, but a tragicomedy," I said.

"A tragi-what?"

"Tragicomedy. It is tragic because . . . well, I don't want to give it away. But it's mostly about the comedy. It's both. Whatever. Just watch," I said.

We watched for about fifteen minutes before Fitz spoke up. I swear, he couldn't keep his mouth shut for very long. In fact, I'm sure he set some sort of record that night.

"So it's a parody," said Fitz. "I like Hamlet. Dude was crazy, but at least he made it entertaining."

"It's absurd."

"Most parodies are," said Fitz.

"No, I mean it was written during the time of the Theatre of the Absurd. Just like the play I'm reading."

Fitz sighed heavily. "If it's about waiting, I don't care to watch. But I like comedy. I prefer comedy, I should say."

"Yeah, you should say that," I said.

He nudged my leg with his leg. I liked playing the literal game with him.

"And based on your favorite movie so far, you like comedy, too," said Fitz.

"I like it when writers pay attention to language. I like this movie because of the writing."

Fitz laughed quietly into his lame sweater. "You might be the only person I've ever met who said they like a movie because of the writing." He leaned forward on his elbows.

"Tom Stoppard said that words deserve respect, and the right ones in the right order might nudge the world a little," I said.

I think he could sense how serious I was because he sat up and nodded without a goofy grin or sardonic response. It was easy to explain to others why I enjoyed writers like Stoppard—they nudged the world a little with everything they wrote. And because I was stuck in obsessions and rituals and ticks and washing and thinking and blinking and coughing and sniffling and retreating into my captive mind, I needed to feel those little nudges. To me, those nudges were more like earthquakes. They woke me from my stupor of thought, my haze of obsessive thinking, and led me to a clearing in the fog.

Words saved me from myself. That might sound corny, but it's true. Without good writing, I'd be so far down that rabbit hole that I wouldn't ever find my way back home. I knew that, and because I knew that, I was aware that if I held on to that kind of writing, that kind of thinking and hoping and believing, then one day I'd emerge from that hole and live a life on the top of the world and not somewhere buried in my disorder.

And maybe even I could move the world someday—just nudge it a little. Maybe I could wear happiness not as a mask, but as a part of my self. The real thing.

"Good writing takes me out of myself. I know that sounds weird. But, whatever."

"It doesn't sound weird, Addie Foster. It's beautiful," he said. He sat back up and stared at the screen. "I'd really like to show you something beautiful, too."

"Yeah?"

"But it's not in the psych ward," said Fitz.

"Don't define yourself by where you are. That would be a mistake," I said.

The pace of my heart increased rapidly. I placed my hand on my chest and started counting, and I think it bothered Fitz. But then he started laughing, loudly, and he rolled off his chair and onto the tiled floor.

"What?" I said, worried. "What did I say?"

He kept laughing until he was crying.

Martha heard the noise and walked over with Jenkins. I didn't like Jenkins. He was an older male orderly with a paunch and these really big, nasty, peppered lamb-chop sideburns that took up half his face. And he had horrible breath—such horrible breath.

"What's going on?" said Martha.

"Everything okay here?" said Jenkins, looking just at me.

Fitz gained some control and sat up quickly, probably afraid of being sent to the isolated part of the ward where they kept patients who were on "suicide watch" or in some other type of special state that required a close eye and more bodies to observe or guide or care or whatever.

Junior turned to Fitz, looking really annoyed.

"I'm fine," he said. "Just two cuckoo birds talking about living in the cuckoo's nest." He flashed a massive, sarcastic grin at Martha and Jenkins.

"We're okay," I said, assuring Martha. She didn't look like she fully bought it, but she walked away with Jenkins and left us alone. Martha un-paused the movie, and the room was quiet again.

"What on earth was that?" I said, leaning into Fitz.

"It's funny."

"It's not funny," I said.

"When you showed up after our failed escape attempt, I took all the anger I had, all the frustration, all the shadows following me around these halls, all the voices talking behind my back, and all that mess up here," he said, pointing to his head, "and I was able to direct it and control it like I never thought possible. I took all that and put it on you. It's not fair, but it's what I did. I shouldn't have, but it seemed to work for a while."

"I didn't know that," I said.

"I know. And here I am trying to talk to you about getting out, about something that matters to me, and you stop to count your heartbeats."

"That's not fair," I said. "I can't control it sometimes. You can't control the voices, can you?"

"You're right. I guess I was just counting on you, but nobody in here is reliable. I'm not. I'd already told Junior and Didi that we were going to try to bust out of here again, but we can't count on each other. You were right. In the end, we're open with nobody. The walls are too high, too deep. Nobody is set up to climb something like that. We just don't have the skill set or the right equipment."

"You're not just asking me because I'm another capable body?" I said, feeling sheepish at making that comment after his about breaking down walls.

"For being so bright, you sure don't recognize when someone has a real crush on you, do you?"

Fitz sighed and sat back in his chair and looked at the ceiling, placing his bandana over his face.

I thought about what he'd said: crush. I was about to count my heartbeats again, but I stayed my hand. *Crush.* It consumed my thoughts. *Crush.*

In that moment, I realized I had unwittingly become some kind of source of hope or something for the other inpatients. Fitz had planned on me for another escape attempt, and he wanted me to go with him because he liked me, not because he needed me. Well, maybe he needed me, but in a romantic way. Whatever. Get over it.

I'd never thought there would be any reason for me to escape because the ward held my redemption. I'd never considered the fact that doing something for the others was a way, or could be a way, of finding answers for myself.

Maybe Fitz was right. Maybe putting my faith in other people would stop me from focusing on my own heartbeat. Maybe I could hold my hand on someone else's chest and listen to that instead. Maybe my heart was figuratively small because I didn't put it in touch with other hearts often enough.

I reached out my hand and placed it on Fitz's chest. He didn't move. He breathed lightly, and the bandana softly lifted, then fell back over the contours of his face. He took the bandana off and looked at me with all this hope. I didn't know what to do with it—it was consuming.

We both turned to the movie and let it fill in the space between us, fill in the part between the seconds. When the movie ended, I looked at Fitz.

"Amazing, right?"

"Yeah," he said. "But I didn't like that they died."

"They had to die. It's absurd, sure, but to make it a tragedy those characters have to die."

Then he turned to his left and shouted, "Shut up!" He glanced at me. "Sorry. You know the drill."

"Who was it? Quentin?"

Fitz gave me a funny look. He shook his head and stood up.

Junior stood up at the same time and threw his chair into the wall next to the TV on the roll-in cart, narrowly missing Jenkins, who was sitting nearby. Junior looked at the rest of us before stepping to the door, only to be restrained by Jenkins, who took him away. Maybe to his room, or maybe somewhere else he could watch him. That left us with Martha.

Fitz sat back down and put his hand on mine to keep me from standing. He could see that my eyebrows were raised and that I was worried about Junior.

"Calm yourself. He does that all the time. Actually, I'm

surprised he didn't break the drywall. He doesn't ever hurt people, though, so don't worry."

I looked at his hand on mine, and he did the same. There was a nervousness in his glance that I liked. He kept his hand there and looked at me.

"Addie Foster. Who knew you were such a fan of words?"

"You knew. That's why I slaughtered you at Boggle," I said.

I worried I'd stepped onto shaky ground considering how he'd walked away from our game weeks before, so I put my other hand on my chest and apologized.

"Don't apologize," Fitz said. "Just let me try to redeem myself tomorrow."

"Deal," I said.

We all separated to our respective rooms after that, and Martha walked with me to mine.

"I see you looking at that boy all the time, Miss Addie," she said. "It's not hard to see that you two like one another."

"That obvious, huh?"

"I think it's cute," she said.

"Gross. Nothing's cute."

Martha opened my door for me, closing it behind me as I walked in and sat on the bed. The moonlight was playing on the wall, a few small shafts of light giving the boring room a little character.

I put my head on the pillow and stared at the slats of light on the wall. I thought about how every good story needs an adventure—and if I was the protagonist, I needed to have something that I was after. Could it be as simple as needing an answer to a question that was truly making me anxious? Could it be as simple as wanting to help the guy with the handsome gap?

I mean, Doc kept encouraging me to do things that I wouldn't normally do, try things I normally wouldn't try. He kept talking about the value of exposure therapy. Think and step outside of the way I was living. Take risks. Be daring.

Well, how was I supposed to do that inside the ward? Maybe Doc was asking me to step outside, literally? I liked that thought. And if I helped Fitz, I would be finding answers for him while also finding an answer for myself about Dr. Morris's question. I mean, I would just be doing what the doctors wanted me to do. Maybe not in the way they meant it, but it's all semantics, right?

After another hour of thinking it through, I knocked on my door.

"Thought you were asleep," said Martha.

"Just need to pee real quick," I said.

I walked to the bathroom, and Martha went back to her desk. I knew she didn't care how much time I took, as long as it wasn't outrageous. I took a detour on the way back from the bathroom and slid a note under Fitz's door. I imagined him smiling that goofy smile as he opened my note.

> *Difficult roads often lead to beautiful destinations. I'm in. Are you? Y/N*
> —*The Comic Character Who Is Way Funnier and Smarter Than the Tragic Character*

I stayed by the door for a minute and heard him laugh on the other side—probably at the over-the-top quote I'd stolen from the sign hanging above Tabor's desk. So ridiculous.

It made me smile, hearing Fitz laugh. I walked back to my room and waved to Martha, then went right back to bed, where I spent the next three hours obsessing over Morris's essay question and thinking about what I'd just agreed to do. I wasn't the type to do something like that. Not me. Not Addie Foster.

Then again, was I really sure what my type was? Was I really going to break out of the psych ward? Well, why in the name of Zeus's beard do they put up all those freaking obnoxious quotes everywhere if they don't want us to listen to them? Why inspire us and meet with us all day, every day, if not to motivate us to take action?

The next morning found me in Dr. Riddle's office. I had a lot on my mind. I was so excited about the idea of my upcoming adventure that I didn't really take note of the schedule I had to stick to in the regular, ho-hum of the day-to-day. I was sure Doc knew somehow, that he'd found the note or that Fitz had confessed. It made me feel jumpy.

The idea alone was keeping me in a state of excited anticipation. Isn't that how it always works? We get all excited about something, and then it turns out that the anticipation was better than the real thing. Oscar Wilde said there are the two tragedies in life: not getting what one wants, and getting what one wants. Makes sense.

I guess my life had kind of worked that way. But I was determined to find out who I was and what I was about. Maybe the real thing would actually be better than the anticipation this time.

"Parent Visit today, Addie. Doubling up on visits this week for the holiday. Are you excited to see your mother?"

"Of course," I said.

Doc started scribbling in his stupid little folder. He had to know something was up. He never took that long to write down morning notes. He was also more chipper than usual. Maybe because he was planning some devious way to get me to confess after already getting the details from Fitz? What a snake.

"Are you writing down the fact that I'm excited to see my mother? Seems pretty pointless, Doc. I mean, how is that going to help me medically?"

He smiled and put his pen down. "I like to write down more than just comments, Addie. I'm writing down notes about your mood at the moment. You seem happy. Again. Still," he said.

"Did you know that there is a ninety-nine percent chance that a breath inhaled today somewhere in the world will contain a molecule from Shakespeare's dying breath?"

"I didn't know that, in fact. Seems like things are okay, though."

"Things are better than before," I said, looking around his desk for the stress ball. He noticed what I was doing. My palms were sweaty, and I balled the cuffs of my sweater in my hands. I tried to think of another random fact to throw him off the scent. He probably noticed that too because he wrote down another note. He had to know something.

"Junior broke it," he said. "Sorry. Don't worry. I'll get another one soon."

Doc wrote down a few more things and then closed the folder and checked his watch. Maybe he was determining just how long he was going to let me sweat it out before he confronted me.

"You have plenty of time for breakfast before the visit. We can talk later this evening. I unfortunately have to be somewhere right now. I just wanted a few moments to see how you were doing."

"Peachy," I said.

"Good."

Doc stood, and I realized he was ushering me out of the

room. Whatever. That was great news. Maybe he didn't know anything about the note. And I was hungry. Yes, I'd put on a couple more pounds. I told myself not to worry about it, but that was only to keep myself from throwing chairs into walls like Junior. How was I to keep from noticing my weight? C'mon.

I ate quickly and didn't talk much. Everybody seemed pretty tired that morning. Leah was eating slowly. She looked defeated, but she also looked like she wasn't in the mood to talk. Didi wasn't there.

Junior was slopping up some applesauce. I never really noticed how bad Junior's acne was until the sun hit his face. I felt sorry for him, having to deal with that kind of thing when people were so judgy about appearance.

At least in the psych ward he didn't have to worry about that too much. Whatever. It's not like the psych ward was some haven of no judgment when the doctors were constantly pointing out things we needed to work on. Actually, no, I was horribly mistaken. The whole place was set up to judge us.

Fitz walked in just as I was finishing up my yogurt. I didn't want to be late for Parent Visit. Then I remembered what Junior had said about Fitz and his mother, and I felt awful. If you ever feel really low about your own life, just look around, right? Get a little perspective.

"I'll be waiting at the Boggle board," he said. "For the rematch."

"Difficult road there," I said.

"Leading to a beautiful destination," he said.

I had to hurry or I would've asked him more about his plan, but it didn't make sense to talk about it then and there. He looked sleepy, and his hair was a mess, which made me snigger as I made my way to the meeting room.

Dr. Tabor was there, helping the parents find their seats. Leah, Didi, and Junior walked in right after me, and each one hugged their parents. I didn't see Wolf. He was probably at the front desk, asking about his horse. I was the only one with one parent there. Well, I guess Fitz only had one parent, but she never showed up.

"Did you get the goods?" Mom asked me.

"I got the goods," I said in a horrible attempt at a Brooklyn accent. "The goods is real nice. The goods is exactly the kind we been after. They gonna sell big. Get me a new load when yous gets a chance. And hurry on that—we gotta get the money to Vinny the Face before we're out on the street."

I had no idea where the made-up narrative was going, but I kept rolling with it because it made Mom smile.

"I see you haven't lost your penchant for tall tales."

"Well, you asked me that like we were in some gangster movie from the '50s. What do you mean, 'the goods'?"

Mom smiled and rested her purse on the table. She had really big brown eyes and short-cropped blonde hair with a streak of purple in the front. She was all about trying new hairstyles, despite my guiding comments. I liked that about her. She had this rebellious side that I was still learning about. Yes, learning about in her, but also learning about in myself. Maybe I was more like Mom than I realized.

"I mean the materials Dr. Morris had me drop off. I think he also had copies of his notes in there. Did Dr. Riddle get you the books and the assignments?"

"Yeah. Thanks, Mom. I've really enjoyed the reading and the

notes. Sounds nerdy, but it keeps me thinking about more important stuff."

"You're getting better, Addie. That is what's most important," she said.

She went on to tell me about her current batch of students and how none of them knew what the Civil War was about or who'd won. I couldn't believe the things she told me about her classroom. Were video games really winning out over the more important stuff, or even the most basic of facts?

I wished I could go back in time to the first Civil War reenactment. Not the real battles, just the reenacted ones. I know it sounds odd, but it would be way better than the real thing because the recreation would have all of the dedication and commitment and none of the death.

Then I started thinking about those late-night infomercials and imagined one for those reenactment types: The commercial would open on someone tripping over an Enfield rifle-musket and cursing, then the screen would go to black-and-white and a giant red X would cover everything and a voice would say, "Tired of having nowhere to store your Civil War memorabilia? Tired of tripping over reenactment weapons and enlisted shell jackets?" Then it would come back into color and show a guy happily sitting in a study with a shelf behind him and all of these prearranged hooks for his Civil War gear. "Those days are over with the new Civil War Shelf-Mate made with military-grade steel!" The ad would have gone on if Mom's face hadn't pulled me from my ridiculous thoughts.

Maybe I really was an outlier, in that I preferred reading to watching movies or playing video games. But I didn't want to assume that—it felt too depressing. Whatever.

Mom had me recount the previous week and what I'd discussed in my various therapeutic sessions. What a snooze fest.

"Does it look like I'm gaining weight?" I said, nervous. I needed to know if she saw it; she was the only one honest enough to tell me.

"You look wonderful," said Mom.

"She says, lying," I said. "You used your Mom voice when you said that, which parents only use when they're trying to protect the child. I get it. You're nice. Whatever. Thanks."

"Honestly?"

"Please," I said.

"Well, I knew you'd be growing up in here," said Mom, leaning back from the table and looking down at my stomach. "I just didn't expect that you'd be growing *out*."

We both started laughing. Only Mom could say that to me and not totally throw me for one. I wiped tears away from my face, and we held hands on the table.

"Thank you for your honesty."

"It's not much. You'll lose the weight in a beat once you're back at it. Either way, it doesn't matter. Don't dwell on it. You still look wonderful. And I mean that," she said. "Honestly."

"Would you mind grabbing another play for me?" I said, wanting to change the subject so I would stop focusing on my appearance. "I think it will help with what I'm doing for Dr. Morris."

"Sure. What is it called?"

"*The Real Inspector Hound*," I said. "Oh, and grab the two on either side of it. I'll need those three for this essay I'm working on." Truthfully, I had no idea what the two books on either side were, hence my vague request.

She agreed to bring me the books. Luckily I'd remembered that I had stashed a few hundred dollars inside the play, months before, when I was trying to save up for my senior trip. Mom said that she'd fly me wherever I wanted to go, within reason, but that I had to pay for anything I wanted to buy while I was there. Considering I was probably going to be in the hospital instead of on that trip, it didn't really matter what that money was used for. And Fitz could use it instead.

Mom was happy to help. She came around to my side of the table and basically lifted me out of my chair and hugged me tight. I sank into that hug. I think she was worried I was sad.

"What's the matter?" she asked me.

"Mostly atoms," I said. "And they're made of subatomic particles." I squeezed her tight to let her know I was doing fine.

"Still my Addie," she said.

I sometimes forgot how lucky I was to have a parent who cared that much. She went on and on about how much progress I was making in such a short time and how proud she was of me and about all the other things going on at home that I'd missed and how I shouldn't worry and that I'd catch up on everything in no time. Honestly, *The Great British Baking Show* was the last thing on my mind.

Six

Junior was in the exercise room sitting on a stationary bike, but not pedaling. He was stationary on a stationary. I'd been in that position before, and I knew how he felt. I should've talked to him, but I guess I wasn't ready to do what Ramirez was asking. Not just then, anyway.

Mostly because I was on my way to defend my Boggle prowess.

I thought about Fitz waiting for me and wondered if I was just interested in him because there were no other options. I mean, I figured outside of the hospital I would still be interested in him, but we didn't go to the same school, so we probably never would have met so maybe it wasn't fair to say at that point. And maybe that's why he liked me. I didn't know.

I figured we were both just having fun and not really looking at what we might have to face outside of these hospital walls. Maybe we'd just walk away from one another after it was all over. Maybe we'd never talk.

No. I don't believe the universe is that lazy. I don't believe meeting Fitz was a coincidence. He was someone I was supposed to meet. Or the other way around. Or both.

Soft light was playing on the coffee table at Fitz's feet. He was leaning back in a beanbag chair and staring at the ceiling. A small overhead fan spun quietly, sweeping short shadows in a soft circle. He didn't notice me walk in, but he looked up when I jumped into the beanbag on the opposite side of the table, throwing up dust all around us.

"What's with the bandana? I need to know," I said. "I keep meaning to ask, but I always forget."

"Apparently not *always*," he said.

"I mean, I can get by with the yoga shirts because they're funny—sort of—but I don't understand the tie-dyed bandana. It makes you look like you're trying to be a rebel from, like, the eighties. And that doesn't work. Then again, you don't own a fanny pack. If you did, I don't think we could be friends."

Fitz smiled and sat up. "Addie Foster. So superficial." He toyed with the fabric of the beanbag, avoiding eye contact with me for some reason. "It's something I had on the day I was admitted. I guess I wear it because it's kind of like a security blanket. I feel weird not wearing it. Stupid, but it's true."

I sat for a minute, thinking about security guards walking around with giant blankets. Stupid. Whatever. I didn't know what to say, and the silence was awkward.

"You know, we have tons to talk about, Addie," he said, shifting in his seat and looking more spirited. "I already asked Dr. Riddle for a day in the chapel this Sunday. He was surprised, but the docs—plural—are never here on Sundays, and it will give us time away from the orderlies and everybody else."

"Chapel?"

"Yeah," said Fitz. "Pastor Michaels offers a sermon in the hospital chapel every single week, even though we always turn it down. I told Doc I wanted to go this week to figure out the cosmos or whatever."

"Why can't we just talk at lunch?" I said.

"Orderlies. Word of this gets out, and it won't work," he said.

"I don't think Martha would care."

"She might. And it's not Martha I'm worried about," he said. "Jenkins almost caught us the first time because we blabbed in public instead of somewhere quiet. He has his eye on us at all times."

"True," I said.

Fitz grabbed the Boggle square and shook the blocks around in the small, encased plastic box like he was playing the maracas.

"Dance won't help you beat me," I said. "That rhythm will only increase my prowess."

"Addie Foster. I can tell I'm in your head. Your palms are sweaty. You're shaking in your slip-resistant booties. I'm going to redeem myself."

The letters fell into place, and he tore the sheet from the top and we started writing. I hesitated before writing my first words. *Spring. Tailor. Sailed.* I didn't want to upset Fitz, and I still wasn't sure if it was his competitive nature that made him split the first time, or if I had done something wrong. He said *warbler* was just a word, but I believe in the power of one word. I let it slide and kept writing.

"Time!" I yelled, shaking the blocks so he couldn't keep writing.

"Methinks the lady doth end the game too soon," said Fitz, writing down *protest* as his final word. He set his pencil aside and sat back in the beanbag chair. I figured we would compare words later, though I could tell by the amount of words alone I'd whooped him, which made me not want to say anything. Fitz was too caught up in the plan to care about the score, and I was too caught up in Fitz to care about much else.

"So Pastor Michaels leaves a half hour at the end of the sermon for people to pray. I also heard that he leaves the room, though he's not supposed to, to allow for the best spiritual experience or something. I don't know. Sounds like the perfect place to talk, right? If we all say we want to go to the sermon, we can discuss the plan without fear of word getting out. Leah can make sure we sound legitimate—she knows the scriptures."

I leaned back and watched the fan spin for a moment before responding. I had always been impulsive, but I'd never gone that far off the path in life. I mean, I watched baking shows with my mom for fun. Maybe that was sad. Maybe it was safe. Or maybe it was just perfect. I couldn't say.

"I don't want to guilt you into this, Addie," he said. Then he started laughing. "That's disgusting."

"What?"

"Shut up!" he yelled to his right, leaning away from me. "I'm sorry," he said. "Not you. You know how Willy gets. Such a jerk sometimes. Trying to distract me from the real thing, right here, right now."

"It's okay," I said.

I started blinking in an alternating pattern because my anxiety was through the roof at the thought of going to a chapel and lying to a pastor about why we needed prayer time or whatever. Lying—to a pastor. C'mon.

My mind felt like an unsettled Boggle board. I kept looking for words.

Church. Prayer. Cheat. Legality. Sin.

I tapped my fingers on my knees and counted, but quickly pushed those thoughts aside and tried to focus on the moment with Fitz.

"A great pleasure in life is doing what people say you cannot do," I said.

Fitz looked over his shoulder, like I was reading directly from one of those annoying quotes posted below the big windows in the hallway.

"It's not from a sign," I said.

"I was gonna say," he said. "I mean, it sounded way better than something on the walls in here."

"That's because it's from an essayist. And it's a thing I've never experienced. I guess it's time to start living the words instead of just reading them."

I was surprised by my own desire to rebel, to run, to seek beyond the walls of the hospital. I was surprised by how much I wanted it. I thought of Mom and the purple streak in her hair and figured I was just allowing my genes to work their way in to my soul, that double helix of DNA spiraling through my chest and curling its way around and through my heart.

"One thing you don't know about me is that my OCD makes me incredibly compulsive," I said. Fitz stared at me, waiting. "So I know this is all going to happen, whether it works out or not."

"Um. It's part of the name, Addie," he said. "Obsessive *Compulsive* Disorder."

"Well, it's not like it's about the obsessions. Not just that. I'm compulsive about everything. If I say I'm going to do it, I always follow through."

"Tell me where to sign."

"What?"

"Sounded cooler in my head," said Fitz. "Like one of those things they say in the movies when things seem to be working out and you want to say something that supports what is being talked about, but in a cool way."

"Very far from cool," I said.

"Yeah." He shrugged. "Worth a shot."

"Nope."

"Addie Foster," he said. "Why such a Conversation Czar? Cut me some slack."

"I'm the epitome of cool," I said.

"That sounds more like a Didi comment," said Fitz.

"True. Where is Didi?"

I picked up the Boggle board and turned it in my hand. After shaking it a few times, I set it down and looked at Fitz. I held my hand over the pieces, thinking about Junior sitting on the stationary bike in the exercise room. All alone.

"Why don't we get together with the others and start working this thing out?"

"Because we all have therapy on different schedules," he said, mimicking a British accent.

"Not really a linguist, are you?"

"Give me a break! I'm trying. Besides, that's why the Sunday sermon is the perfect time to meet. Group Talk, movies, food— they all bring us together, but none of them bring us together in the safe way that we need. Also, no orderlies."

"Speaking of all of us," I said. "I didn't see you during Parent Visit."

I didn't want to let on that I'd been given information on the sly, so I tried to pretend like I had no idea why Fitz hadn't been there. I wanted to see what he'd say. Like, maybe he'd let on more about San Juan Island or something.

"Yeah," said Fitz. "My mom couldn't make it this week. And by next week we should be out of this place."

He looked defeated. I felt awful. I wondered why Fitz would lie like that. We were all dealing with some pretty heavy stuff, even if it was just waiting for a horse or whatever, but it seemed odd he'd lie about his mom when we'd been so open about everything so far.

But he didn't talk about it again.

Sunday rolled its way in much more slowly than I had expected. I guess because I'd spent most the week thinking about the upcoming planning session. We all spent the week thinking about it, I figured.

Group meetings that week with Tabor were stagnant because we kept looking at each other in furtive glances, fiddling with things, trying not to let on that anything was amiss. I knew Doc wasn't aware of our plan, but he still wrote a bunch of notes in that stupid folder, probably about how I seemed closed off or something. I read way too much into everything we did and heard, into every visit with Doc. He'd ask how things were going, and I'd curl the cuffs of my sweater in my palms and wonder if he knew. Of course he knew! My anxieties sloshed around in my mind endlessly.

Ramirez just kept telling me the same things: I needed to expose myself to uncomfortable situations and learn how to deal with the aftermath. I'd been trying this thing where, after I felt a compulsion, I wouldn't blink or go to the bathroom to wash my hands until I'd waited ten seconds, then thirty, then one minute, then two, then five, then ten. I got up to fifteen minutes, and eventually I'd forget that I was supposed to wash my hands. So, in that regard, that behavioral stuff was changing things.

I spent most of that week waiting in my own mind. I kept thinking about the characters in *Waiting for Godot* and why they were okay with waiting, playing out absurd rituals and mocking the engine of silliness around them, rotating hats and joking about everything instead of confronting the real reason Godot didn't show up or asking *why*. The only thing they are sure of in their life is that they are waiting. That's it. Waiting for Godot to show up. They say life will end if he doesn't show. They talk about leaving. But they don't move.

Dr. Morris's question was on repeat in my mind: *What are the characters waiting for, and why is it significant that it/he/she never shows up?*

Anyway, on Sunday, Pastor Michaels showed up. I guess I'd never really noticed him because he only came around once a week—and usually only for a brief moment in the morning to check if anybody wanted to join him in the chapel for a short sermon.

I wonder if Michaels thought that he'd received some crazy amazing answer to his prayers when he walked into the ward that Sunday and saw six inpatients patiently waiting for his arrival. Hallelujah! They're finally listening!

"I don't know whether to see y'all as angels, or make my way back through that door," he said, smiling.

He had this soft drawl to his voice that was kind of comforting.

"I told them you offered sermons for anybody interested. Every Sunday. Like clockwork," said Fitz.

"Still true," said Michaels. "But I seem to recall that the last time I saw you, you yelled country song lyrics at me and then walked away," he said, looking at Fitz. Then the pastor laughed. "But I'm not one to question true conversion or its process. Come, ye children of the Lord, let us walk to the chapel."

The pastor was really tall and lanky with an awkward gait and limbs that looked too long for his body. He looked like one of those twig bugs but with a suit that had shoulder pads too big for his frame, making him look even more ridiculous. He had soft eyes and round glasses and was balding, like Tabor. His ears were huge. He carried a Bible and would hold it across his stomach with both hands when he spoke. He had this massive underbite, and it always seemed like he was contemplating something.

I wondered if it was because his world required a different type of understanding, a different kind of language and communication between believers or something.

The walk to the chapel was pretty quiet. The halls were lined with garish oil-painting portraits of people with phony-sounding names on gold placards below their pictured, floating heads. Most of the placards also had a title before the name, depending on how much money the floating head in that painting had donated.

Some of the hospital wings were even named after those donors. Even the parking structure had someone's name on it. What a wonderful tribute. Give me a break. I bet they allocated rewards based on the amount donated because—a parking structure? C'mon. That person must have offended somebody or donated the money in all pennies. They got the shaft, for sure.

I wonder if they handed out plaques for small donations, like you got a brick on the outside of the building or something. Or maybe there was an *Alex Steiner* gold plaque screwed into one of the toilet stall doors because he only donated a five-dollar gift card. Big deal. Not worth it.

Still, I was grateful for the money they gave to help people. Not a bad way to spend, in my opinion.

What would I get my name on?

"If you donated money, what would you want named after you?" I whispered to Fitz as we shuffled along.

"Probably the game room. Maybe the pharmacy—lots of good medication jokes to be had there. You?"

"Probably prosthetics."

"That would cost you an arm," said Fitz.

"Too easy," I said. "But at least I'd know I had a hand in their recovery."

"And a leg," he said.

"I'd make them put my name on all the prosthetic eyeballs, too."

"Why?" said Fitz.

"Beauty is in the eye of the beholder."

Fitz laughed, and Michaels turned around and eyed us.

"That's awful. Beauty is in the eye socket of the beholder, more like. But I'd lose an eye for that," said Fitz, grabbing my hand and giving it a quick pulse.

I had a hard time concentrating when he did that. I started blinking at my alternating steps set against the reflective tile floor. I was so happy, and cleared my throat in sets of three, trying to stay calm, as Michaels turned back to check on us again.

After a few detours and up a flight of stairs, we walked up a ramp and into a small chapel. The doors had small, latticed, stained-glass windows on either side. I wasn't sure what religious moments were being depicted, but it looked like a lot of angels were doing a lot of talking to surprised people who were on their knees. A few people were holding books, and a few more had walking sticks or canes or something.

One that I really liked showed a boy on his knees with a pillar of light shooting straight down from the sky to the forest floor. It looked like it would be a pretty cool experience: like, unmediated truth straight from the head honcho. Pure truth. Beam me up! That's what I wanted to yell.

We filed into the room. There was a close, stifling smell, like mildew. There were five rows of really old wooden pews with their corners chipped and smudged, all lined up facing the lectern. Higher up there were these really cool latticed, handblown glass windows with little bubbles in the panes. The windows let in these cut-up squares of light that scattered themselves all over the chapel—little blocks of warmth spotting the floor.

Pastor Michaels pointed to the pews and told us to relax. He asked for our names first and hurried through them. Well, except for Leah. He made some joke about her being Jacob's wife and about how she stole seven years from her sister, Rachel, in a trick and then threw his head back like it was some hilarious joke. I didn't get it, but Leah smiled and laughed a little. I figured she knew the stories because her mother dropped off prayer beads for her one week.

She rubbed her hand through her hair and quietly stared at the stained glass. I thought she looked more upbeat since the last time I'd seen her. It was odd, seeing growth in other patients simply through body language.

The chapel was taller than I expected, but still cramped. Candles lined one side of the room below pictures of prophets or saints or something. Each pew had a hymnal resting on it. I didn't know any religious songs, but thankfully the pastor didn't ask us to sing. I imagined myself in that moment as some preacher on a soapbox at some revival, hollering from my tent about the truth, getting good followers to come my way.

Pastor Michaels stood at the lectern and looked at us, probably wondering why we had decided as a group to seek religion that day. But I think he was more eager for an audience than he would ever let on, so he spoke after a beat.

"I honestly didn't plan a sermon because I never get a response from your group, even though I set aside an hour every week for the adolescent psych ward. Sorry," he said, realizing he was talking to us and not thinking about these things to himself.

"I've been reading about Job lately. Y'all heard much of Job? I think his faith and determination and love in the wake of such incredible trials is something we can discuss and learn from."

"He's the guy that got, like, buried in crap," said Junior. "Right?"

I saw the pastor wince at the horrible word choice, but also kind of smile because it was such a colorful way of describing the situation. Junior didn't seem to notice or care.

"I've never heard it put that way, but yes. Job was buried in misfortunes brought on by a loving God. I know it doesn't seem loving, but look at the way Job responds. It's beautiful. He lost everything, and still he praised his Lord."

"Quite a shakedown," said Fitz. "Am I right?"

I sniggered and covered my mouth and tried to look away or like I was praying by dipping my head behind the pew. Pastor Michaels coughed, but it seemed like a fake cough designed to fill the awkward moment after Fitz's comment. He opened his Bible and was about to read when Didi yelled, *"The Fresh Prince of Bel-Air! Gilmore Girls!"*

The pastor looked shocked, so I quickly explained to him what Didi was dealing with.

"Pretty good choice there on the first one, Didi," said Fitz, under his breath. "I can't comment on the latter because I've never seen it."

I saw Didi smile at Fitz.

After that, the sermon was pretty uneventful, and felt more like Michaels was reading straight from the Bible rather than actually discussing the doctrine or teachings or whatever with us. He didn't seem to mind that Leah was already praying near the candles in one corner, ignoring his sermon. Fitz was responding quietly to remarks from Lyle or Toby or Willy or whoever for a while before going quiet.

I looked up at the handblown glass windows and watched the light play off the small bubbles. I wondered how that air got trapped in there. Then I thought of how intricate even something as simple as a window is when it is all boiled down or whatever.

"You believe in God, Addie?" Fitz whispered to me.

"I don't know," I said. "Does He believe in me?"

"That's a good question," said Fitz. "I bet He does."

We were silent for a while until the pastor spoke of how Job blessed the name of the Lord even after all the awful things that had happened to him.

"Do you believe in forgiveness?" said Fitz.

"Of course," I said, surprised by the question.

"Yeah, but what if it's something really awful. Do you think someone can be forgiven for that? I mean, like, really awful," said Fitz, shuffling his slip-resistant booties anxiously.

"How awful?"

"Unforgivable," said Fitz.

"Is there such a thing?"

"I want my horse!" said Wolf.

"I'll find you that horse one day," said Fitz. He winked at Wolf. "Never mind," he said to me, returning to our conversation. "Just curious."

"Ask the pastor," I said.

"No. It's okay. Just wondering is all. More of a private atonement, I guess."

I contemplated Fitz's question while the pastor droned on about Job and his awful situation. Fitz dipped back into speaking to the voices he was hearing. At one point, he lay face down on the pew and shouted, "Shut up, Willy!"

"It's okay," I said, both to Fitz and to the pastor, who looked surprised.

After the "Amen," the pastor spoke to us in a more conversational tone. Weird how he was able to flip a switch like that. Whatever. The sermon had been better than milling around the ward, looking for something to do.

"I believe the good Lord would like to hear from each one of you. For that reason, I'd like to leave the last portion of our time to you and the Lord. Nothing more important than a one-on-one with the heavens. I promise you He is listening, and He will respond. Knock, and He'll open. Ask, and ye shall receive." He folded his hands over his Bible again. "I'll be right outside if you need help praying. I'd love to kneel down with you. When you're done, I'll walk y'all back to the ward."

The stained-glass doors creaked closed behind Pastor Michaels. His large, thin frame shadowed the doorway. Leah walked back from the row of candles. Didi and Junior joined me and Fitz, who was holding his finger to his mouth to make sure everyone stayed quiet. Wolf stared at the ceiling like he was in some sort of a trance.

"Alright, everybody," Fitz said, rubbing his hands together, "let's get things moving, and soon. I'm thinking that we can get out a week from tomorrow. The Monday movie will provide us the perfect opportunity. We only need a couple things. But first, I need a count of who is planning on exiting? Addie's in," he said, smiling at me. "And you all know I'm halfway out the door already."

"I'm in," said Didi. "I mean, I'll help, but I don't feel like leaving."

"Yeah, I'll help," said Junior. "I want to see the looks on the faces of the doctors and orderlies when they figure it out. That's all I need. But I don't want the same assignment as before because I don't want to mess it up again."

"Wasn't your fault," said Fitz.

"I'll help if I can," said Leah. "Actions speak louder than crossing a bridge when you come to it."

Wolf didn't say anything, so we had our numbers.

Honestly, I was kind of hoping Junior would join us on the outside because he was a big guy and pretty stable—as far as psych ward inpatients go, anyway.

"Perfect," said Fitz. "Okay, it will be similar to last time, but I've added a couple things that should help. First, we'll need somebody to volunteer themselves for suicide watch." Fitz stopped. "Wow, that sounded awful."

"Yeah, that doesn't sound like a good part to any plan," I said.

"That's not what I mean. Or, that's not what we need. Well, we need it, but . . ."

"Spit it out," said Junior.

"If we have someone on suicide watch, that person gets two orderlies to watch them. That way, when Addie and I break out later that night, we will only have to slip past one orderly."

"Smart," said Didi.

"Thanks," said Fitz. "But we still need a volunteer."

Junior smiled. I didn't know much about the guy, but I could tell he was enjoying the idea of a breakout. I think it made everyone pretty giddy—there's something about doing what we're not supposed to do, like the essayist said, that packs an adrenaline punch, like a cocktail of happiness and eagerness and hope.

I realized I hadn't really thought about what we were going to do once we were on the other side of the hospital walls. I knew Fitz wanted to go to San Juan Island, so I guessed we'd start there.

"I'll do it," said Junior. "Just let me pick the movie for next Monday. Unless someone has another movie they already got approved?"

Junior looked around, but no one spoke. The floor was his.

"I have one in mind. I know it will make me angry. I need to be angry if the suicide watch thing is to be believable. I don't think they're ever worried about me killing myself, but I know they get scared I'm gonna hurt someone else, is all."

"Excellent," said Fitz. "Well, not excellent that you would hurt someone, but excellent that we have our guy for the job."

I laughed at this new version of Fitz—this man planning what seemed like some incredible heist, when it really just amounted to surprising a few orderlies and outwitting some doctors who'd never prepared for a breakout because most psych ward inpatients have nowhere to go. Right?

And if they do have somewhere to go, they're either not

capable of getting out or don't have the nerve. I guess a number of factors were at play.

Fitz started in again, still rubbing his hands together. He looked a little sweaty, and I saw the hairs on the back of his neck curl in that wet shine.

"Okay, we'll also need somebody to swipe a keycard from an orderly," he said. "This is the trickiest part. We'll need to swipe it as we are led back to our rooms. The shorter the time the orderly is without their card the better. Otherwise, they'll notice it's missing. Since they only need it to get in and out of the pharmacy and the ward itself, we have to make sure we don't take the key from the orderly who is on pill duty that night. Who is it? Anybody know?"

"It's Jenkins," said Leah. "He's on pills every Monday."

I hugged Leah close to me, and she had this big grin on her face. I think we all felt a little giddy, but didn't know how to express it. It was like some odd feeling of community among the most random assortment of people ever. That's how it felt, anyway. Hey, I figured the pastor would appreciate the fact that we were getting along so nicely during our prayer time.

"Okay, so somebody needs to swipe a card from either Potts or Martha," said Fitz.

"I can help with Martha," I said, surprised by my own eagerness to help. "I'll need your help though, Didi. You'll need to distract her."

Didi grinned and started flapping the ears of his fur hat up and down rapidly. "This kind of distraction?"

Leah laughed at Didi's ridiculous motions. Wolf even looked our way to see what was going on.

"Maybe something a little more engaging," I said, smiling. "But that would work, I'm sure."

"Perfect," Fitz said. "You two plan the keycard swipe, Junior gets on watch, and the only thing left is the main doorway, where it sounds like Potts will be. Is that right?"

"Sounds right," said Junior.

"So we need Potts to leave his post for a short spell. Just a minute or two."

Nobody said anything for a moment. I could hear the echo of our heavy breathing in the tight space of the chapel. The air smelled of sweat and anticipation.

"I can do it," said Leah. "I already lit a candle for us. *No te preocupes. Estamos listos.* Trust me. We're good. *Los Santos* are with us."

"You don't have to do anything," I said to Leah, but she made a stern face and looked at Fitz.

"Let me do it," she said. "What do you have planned for Potts?"

"Well, it's mostly watching the clock. Addie and I will leave our rooms at exactly eleven forty-five. We'll both say we need to use the restroom. Martha is super flexible about that stuff. Anyway, Addie will use the restroom and grab her stuff—we'll have to hide our clothes for the outside behind the toilet during the movie at some point—and then she will tell Martha she forgot to take her pill and needs to check with Jenkins.

"I'll use the bathroom and then tell Martha I need to check with Jenkins about Riddle's request for my morning pill or something more specific. I'll think of something better.

"And that's all false, of course, but Martha won't care enough to stop me. Then, Leah, you need to make your move. You'll need to get Martha to open your door—say something that surprises her or makes her worry—and then just take off. If you head to the bathrooms, you'll pass right by Potts. He won't know Martha is behind you, because she's slow, so he'll take off after you. That will give me and Addie the minute or two we need.

"You'll just dead-end in the game room, and Martha and Potts will walk you back to your room. Now, I still haven't figured out what you should say to Martha. I don't want a second person on suicide watch, or they'll have to bring in the on-call nurse."

Fitz sighed, his chest lifting and lowering like a giant bellows. I could tell he was nervous about things working out correctly.

"What if Potts doesn't chase me?" said Leah.

"Then I'll have to distract him, and we'll run away from him anyway. Not ideal, because then they'd know and we'd lose ourselves a couple hours' head start, but it would have to do," said Fitz.

I started worrying about the night after the escape. I mean, it didn't sound like he'd thought of where to sleep when we got out. I made a mental note to talk to him after our chapel visit. I thought I had enough money for a hotel or motel or something—assuming Mom brought the books I'd requested on her next visit—and it's not like Fitz and I had sat down and done a break-out-budget by the hour or whatever.

It made me think again of one of those corny late-night ads: "Need to break out of your friendly neighborhood psychiatric ward? Try *Phil's Bills*, the most user-friendly break-out budget available, created by our own former SEC accountant, Phil Sumpter. It will help you dole out your money each day for street meds and low-cost beds. But wait! Order now, and get *Phil's Dills*, a whole jar of his homemade pickles canned and seasoned in Aubrey, Texas—all garlic, no brine! And if you order by midnight, you can even get *Phil's Skills*, a guide on how to budget once you're on the outside and free of that pesky hospital gown!"

Leah brought me back to the present.

"Martha won't put me on watch," she said. "I know how to tease her. But I'll make it seem serious at first."

It seemed like we were putting a lot of faith in Leah. But there really wasn't another option, and I knew she had the gumption to make it happen. Didi and Junior were already doing something, and Wolf wasn't really involved.

Having three people ask to leave their rooms might surprise Martha. I didn't think she'd do anything different, but it might make her the slightest bit suspicious.

Thankfully, Martha was the sweetest person ever. She liked lights out at night so she could read in peace. She was all about these romance novels that took place in space. She called them space operas or something. It made me imagine alien-robot hybrids singing opera songs to one another on some distant planet. So weird. Anyway, if you had to use the restroom she usually just waved her hand and kept her nose in whatever book she was reading at the time.

If you asked to use the bathroom more than a few times it bugged her, and she'd say no, but that was only because it would cut into her reading time. She was selfish in that way, but we're all selfish in our own ways, I guess.

Martha hated being on suicide watch because she wasn't allowed a book—there was a strict policy about all eyes on the patient or something. But because Martha was the most senior orderly, she was always able to claim her standard position on night watch near the rooms. That way, she didn't have to deal with the main door and any visitors, or be stationed at the pharmacy, logging doses and taking notes each night for the morning staff.

"Looks like we're all set," said Fitz. He got another goofy smile on his face and looked at me from beneath his curly hair that poked out from beneath his bandana.

"I want my horse," said Wolf, bowing his head.

"And somebody work on getting Wolf that horse, okay?" said Fitz.

"Why don't you find him one on the outside?" said Junior.

Pastor Michaels walked back in and surprised us. We were still sitting in a circle when he entered, light pooling around our bootie-clad feet.

"A group prayer. Y'all are taking nicely to this. Why don't you make sure and stand by that door again next week, and I'll have something special planned for your group about prayer. Ain't nothing better than an earnest and honest plea to the Lord," he said, holding his Bible over his stomach. "Let me walk you back, now." He gestured with his right arm, motioning us to rise and leave.

I watched as Leah whispered something to the candle she'd lit earlier, then she joined our group. Behind her, a few candles burned low in their cups of wax, and I wondered what my life would be like: would I get blown out, or flicker and come back stronger? We all flicker; it just depends on how willing we are to emerge again, and with how much light.

As we neared the door, I stalled and dropped back in the shifting group of people to find myself next to Fitz, near the back. He stood close to me as we walked the hallway. The hallway was crowded with other doctors and people visiting their friends or family or whatever, which, it turns out, is exactly what we needed. That way the pastor didn't keep a close eye on us.

I felt Fitz's warm hand touch mine. My heart raced. I think he saw me glance at my watch because he squeezed my hand again.

"Don't count the beats," he said, smiling.

"Wasn't going to," I said, squeezing his hand back.

Seven

The next morning the sky was bouncing with rows of bright clouds cruising through the blue, like some race to the horizon. There were these small rays of sunlight trailing down the hospital windows that turned as the clouds drifted past.

Wolf was standing near the entrance to the psych ward and quietly repeating, "I want my horse." I considered talking to him but realized it might only lead to more anxiety. I understood routines all too well. Rituals—the absurd nature of their repetition.

As I made my way to Doc's office, I saw Leah curled up with a book near the fake plants in the study room, but it didn't look like she was all that invested in her book. I stopped by to visit, even knowing it would make me late for my session with Doc. Whatever. He'd get over it.

"What are you reading? Looks cool," I said. "And I love the new hair color."

"Thanks," she said, rubbing her buzz. She'd dyed a streak in one side of her hair, probably for a day visit with her mom, who probably wanted to help her stop obsessing over the short hair. Really, though, the girl pulled off the look.

"I almost dyed once," I said. Leah looked at me in surprise. I waited a beat. "But I didn't think my hair would look good with the new color."

She laughed. That's what I lived to see—a genuine smile on another face. She had her knees pulled up beneath her oversized shirt that she usually wore to bed. Look, it's not like people really got "ready" for the day in the psych ward. In fact, we rarely wore anything but sweats and a T-shirt. On cold days—okay, every day—I grabbed a sweatshirt as well, but the dress code was non-existent. Even the orderlies wore the same thing most days. It was probably nice for them, in fact, not having to worry about that sort of thing.

"It's a book about whales. Kind of cool," she said.

I nudged her a little with my shoulder as I sat down next to her and curled into my own body, the shared warmth a nice thing on a cold morning. "You okay?"

"I am. Just thinking, is all."

"Yeah? What about?"

"Whales. Like how much they eat and stuff. A baby whale gains two hundred pounds a day for the first year of its life. Cool things like that," she said, rubbing her hair as she finished her sentence. "And when they die, it's called a whalefall, and they make it so other fish can live on their body for hundreds of years. I don't know how that works."

"I've gained so much weight here, I'm starting to feel like one of those whales," I said, standing and lurching forward, mocking a slow step and undulating motion.

Leah laughed as I made a fake whale call by singing in loud, prolonged rhythms with my mouth in an *O*, and swam away. "I'll seeee yoooou at lunch, Leeeaaah," I said in my whale voice.

She kept giggling as I wandered away. Yes, I was smiling. Yes, it was because I was able to put a smile on Leah's face. Yes, I lived for moments when the psych ward and the complexities of life and the stresses of recovery melted away, leaving behind a smile and some genuine laughter.

As I knocked on Doc's door, I thought about what Leah said about whales dying and making life for other fish. Like, I guess the vegetation would be greener the closer it got to the body, right? The fish a little happier, the world a bit more certain knowing it had this whale to keep it alive for hundreds of years. It was pretty amazing.

It was all I could think about, this life-giving-life to others for hundreds of years just by the presence of a body, the soul removed, the physical left to molder. How much life could be sustained off whatever I would end up leaving this world?

I settled into the chair across from Doc, who already had his stupid folder open, already doing his doctorish moves with his glasses.

"Your mother dropped these books off yesterday," he said, handing me the play I'd requested. Mom had indeed delivered *the goods*.

It was then that I started to get nervous again. Like, I'd tried my best and done quite well in forgetting about the breakout planned for that evening, but seeing Doc and the book with the money hidden inside it brought it all back. The week had really cruised by, but that tends to happen when your life is set in a routine that plays out like clockwork. Or as Leah might say, like the broad side of a barn. I started curling the sweater in my palms. I worried he knew everything and that his folder was just open so he could write down my confession or whatever.

I started tapping my left foot in seven-step patterns, blinking my right eye in sets of three, and clearing my throat after each set of the foot-eye combo.

"Ticks trying to keep you busy, Addie?" said Doc. "Have they kept you up at night lately? Is it worse today for some reason?"

He had to know something. Maybe he'd met up with Wolf, and Wolf had stopped talking about his horse long enough to tell Doc everything we'd said in that chapel. Maybe Leah wasn't really thinking about whales, but was relaxed because she spilled it all and felt relief from that weight being lifted off her conscience. Maybe Fitz had yelled it to Toby or Willy or something. I didn't know how to proceed without giving myself away, so I grabbed the new stress ball and began pushing on the giant, fake smile.

"Just one of those mornings," I said, offering a boring platitude and hoping Doc bit.

"That's okay. It doesn't mean you're sliding back. We all have those days sometimes."

There he went again with the first-person plural, like *we* were all dealing with the same OCD that kept *us* washing *our* hands and tapping *our* feet and clearing *our* throats and blinking *our* eyes in three- to seven-set bursts. Whatever. He had no clue. Whatever clue he had came from those manuals he read.

"In fact, you might be feeling more anxiety because you're looking forward to getting outside. It will be a nice break from the ordinary."

Of course. He knew. He knew my anxieties were because of the breakout. *Nice break. Breakout. Outside.* He knew. Who told him?

"What do you mean?" I said, hoping I was wrong.

"Group Talk today is in the yard. It's a nice day, and I told

Dr. Tabor to take everyone outside near the big pines to soak up a little sun."

I had to get out of that office or I'd totally fall into my anxieties and slip somehow. I wondered what I could say to get Doc off the topic, but I also wasn't sure if anything I said would let me leave earlier or just make him write more notes in that folder. I decided to give it a shot. What could it hurt? I was already sweating, and I had to kill time and distract myself from the evening plan, something I was totally freaking about because I wanted it so bad. For Fitz, sure, but for me, too.

"Last night I couldn't really sleep," I said.

Doc looked over his glasses and set his pen down. Finally, some eye contact. You'd think they'd start with that. You'd think, sure, but you'd be wrong.

I decided to tell Doc the truth of why I couldn't sleep—and it wasn't just because of the breakout. Oddly enough, the breakout and thinking of Fitz had reminded me of my physics class in high school where Mrs. Peddle had taught us about light particles. Sounds odd, I know, but that's what kept me up the night before, so I figured I'd let Doc use all his doctorly wisdom to poke and prod and see what stuck and what made sense.

"Why is that? Counting? Did you feel you needed to wash? Ticks?"

"Usually this is where I'd say 'Yep.'"

"But you're not saying 'Yep,'" said Doc.

"Nope," I said.

"And why is that?"

"I kept thinking about this experiment one of my teachers told me about. And it made me think of light. Did you know that the light we see from the stars is hitting us after years of travel?

We are literally looking back into space-time, and the light from some of the stars is years old, and *just now* reaching us. So cool," I said, getting caught up in the idea. "Like, something that is dead and gone can still light up our world. What *was* can still be an *is* if we put ourselves in the right place."

"Seems like a good thought to keep you awake," said Doc.

"Right, but then it got me thinking about my past," I said, kind of lying. I say *kind of* because I'd really been thinking about Fitz and how he'd asked about being forgiven and said that he had to make a personal atonement. To me, it sounded like Fitz was trying to rewrite his past, or change it somehow.

Doc was scribbling away in the folder and not looking at me, so I paused to see how long it'd take him to realize I was waiting for him. He finished a sentence and looked up, like, wondering what happened to the recording or something. Sometimes I wondered where he learned, or didn't learn, his bedside manner.

"Anyway, I started thinking about this experiment called the double-slit experiment. My teacher, Mrs. Peddle, said that observing a particle now can change what happened to another particle, but in the past."

"That doesn't make sense," said Doc.

I don't know why, but something about him not understanding what I was talking about made me giddy. I realized I had stopped trying to squeeze the guts out of the stress ball and was actually quite calm. It was a wonderful feeling.

"That's what I said in class. Mrs. Peddle said scientists are only dealing with a fraction of a second right now, but they are hoping to use that theory on light from distant stars. I still don't get it. But what if the present could change the past, even if only for a fraction of a second?"

Doc set his pen down again and rubbed his beard. It was a normal sight, but this time he had a little more expression on his face, his eyebrows knit and lowered. He bit the side of his lip and sighed as if in deep thought.

"In a purely mathematical world," he said, "perhaps we could talk about that theory. But in the world we live in, I don't see that as possible, or even probable, though I love the idea, Addie. Your mind is clearly working on a different plane than most."

"I can never stay awake on planes. I'm not a good traveler."

"I mean, on a different level," said Doc.

"I know what you meant," I said, smiling.

He smiled back and shrugged with a small laugh. He started scribbling in the folder again, and I wondered if I was being silly in thinking that helping Fitz change his past was possible. I knew the experiment was just that—an experiment, totally just theory—but what if understanding more about it could help me with Fitz? What if what I did right now with Fitz changed, maybe not his past, but at least the way he looked at his past? What if I could help him with that personal atonement he sought? Maybe I wasn't supposed to help, but I didn't know what else to do. I felt like an adventurer who finally had a goal that was worth pursuing. Like I was worth it.

I was all caught up in those feelings and thoughts, and my ticks returned as all my anxieties rushed back. Would breaking Fitz out hurt or help his situation? I wasn't sure, but I was sure I wanted to be with him wherever we decided to go and whatever we decided to do. Just as I started tapping my foot, I heard Didi right outside of Doc's office shouting, *Home Shopping Network! QVC!* I started laughing but tried to cover it up with a cough. Doc smiled.

"It's okay to laugh. I've never heard those two before. In fact, I need to catch up with Doug, so I hope you're okay with our time being a bit shorter this morning. Mind telling him to come in when you leave?"

I stood, perhaps too quickly, too eager to get out of his office and away from his stare. Doc cleared his throat, and I wondered if he was going to say one last thing, like "You'll never get away with it." Like, he was waiting to see if I'd be honest after giving me every opportunity to talk about it, and he finally had to lay down the law or whatever. But all he said was "Make sure you keep track of these thoughts. I want to talk more tomorrow about this idea of changing the past. It's a wonderful thought, Addie."

My whole body relaxed, and I sighed as I turned the corner away from Doc's office and shouted Didi's way. I wondered how everyone else was handling their morning, and how they were dealing with keeping the secret a secret. I saw Wolf rocking back and forth on his feet near the entrance and realized it might be easier for some to keep a secret than for others.

The moon was still visible in the sky. I stared at it and thought about the light reflecting off the moon from the sun and wondered just how long that light took to reach me. How many minutes? How many years before the starlight reached us on earth? I wondered if there really was a man in the moon, and if so, did he have a handsome gap? Probably not. There's only one Fitz.

Eight

Screenwriters should stop going to the same school, or at least stop writing the same stories. The movie Junior picked— *High School Musical*—got louder as the students broke out into a simultaneous dance and song after tearing up their midterm exams or something. Nobody dances like that in school. Nobody dances like that anywhere, really. I understood why Junior hated this film. I almost threw up, but controlled my gag reflex and looked at my feet until feeling came back to my stomach. Just kidding, it wasn't that bad, but it did seem like a very tired narrative.

Another student on screen began preaching about the finer points of life, and why the other students had missed out on those good things for so long. They all agreed to fight the powers that be, one dance at a time, smiling their way to a restructuring of enforcement. How vogue. At least the lead actor was kind of attractive, so I daydreamed about being in that school and meeting him. Then I saw Fitz and realized I already had that. I know, I know, way too mushy. I agree.

Fitz was wearing his *Namaste in Tonight* shirt—seriously, we had maybe four different shirts and a couple pairs of pants, nothing spectacular—and I commented on the irony of his clothing choice considering tonight was the night we were escaping.

On screen, one of the students swiped something from the teacher's desk, only for the teacher to immediately notice it was missing. It was a playful gesture, but it made me nervous.

"Isn't Martha going to notice that we never returned from our different errands or whatever?"

"I'm not worried about Martha," he said.

"Why not?"

Fitz started laughing. "Willy, that's a good one. I think you should tell Toby. I'm kind of busy. Sorry, Addie," he said.

"No worries. Can you tell me?"

"I could tell you, but then I'd feel bad. It's kind of lousy."

"Okay," I said.

"Maybe later, Willy," he said, motioning for Willy to take a hike. "Sorry. But getting back to what you were asking: Martha will have to work on an incident report with Potts because of Leah's running. It won't be anything serious, but you know they have to report all of that. Martha is forgetful. And even if she does notice, we'll be long gone."

"Speaking of long gone," I said. "Where do you plan on staying tonight when we get out? We have to think of these things, or we'll really be up a creek."

"We'll take a bus to a motel near where the ferries launch to the island. We'll be fine," he said, slouching in his chair. "Won't we, guys?" He leaned to his left and nodded his head and kept saying things like, "Yep, sounds good," and "Wouldn't have it any other way" until I hit him in the arm. "You've got to understand that we won't be alone," he said, smiling at me.

I was glad Fitz was able to make light of his situation. I think I'd be terrified knowing I would never be alone, that those voices would always be there. I guess we all have an interior monologue, but for it to be so insistent and loud and populated would be impossible to ignore. Maybe his life was a series of interruptions, and he lived in the space between. He lived in the spurts and spats between the longer moments of conversing with the imaginary group that followed him everywhere.

Maybe Doc was confident he could rid Fitz entirely of those intrusions, but I doubted it. If this was the best Fitz had ever been, I figured he would never really get past those other voices in the background. It made me sad. I rested my hand on his briefly.

"My heart is like a freaking hummingbird," I said.

"Then I'll go first," he said.

Fitz asked Jenkins if he could walk him to his room—I didn't hear the excuse he gave, but I started thinking of how I was going to have to trick Martha. I didn't know what to do. Why hadn't we planned better what we were going to do? At least we'd thought of breaking our pills in half the day before. That would buy us at least one day on the outside before the tremors hit.

Fitz returned ten minutes later, just as the students on the screen were breaking into song in the gym after passing the basketball around. They all looked so happy; it was actually quite wonderful. But it was so easy to see through those masks. Everyone wears a mask, but actors get to change theirs constantly. I kind of envied the way they played different parts and got to live different lives. They could empathize with so many types of people, of personhood. If actors were the opposite of people, what did that make me? A series of masks, maybe.

"I'm so nervous," I said, alternating my blinks at a rapid rate.

"I didn't do anything but go to the bathroom," he said.

"What?"

"It was a dumb idea to try the change-of-clothes thing," he said. "It's too obvious. Why didn't we think of that? Of course they'll notice we walked into our room with nothing and came out with a bundle under our shirt or something. So stupid. But I did grab our pills. I can pocket those."

"Good. The pills are the most important thing. It's not like we need the extra clothes, right? I mean, we'll need to stop some-place for shoes either way."

Fitz smiled and flashed that handsome gap.

"Luckily you won't get too many looks in Seattle for walking around barefoot. But I agree, we should get something for our feet."

I wanted to keep talking to Fitz, but I was too nervous. I tapped my hand on each leg seventeen times and then repeated the process. I asked Martha if I could use the restroom so I could wash my hands, and she obliged. When I got back, the movie was reaching the closing scene where the students were dancing on some massive stage in a giant auditorium or something. It looked ridiculous.

"Sure is true to life, isn't it?" said Fitz, loud enough that Junior could hear.

"Just like my childhood," I said, just as loud. "I always danced in class when I wanted to really feel alive."

As the credits rolled, I realized I hadn't spent enough time emotionally preparing myself for the chain of events that was about to be set in motion with Junior's outburst.

I wished we had spent another few weeks planning everything or had gone over the details more, but Fitz was adamant about the timeline for some reason, and he still wouldn't tell me why. Maybe I was wrong to trust him, but at the time I only knew he was desperate and I wanted to help. I wanted to find out my own answers, too, for Dr. Morris and for myself. Maybe I was more selfish than I let on. Whatever.

Junior stood up just then and heaved a chair into the wall— harder than usual. He broke through the drywall. He knocked over another chair just as the orderlies stood and walked his way.

"Where's a knife?" he yelled, lifting another chair over his head. "I'm gonna rip their cute little faces out of that screen! *Nobody* is that happy!"

The orderlies backed away, and Junior threw a second chair into the wall. Jenkins grabbed Junior, and I could tell that Junior was strong enough to break free but chose not to. He fought it off for a while to really sell it, though.

He looked at us and winked as the orderlies dragged him to the door. He kept shouting about a knife to make sure he'd go on suicide watch. I could tell he was not legitimately mad, and that the knife comment was just for show.

Junior was still shouting as Martha turned off the TV and motioned for us to line up at the door. Didi couldn't stand still, and I saw him raise his eyebrows as Martha came closer. He started flapping the ears on his hat and singing some opera song I'd never heard. But knowing Didi, he'd probably claim he wrote the opera himself years ago and that it won a bunch of awards. Like, all the awards.

Martha told Didi to calm down, so he took his hat off and started swinging it around. He leaned back, yelping and shouting, "Gotta get me that eight seconds for a score!" and acting like he was holding onto a rope like a true bull rider. Didi then dropped his hat and looked at Martha and started running around the room, flapping his arms and yelling, "Fly like butter, sting like a flea!"

Martha looked super annoyed and waited for him to stop. But he didn't.

His whole act was way over the top, but Martha wasn't going to question Didi because then she'd have to log his outburst in the shift notes that night. She bent over to pick up his hat, and it was time for me to get her keycard.

Leah was supposed to help, but she stayed in her seat and looked nervous. I didn't want Martha to hear or feel the keycard being clipped, so I stood there unsure of what to do.

That's when something happened that I am still not quite sure how to explain because it went against everything I knew about the guy: Wolf looked at me, then at Leah, then took off in a sprint in Junior's direction yelling, "Hi-Ho, Silver!" as he jumped onto Junior's back. He started yelling, "Hyah! Hyah! Go, boy! Hyah!" as he kicked his feet into Junior's ribcage like he was spurring a horse.

I almost didn't get the keycard because I was so shocked, but as Martha turned to help with Junior, I grabbed the card. I know she didn't feel it because she was so surprised by Wolf's outburst, as we all were, I'm sure.

It looked like Junior was laughing but still trying to maintain his serious and angry demeanor.

That's when Leah stood up, perhaps encouraged by Wolf, and screamed at the top of her lungs. I quickly covered my ears like the rest of the group. Well, except for Wolf. He was still shouting, "Hyah!"

The scream brought Martha running back our way. She

looked at Leah, who was standing next to me, with a shocked expression.

"I just was curious how loud I could scream," said Leah, her face turning pink.

"My goodness, child," said Martha. "You were all acting fine during the movie. And it wasn't even a good one. Now you're on one—all of you. I wish you had smiles like those kids on the screen. And quit all that yelling and flapping," she said to Didi.

"*The Magic Schoolbus!*" said Didi.

I don't think Didi meant to say it, but it seemed to fit the moment just fine.

Martha just shook her head and gave Didi back his hat. She opened the door, holding her hand out to lead us into the hall-way.

Jenkins had Wolf under control, and Junior was on his way to the suicide watch room.

Everything was working out just fine—and that made me nervous. No plans ever work out that smoothly.

Who would have guessed Wolf would come through for us? Wow. Maybe Wolf was a lot more coherent than any of us thought. He never let on that he was listening to what we had talked about in the chapel. In fact, he always looked so unin-terested that we all thought he just walked around with us and nothing more. Turns out we were wrong, and it was nice to be wrong about Wolf.

I was sure the other slip-resistant bootie was about to drop. Like, Martha would notice her keycard missing, or Wolf would suddenly start saying something other than asking for his horse and totally give us all up.

But that didn't happen. We walked to our individual rooms

and sat in silence for over an hour. I stared at my watch and was careful to move every few minutes so I didn't fall asleep. The pills I was on made me quite sleepy and hungry. I flipped through *The Real Inspector Hound* and made sure I'd found every bill hidden in the pages, and pocketed the cash.

I'd probably put on a few more pounds over the last week, but I was careful not to speculate or feel my stomach or anything. Wasn't worth my time. I'd already spent hours talking with Ramirez about the weight gain, and he kept telling me different ways to handle those intrusive thoughts. I'm not saying it all worked, but I was getting better at keeping my hands by my side and leaving my stomach alone.

I decided to read because I had to keep my mind from wandering back to my anxious thoughts of the escape. It was difficult because I had the keycard in the pocket of my sweats, and I kept turning it, my palms hot. I wanted to wash my hands after holding the keycard, but I waited because the plan required that I wait.

To keep from obsessing, I opened up *Waiting for Godot* and read more about Vladimir and Estragon, and I was just getting to the scene where they started swapping hats in this really fast-moving part when I looked at my watch and realized it was almost time.

It was tricky reading by moonlight, but when I'd tried turning on my light, Martha shouted, "Lights out!" But that was good news: Martha was out there reading, which meant that Potts and Jenkins were in their places too, most likely.

I considered writing Martha a note, just to let her know that we would be okay and that we were sorry about putting her through all of this. But I didn't. I regretted it later, but at the time

I was too nervous, too worried she might find the note before we got far enough away from the hospital.

Five minutes later, I knocked on my door.

"Bathroom," I said.

I could hear Martha's heavy sigh on the other side of the door, and I listened as she struggled to get up from her chair. It sounded like quite the ordeal, shifting papers and gasps and grunts.

As I walked to the bathroom, I heard Fitz knock on his door, and Martha told me to hurry. She turned away, and I realized I wouldn't have to tell her I was seeing Jenkins about my pill or anything. I walked past both the pharmacy and Potts, who looked like he was reading something on the computer.

Fitz was in the process of making up some story about needing to see Jenkins about his pill when I heard another knock: Leah. I was amazed everything was moving so precisely. When in need of precision, courage, and proper execution, just look to the adolescent psych ward. That was probably a pretty popular phrase, right? I bet it's on some poster in the offices of all the most powerful CEOs out there, or used as a movie tagline. Or it should be.

Fitz turned the corner and walked my way just as Martha was nearing Leah's door, or so I hoped. I mean, I couldn't see Martha at that point. We stood behind a fake ficus tree near Potts's station by the front door and hunched into the shadows. Thankfully the hospital was all about conserving energy, so only half the lights were on at night, making it easier to hide.

I felt Fitz's body heat and smelled his scent—all guys have a scent. I'm sure all girls do, too, but it's impossible to know how you smell, right? Anyway, we both watched as Leah came booking around the corner at a full sprint. She was a fast little girl. Her feet padded against the tiles as she zipped by the front desk and down the hall. It was nice to see her leg it like that.

Potts almost fell off his chair when he heard Martha scream Leah's name. He opened his door and took off after Leah, who was laughing, and I almost laughed out loud with her.

Martha came huffing around the corner and looked annoyed and tired and maybe like she thought it was a little funny that she was chasing a girl at midnight down a hall in a psych ward. Martha shouted Leah's name again, and it's the last thing we heard.

Fitz and I were out the door.

I had the keycard in my hand. "What are we supposed to do with this?" I whispered to Fitz. "She'll notice, and we'll be caught before we get anywhere."

I'd spent an entire week after our Sunday talk coming up with plans for numerous scenarios that were not probable but simple and maybe even likely. But, of course, I hadn't planned for this specific moment. And, of course, we'd missed a few things. Isn't that always the case?

"Slide it back under the door," Fitz whispered.

"What? Why?"

"If you slide it far enough, maybe she'll think it fell off while she was running after Leah. Hurry!"

Fitz grabbed the card and slid it as far as he could. Moments later, we heard Martha's voice from down the hall. We took off in a sprint, only slowing down when we reached the elevator bank.

"We just walk out the door?" I said.

"To the ER. Then out the door," he said. "Nobody looks twice at people leaving the ER in a sad sartorial state," Fitz said as we rode the elevator down to the main level. "Pretty good word, huh? Sartorial. Picked it up from *Ninja Assassin Protocol 4*."

I was blinking so rapidly that I only caught glimpses of Fitz. The elevator doors opened, and Fitz walked me to the ER. He could tell I wasn't doing so hot. I took deeper breaths and gathered my emotions before we stepped into the lit hallway of the ER. I knew there would be a lot of people, and I couldn't show any signs of abnormal behavior.

Fitz held my hand and walked with purpose. "If you're confident," he said under his breath, "nobody will think twice about what you're doing or why."

And it was true.

We walked right out the door, slip-resistant booties and all.

We walked into a breezy, starlit night and didn't look back.

Okay, that's not entirely true. We looked back when we were a block away. The night was a bit colder than I'd expected it to be, but the temperatures in Seattle could be just as mercurial as Fitz, changing by the minute. I told him we should hurry to a bus before word got out that we'd escaped. I wanted to be indoors somewhere before planning our next move.

"Look at all those stars," he said, still holding my hand.

"We're free of the hospital, you know," I said, looking down at our hands.

"And?"

He smiled, and I felt all my insides come untethered. My heart picked up its thrumming pace.

"Let's get to a motel. I have enough for maybe two nights, as long as we're not too spendy on our shoes. I'd like to get a better sweater, too. I bet it will be colder tomorrow." I had on my usual gray sweater, but it was pretty threadbare.

Fitz hugged me to him, and I felt myself relax in his embrace. "I'll keep you warm," he said.

I didn't look up, but I could feel his heart beating against mine. I wanted to stay there forever, but we had to keep moving.

He seemed to know where he was going, so I followed Fitz and smiled at the way he walked so confidently with my hand in his. We were able to find a bus, but the driver only knew of one motel near the ferry. It made our choice pretty easy.

It was a longer ride than I'd expected, with a lot of stops thrown in, but I'd always enjoyed watching people get on and off the bus. It was this odd form of people-watching where I could give them narratives and imagine what their lives were like when they stepped past the sighing doors and back onto the pavement of reality. It was kind of inspiring, in a weird way.

"You guys warm?" said Fitz, looking at the empty seats in front of us.

"Are they acting cold?"

"Just Lyle. He's a snowflake," he said, then wrinkled his brow. "Maybe that's the wrong term. He's a delicate flower."

"At least they made it out of the hospital," I said. "I was worried that Willy would get his long braids stuck in a door or something."

Fitz just smiled and rested his hand on my lap.

I mean, like I said, I was never really one to break the rules. I was always home on time. I always slept in my own bed or on the couch by our family dog, Duck. So being on a bus with a boy in a city I'd only traveled through during the day with Mom was like being in the Twilight Zone. I didn't know how to get a read on the emotions, the colors, the scents, the lighting, or the other people we saw who were just going about their daily routines.

When we arrived at the motel, we stepped off into a much colder wind. The blinking neon sign a hundred yards away had only half of the letters working — *TEL*. The bus drifted back into the nighttime sounds of the city. I smelled cheap, fast food and the salty ocean breeze.

"Let's hurry," he said.

"Wait," I said, grabbing his arm. "If the orderlies find out we're gone, they're going to look to any form of transportation we could have taken. If they find that driver, he'll point out exactly where he dropped us. It won't take them long to take two and two and two and stack it all up to six."

"You love your numbers," he said.

"I'm serious."

"I know," said Fitz. "And you're right. Man, I'm so cold!"

I thought of running into the motel and asking about other accommodations in the area, but then realized that wouldn't work either. If the person working at the desk remembered telling two young people where to stay, then the trail would still be fresh for the police or whoever would come after us. At that moment, I imagined the police handing hound dogs some of our clothes to get our scent. Stupid, I know, but whatever.

"Usually motels are in groups. Let's just keep walking," I said.

The wind cut right through me. I had on sweats, but neither of us had any shoes on. Hopefully the people at the front desk wouldn't look too closely or care too much. Hopefully Fitz was right about people in Seattle not worrying about that kind of thing.

Fitz's hair was all over the place, and I realized that his bandana looked even stranger outside of the hospital. Everything did, except maybe his shirt. Funny how that worked out. He used his body to try to shield me from the breeze, but eventually we just walked side by side at a fast clip for about four blocks before we saw a faded sign for an inn another half a block away.

I jumped a little, excited by the idea of any respite from the wind off the churning water.

We hurried to the front desk of the inn and found that the rate for one night wasn't that much more expensive than the motel. It probably meant the room wasn't all that nice, but all I wanted was a warm bed and a warm shower.

There was no clerk at the desk when we arrived. I rang the small bell, and we waited. It was one of those obnoxious tabletop bells that seem more like you're insulting someone rather than just attempting to get somebody's attention.

A short man walked in, looking sleepy. His tie was loose and askew, and two buttons on his shirt had popped off. We stood close to the desk so he wouldn't be able to tell that we didn't have any shoes or luggage. Maps of the islands were spread out beneath a thin glass plate on the countertop, finger-smudges all over the little dots of green and large swaths of blue beneath. I traced the lines of the ferries from port to port until the clerk finished logging onto the computer.

"One room," Fitz said.

I blushed and looked away. The clerk looked at me and then at Fitz and told us the price. He was maybe a year or two out of high school, and even that was a stretch. He didn't seem to care about our ostensible rendezvous.

When I handed over the cash, he gave us another odd look, but passed us the key and told us where the elevators were and when breakfast would be served, then he headed back to the dark office where he would most likely go right back to sleep.

The room was garish and dirty. Loud and shiny decorations attempted to mask the awful smell of mushrooms and the beer stains on the walls and the floor. There was a nautical theme to the room, fitting seeing as we were near Fidalgo Island, with windows looking out onto the streets that led to the water.

"We got lucky," I said.

"Very lucky," said Fitz.

"What were you going to do if I hadn't gotten the money?"

"Probably find some homeless shelter or sleep in one of those ATM portals that close off. I don't know. It wasn't the first thing on my list," he said.

I plopped down on the bed. I was so tired that it didn't fully register that there was only one bed until Fitz sighed and dropped next to me, his body like a massive boulder hitting a rickety cot. His weight tugged at me, pulling me closer into the large indent our bodies made in the cheap mattress.

"We got lucky," I repeated. "Doesn't mean you'll get lucky."

"So presumptuous."

"Well," I said, waiting for his response.

"It's the universe," said Fitz. "Knows it owes me one."

"So arrogant. Classic tragic character flaw," I said, smiling.

We both stared at the ceiling for a while in silence. I could hear his breathing and his heartbeat, and I started counting the number of beats, the blinking on and off with each alternating aortic push.

"We could watch a movie. Oh, and I'll sleep on the couch. I'm a gentleman, after all," he said, smiling. "Lyle, I'm not in the mood. Yes, I think you did a fine job earlier today. Thanks for taking a minute to talk to me. Go write some lyrics or something." Fitz waved to his right, as if motioning someone away.

"It's the middle of the night," I said.

"Addie Foster. You're supposed to be the comic character. You should say something funny instead of denying a movie. Shut up, Toby!" He laughed and rolled on his side and rested his chin against his hand. "Country singers. They ruin every possible romantic moment, don't they?"

"We're a mess," I said.

The awkwardness of being alone with Fitz outside of the hospital was gone, and I felt comfortable just lying next to him, tapping my hand on the bed and blinking in my usual pattern. I waited a few minutes before talking, hoping he'd say something first.

I wanted to ask him more about San Juan Island. Like, maybe since we were finally out, escaped, free, we could discuss why the island was so important to him, and why he had to go there before the middle of November. But I was too nervous, and I felt gross being in that germ-riddled room.

I rolled off the bed and went to shower. When I came back, Fitz was on the couch, totally out, snoring like an old car engine starting up on a winter morning. I climbed into bed and tried not to think of all the people who had slept in that bed before me.

The sheets smelled like musty books in dusty boxes in the attic at home. I was wary of how often the sheets were washed, or what might be crawling around inside the mattress, but I tried to shrug off those thoughts and sleep. It didn't work.

It didn't help that I kept thinking of how dangerous it was to let Fitz into my life. I considered waking him up to tell him that he shouldn't get attached to me, that we wouldn't end up together because we had too many issues to deal with outside of just normal living, normal loving. But I let him sleep.

At some point in the night, I realized that I had free access to a sink and soap and no Martha to stop me. That was dangerous. I kept thinking of all the messy bodies that had made their way to those sheets—sweaty bodies, bodies with dead skin flaking off everywhere, bodies with other bodies. Fluids. Ugh. Gross.

I took another, longer, shower and ended up laying down on top of the sheet. I know it really didn't make a difference, but it was the only way I could justify being anywhere near that bed. And that's when I heard it. It was a sound that I'd grown to love as a child, and one that always made me feel nostalgic, made me think of home: a foghorn sounded, sending its yearning call into the foggy night.

Nine

Maybe calling it a continental breakfast just means you need to have cheap orange juice and stale muffins and a waffle maker. At least here there was the option of little cereal pouches and some type of yogurt or whatever.

"Grab it to go," said Fitz.

He took a banana and a cereal pouch and a couple muffins and stuffed them in one of the little paper sacks at the end of the counter. As we left breakfast, I remembered that we only had half of our medication, and only enough for one day. I mean, I always took my meds before or after breakfast, and in that moment, I worried I might feel the absence of the missing half. It made me worry. What would skipping my full dosage do to me? How would my body react? Even scarier was the thought of what it might do to Fitz, to his mind.

I tried to push that stress away as Fitz took his half of his medicine and grabbed my hand, and we hurried to the old oak door and stepped out into the bright morning, the sun burning off the inlet fog.

I relished the feel of real sunlight on my face after being inside for so many weeks. We didn't get much outdoor time at the hospital, and if it was offered (read: rarely), it was only a small visit to a tiny courtyard enclosed by hospital walls. At least Doc was making some inroads by having Tabor take Group Talk outside, but that wasn't enough for me. And the sun never truly reached its warm fingers into that small courtyard. At least not while we were there.

We walked closer to the water, and Fitz started asking passersby about a secondhand store. The inlet was echoing the loud sun booming over my head. It made my heart beat fast, but in an excited way. I put my hand over the pulse and imagined some muscular fist opening and closing.

Have you ever seen a heart beating outside of a body? I have. Doc had this video. It was nuts. He let me watch it because I kept nagging him. Your heart is this crazy strong muscle that flexes and flattens and fills again a hundred thousand times a day. It has all these nerves that keep it pumping.

"Got it," Fitz said, snagging my hand—and my attention—again.

"Aren't you enjoying this sun?" I said, surprised he was in such a hurry.

"We can take all the time we want once we're on that island," he said.

A breeze pushed against my body, and I decided to let my hair down and let it wander in the wind. I shook it out and tried to keep pace with Fitz.

"Whoa!" he said, stopping when he saw my hair loose.

"What? Never seen a girl with hair?"

"Addie Foster," he said. "The face that will launch one ferry boat."

I smiled. "I didn't know you'd read *The Iliad* or *The Odyssey* or anything that wasn't about the protocol of ninja assassins."

"So quick to judge, Addie," he said with a giant grin. "You've got to tell me what kind of conditioner you're using because, girl, it's working." He snapped his fingers with sass. "Tell me that's not a mask, Addie. Tell me you're not acting. Tell me something that reminds people why it's nice to smile."

"Let's just get our clothes," I said, blushing.

"Oooohhh. *Now* we're in a hurry, huh?"

We walked to the outer banks of the small clip of land where the ferry launched for the islands. It was oddly pleasing to have a sensory experience that was incredibly normal, yet had been absent from my life for so long. Just everyday stuff—doors opening and closing, people talking, the smell of fish and fried food, airplanes scudding through the sky, kids zipping past on skateboards, kites in the air, Frisbees, dogs barking, bells over doors ringing.

"Where are we going?"

"A thrift store is up here, apparently. It's the only one around. Run by the Episcopal church. We'll see what they got, then make our way to the ferry."

I checked my watch and frowned. "Did you turn off my alarm?" I said.

"Yeah. You were in the shower, and it kept beeping. Why do you need an alarm? What's it for?"

"It reminds me to take my pills," I said. There it was again, that red light going off in my mind. Wait. That red light appearing, not going off. On. Turning on.

"What?"

"My pills. I'm worried about the fact that we only took half."

152

"It's one day, Addie," he said.

"I'm going to be so sick later today," I said, dreading the inevitable stomach lurching and empty feeling I got whenever I forgot my medication—the same feeling I felt the day before when breaking the pills in half. Would it be worse because of the new environment? I had no way of knowing.

"I like having a clear head," he said. "I think better when I'm not on so much of that garbage."

I thought about reminding him that he was doing better than ever before because of those very pills, but decided not to say anything. I guess he was right. It was only one day and half the dosage. But it didn't stop my mind from sending stress signals to my heart and tightening my chest whenever I thought of him without his pills. I'd only known him with those pills. Who would he be without them? It's not like he hadn't dealt with those emotions before, though, right?

It worried me, but the outing was moving, so to speak, and I wasn't able to slow it down. I mention that so to speak. I speak, so to speak. Too much momentum. I tried to stay in the moment and move on.

The sun was starting to rise behind the evergreens, and it threw some pretty crazy shadows all over the rolling landscape. I enjoyed the sun as little beams hit me and warmed me all unevenly. I noticed Fitz was sweating more than usual, but wasn't sure if it was the lack of medication or his anxiety about whatever awaited us on the island.

When we stepped into the store, I squinted so my eyes would adjust to the cheap, fluorescent bulbs. I hated fake light.

One wall was lined with suits and blazers and ties and dress shoes all in the most ridiculous array of colors I'd ever seen. Most of the clothing was far too bright to wear, no matter the comfort level or functional appeal. Not the best options. But I walked down the women's side to find, surprisingly, some really pretty sundresses and some nice shirts.

"People are calling this secondhand?" I said.

Fitz popped around the corner wearing overalls and a straw hat, and I started laughing.

"Truly. Walt Whitman himself," I said.

"My namesake, in a way," said Fitz. "Just wish I had a stalk of wheat I could hold between my teeth. And a banjo. Lyle is over here laughing, and Toby is telling me some clean jokes for a change. Thanks, guys," he said, calling out to the empty space behind him. He started dancing a hoedown-type jig and lifting his knees as high as they could go and slapping them and yipping. Yawping, Whitman would say.

"Just don't go throwing all your clothes off and rolling in the grass," I said. "Don't go full Whitman on me."

"What?" He stopped dancing and raised his eyebrows and tilted his head.

"Have you never read Whitman's poetry?"

"Only the 'Captain, my captain' one."

"Well, he usually takes off his clothes about halfway through his poems and starts rolling in the grass," I said. "Not saying it doesn't sound freeing, but I'd like not to make it too obvious that we are escapees from a mental ward."

We both said goodbye to our booties. What a sad parting! He decided on flip-flops because they were cheapest, so I went the same route.

Fitz turned back to the men's side. He found some soft gym shorts and a nice big sweatshirt that said *I Love My Grammar's*

Synonym Rolls! It had this cheesy cinnamon-roll man leaping in the air with a giant smile, clicking his heels together. It looked dumb, but it also looked warm.

My sweatshirt said *Silently Correcting Your Grammar*. I liked that it fit with Fitz's choice. I imagined that both shirts had been donated by the same couple—a couple who had also worn them ironically. I already had good sweats on.

"At least your shirt fits your personality," he said.

"Yours is lame, but at least it has a cute roll on it," I said, smiling.

I saw Fitz pause and stare over my shoulder. When I turned, I saw that he was looking at a toy model airplane. It was this really cool looking 1920s biplane that was covered in this gorgeous yellow with bright green lines, kind of like what the water looks like when those phytoplankton make it all neon and alive at night, all that light cruising through the waves. That kind of light I can get behind. That kind of light is worth watching for. That made me think of blue whales eating nine thousand pounds of krill in one day.

"Sometimes we'd grab coat hangers and pretend to fly around the apartment and use these bogus pilot codes and jump off the couch and knock into one another and make fake radio static in our arms and get spit all over the floor and laugh about it," said Fitz.

I was the only person near him, but it didn't seem like he was talking to me.

"Who?"

"Quentin," he said. "Let's hurry!"

He grabbed my arm, and I realized he was not interested in

talking about Quentin at the moment. *Quentin.* I couldn't get away from that name. I wanted to know more.

After paying for the clothes, I saw that we probably only had enough for the ferry ride and maybe a couple more meals, as long as it was fast food or something reasonably cheap. Thinking of food made me double over near the store entrance. My mouth was sweating, and I felt like I was about to throw up. It never happened, the actual throwing-up part, but I was on edge the rest of the morning, my stomach twisting and rolling like waves near the breakers.

A breeze rolled in, heavy with salt and carrying a strong chill.

"You know we can't *get* cold?" I said, thinking back to something Mrs. Peddle had once told me.

"What do you mean? I got this sweater because I plan on things *getting* cold."

His eyes looked amazing in the sun. Like, the gray had these small bursts of bright blue speckled throughout, and he looked noticeably happier, shining, like his soul was trying to step out of his body or something.

"No. You can never really get cold, you just lose heat. Our bodies lose heat."

"That's pretty awesome," said Fitz, still clearly mulling it over.

I looked down at my feet as we hurriedly walked past the passersby. I realized I would likely never wear these bright-pink flip-flops outside of this odd and beautiful time of my life when I was free of the psych ward with Fitz. I stared at the flower between my toes.

When we arrived at the ferry docks, I looked into the muddled light where the water met the sky. I kept my head down and looked over Fitz's shoulder, expecting to see cops walking around and talking into the radios on their shoulders, reporting to some-one that they'd found the missing inpatients wandering the docks. I curled up the sweater sleeves in my hands, and we kept walking.

We finally boarded the ferry, and I watched the shifting wa-ters roll out beyond our sight. It was majestic.

I heard the sea terns making their swooping calls. The sun hung in a corner of the sky, reaching its long fingers of fire into my hair and onto my face and chest and arms and legs. I held my arms out, and Fitz started laughing.

"Sit down, you weirdo," he said. "Not today, Willy!" he yelled over his shoulder while simultaneously reaching his hand out to me, offering me a seat. "Sorry."

"I'm used to it," I said. "I'm sorry you have to deal with it. Is it worse since you only took half of your regular dose?"

"A little," he said. "But I think clearer. It's like, I get more annoyed by the disturbances, but those moments between those disturbances are so clear that it makes it worth it for the short periods of clarity. It's worth it for today. Maybe not for the long haul, but at least for today."

I sat down in one of the cheap plastic seats on the top deck of the ferry. It was remarkably bright out for a November day, the sun booming overhead, and I wondered what kind of weather we were in for later in the day. I rolled up my sweater in my hands again and began tapping my leg as the breeze continued to kick off the water. Fitz wiped away more sweat from his forehead.

"Speaking of today," I said. "Time for some answers, Fitz."

"You know, sometimes finback whales make calls to their family, and their calls can be heard from over three hundred miles away. That's the truth. Three hundred miles. Imagine that," he said.

"Don't deflect," I said. "I read Leah's book, too. It's amazing. But you need to be honest with me right now."

"I'm not deflecting. I'm getting to it. Just let me do it my way," he said.

I slouched and tilted my head back onto the shoulder rest, my face looking straight up into the cornflower-blue sky.

"Okay," I said, sighing.

"I read that it was because of how dense the water is when you get super deep in the ocean, and the channels fix the sound to some crazy range, and because sound moves much faster in that kind of environment."

"That's pretty cool," I said. "So would sound move faster during a rainstorm?"

"I don't know," said Fitz. "I guess when I think of Quentin and San Juan Island, I think that maybe if I say 'I love you' and 'I'm sorry' or something like that, somehow it will eventually reach him wherever he is now. I know it sounds weird," he said, looking down at his hands.

"Not weird," I said. "It sounds really cool."

He pulled his bandana off and rolled it around his hands. "Look, Addie, can we talk about this on the island?"

"Of course," I said. "All we need to do right now is to calmly enjoy the ride."

"And not mention split infinitives," he said, motioning to my sweatshirt.

"Ugh. Grammar Nazis are obnoxious, if."

"If what?" said Fitz.

"Oh. Nothing. Just thought I'd end my sentence on a preposition."

"So you have a proposition for me? Are you proposing, Addie?"

"I said preposition."

"I know," he said, smiling. "Just messing with you. Something my old Grammar taught me." He pointed at the cinnamon-roll guy on his sweatshirt.

I laughed, instantly thankful to have conversations with somebody who was able to keep up. He didn't stall for one moment between his replies, and I realized that I had possibly met my match.

Possibly. Maybe. Hopefully.

We stepped inside to get something to drink. The overhead speakers burbled as the ferry guide from the top deck started to talk about the interesting sights to see and the wildlife in the area.

The boat was pretty warm inside, but I was worried if we stayed too long we'd get used to it and not go back outside to watch for whales or other wildlife. I mean, it'd be easy to sit inside and look out a window, and we could've just turned on the TV to some animal show if we were really going to be lazy. So I told Fitz we should go back outside and watch from there.

The guide was spouting out all these facts about the islands of the Pacific Northwest and telling us about the different types of birds and animals we might see and how to tell which species they were.

"To your left you'll see Steller sea lions," said the guide.

We looked over to see these little bodies undulate below the surface of the water.

"If you look closely, you can see a couple western grebe out beyond the rocks on your right," the guide said.

I didn't know what he was talking about, but I saw two birds out there that looked like ducks but with red eyes. I think our guide expected tips or something because he seemed way too cheery for that early in the morning.

A few minutes later, Fitz and I were standing at the railing, at the bidding of our new friend, the guide.

"The common name is 'killer whale,' but they are also known as orcas. A group that size is called a pod. It's pretty rare to see them because the ferry makes so much noise," the guide said.

The guide kept talking, but we weren't really listening. I watched the massive creatures slide through the water and spray into the air and dip and swerve and glide. It was beautiful—a group of slippery, black bodies moving through dark sheets of blue.

Their bodies were just small dots after a few minutes, like a sentence written on the horizon, oddly punctuated with ellipses every few words. They were moving up and down, like black buoys floating away, like Morse code but in the water. Long. Long. Short. Short. Short. And then there was just this odd quiet and stillness, a flat line of ocean, a sentence deleted.

"There are breeding bald eagles every mile or so, and you can likely see a few nests of peregrine falcons—they can reach more than two hundred miles per hour in a dive. You also are quite likely to see trumpeter swans, depending on your destination on the island," said the guide.

I wanted the guide to stop talking so everyone could look at all the amazing scenery. Although, I guess some of the things he said were pretty cool. I mean, two hundred miles per hour? It was something I couldn't quite grasp without seeing it. Then again, a lot of my life was ungraspable.

"Will we see any blue whales?" I asked.

I figured it probably wasn't likely, but thought I'd check.

"There's an extremely small chance you'll see a great blue whale," the guide said. "Probably one in five hundred thousand or so. Not good odds. But I can tell you a little about the blue whale. It can grow to be over one hundred feet long." And then the guide said something I'd read about before, but hadn't registered until that moment: "In the right conditions, the blue whale can communicate with other blue whales up to one thousand miles away."

"Whoa," said Fitz.

"No way Quentin is that far away," I said, looking at Fitz.

"Yeah," he said, his gaze far away. "Yeah, I bet he can hear me. I hope he can hear us."

I told Fitz everything I knew about whale hearts, and then about hummingbird hearts and how they're as small as the tip of my pinky, and how they beat crazy fast against their super-thin skin, and how they never really slow down because it makes them too cold and too weak.

He told me more about the sound channel deep in the ocean, and I let his voice mingle with the call of the terns. I drifted off into some trancelike state where I heard nothing but the breeze and felt the hopeful strength of the day.

We arrived at San Juan Island and stepped onto the dock that was covered with oil-wet slicks. The slicks were all spotted, and the pencil-thin beams of sun wrote rainbows over the weather-beaten wooden dock.

I looked at Fitz. He was smiling and walking my way. It was one of those moments that I wanted to stick, so I took a mental picture to keep rolled up and stored away in a safe place in my mind. I mean, the museum of my memory had rooms galore, and tons I hadn't ever visited in my entire life, but I wanted to store that memory in a place I could visit often. A room I knew well, where I could set up some comfortable chairs and visit whenever I was feeling down.

"We made it!" I yelled, jumping into his arms. "We made it to the island!"

Fitz spun me around and laughed at my enthusiasm. I wasn't sure exactly what the island meant to him, but I was thrilled that our plan had actually worked.

"This way," Fitz said, grabbing my hand, still smiling.

I still wasn't used to his touch, but I wasn't about to stop him from holding my hand. C'mon.

We walked near the shoreline for a while, passing these gorgeous Pacific madrone trees. I kept looking up at the birds, their wings swishing in the air, their calls sounding out into the clear sky.

"Can't you tell me about these birds?" I said. "As our resident ornithologist, I mean."

"Hah. Hah," said Fitz in a mocking tone as we continued our stroll through the trees and the tall grasses sighing in the wind.

We walked along the coast for a long while and came upon a copse. Fitz led me up a small rise and around another grouping of trees and then said, "Wait here."

I did, shifting my weight from side to side, and tapping my legs.

"Follow my voice!" he yelled after a few minutes.

I stepped around a tree and walked over another small hill and saw the ocean and a small piece of land jutting out in the distance, but nothing else.

"Where are you?" I said.

"Step forward," he said, then yelled, "*Holy C-SPAN!*"

I laughed. "Did you bring Didi with us?"

"I thought it was better than cursing," he said. "Wait till you see this."

He sounded surprised. I was right on top of his voice but couldn't see him over the ledge of grass at my feet.

"Sit down right there. That's where I slid down. You'll be safe," he said. "Yes, she will, Lyle!"

I heard him cuss under his breath at some other voice. His outbursts were getting more frequent, his sweating more copious, and I saw him shiver and hold himself tightly. He seemed more distracted than usual. But I had also been blinking a lot because I was nervous and anxious and imagining the police were on the lookout for us or something. Whatever.

It didn't look like we were too high up or anything, so I did what he said and sat down and scooted forward. It got my butt wet, but it's not like that was a big deal or anything. I slid down just fine.

Fitz caught me in his arms and then spun me around before putting me down on my feet.

We were in this amazing alcove totally empty of any people as far as I could see. Instead, there was this massive skeleton. I wondered if it had once been a blue whale because the head alone was as big as the entire game room in the hospital. I mean, the length was unbelievable, and the bones were bleach-white and strewn all over, moldering on the ground.

"No way," I said, walking to the bones.

"I know. That's what surprised me," he said.

I went and lay down in the chest cavity and rested my hands on my chest and looked up through the bones at the blue sky and the thin clouds passing over. I thought about my heart, and Dad's heart, and Mom's heart, and Fitz's heart, and wondered at their different sizes. I bet mine was smallest, but I wanted it to be more, to be bigger, to house more people and more love and more hope.

"You know, certain yoga positions open up the heart more," said Fitz.

"You're full of it," I said.

"It's true. Those shirts are not just for show."

He sounded sincere, but I wasn't convinced by his confident tone.

"Only, I don't want to be in a position where my heart is more open because I don't want anybody to see what's in there," he said. "Or what isn't in there, I guess. I don't like the idea of being vulnerable like that."

"The V-word? Are you okay, Fitz?"

"It's not like we're in a play or onstage now, Addie. Nobody's watching us, you know?"

"And?"

"I could fit thousands of my own heart inside that whale's chest, but it wouldn't matter. I am the one still living, and my heart is the one still churning in my chest, sloshing around all my shame," he said.

"What?"

Fitz kicked sand into the air and yelled something at Willy, then turned back to me. His face was pale and rigid and unblinking. He held his stomach and looked like he might hurl. He coughed, then composed himself and stared into the sky.

"Quentin," he said.

I looked out at the massive bay of gorgeous water. There were tons of birds doing this amazing thing where they circled above the swells and then, when they spotted a fish, they dive-bombed into the water at this incredible speed. It made me want to watch from beneath the water, to see their bodies shoot through the blue, leaving a trail of bubbles.

I hesitated, then said what I was thinking. I was tired of being left out, tired of feeling like he was hiding something. "What happened to your brother, Fitz?"

"It's just, I haven't been able to really say goodbye to Quentin," he said, looking at his feet. "I mean, they let me go to the funeral and everything, but it was so rigid, so structured, with the program and all. So freaking structured. I never really got to say a proper goodbye. And this is our place."

He looked out at the endlessly restless water.

"And I'm sorry, Quentin. I know it's a stupid adage, but I often think about bad things happening to good people. Sorry it's not more colorful than that."

I didn't say anything.

"This month marks the anniversary of his death," said Fitz. "That's why I tried to break out earlier. I wanted to come here because it's the year Quentin would have been old enough to join the San Juan Islands Birders Club. He wanted that vest and those binoculars with the logo on them and that little pin so much. It came with a book and a checklist and everything. Sounds silly, but it means a lot to me because it meant a lot to him."

"That doesn't sound silly at all," I said.

Fitz walked over and sat next to me in the chest cavity of the whale bones. He rested his head in the sand, and we both stared into the sky.

"Mom took us to San Juan Island every few months to run

around and explore the coastline. Quentin always brought this little notepad and these really cheap binoculars. He liked looking for birds. He knew everything about them. Quentin's favorite bird was the Kirtland's warbler. He said it was like the LeBron James of birds—everybody wanted to get a picture of it. At the time, I didn't think about the fact that it was kind of an odd hobby for someone so young. At the time, we only cared about having fun.

"So we visited the island years ago and found this secluded alcove. This one we're sitting in right now. Nobody was ever there. Here, I mean. Nobody is ever here. Anyway, we fashioned these wings out of leaves tied to sticks, and we'd hold them and flap them and take turns jumping off this lip, either into the water over there or into the sand along that ridge where you first dropped into the place. It was stupid and fun. It made Quentin so happy. It made me happy, too," he said.

Fitz stopped and took off his bandana. He bunched it up in his hands.

"You don't have to tell me if you don't want to, Fitz," I said.

"No. It's fine. It wasn't you. It was your Boggle word: *warbler*. That's what upset me weeks ago. Sorry, again, for being so rude," he said.

I turned and looked at the small dots of sand freckling Fitz's face. His curly hair was covered in sand. I'm sure my hair was likewise a mess of sand and sea air. I liked that we matched.

We were both quiet for a minute. Then Fitz said, "That was the fall I started hearing voices. I'd just hit puberty—I know, you probably thought I was born with a voice this deep." He looked at me briefly, then back to the sky.

I was aware he was trying to put on the comedy mask, but it wasn't working. Those small gestures to swap masks never work in the face of something so persistent. It's impossible to hide some things.

"And I felt that if I missed this year, it would be what would tip the scales of depression the wrong way."

I rested my hand on his chest, and he let the bandana drape over his face, like he didn't want me seeing him as he told the rest. He breathed, and I saw the bandana stir.

"I heard a voice tell me to push Quentin off the ledge," he said. "It was something we always did, so I didn't think much of it, though it scared me because I didn't know where the voice was coming from—*who* the voice was coming from. But he wasn't expecting the shove. We always yelled, 'Think like a bird!' before the push, or something like that, but I didn't say anything that time. I just pushed him. He slipped, and . . . he landed weird. It was an accident."

He took the bandana off and stood up and stretched. We both stared at the water for a minute.

"I'm so sorry, Fitz," I said, reaching out my hand.

He didn't reach back. It was awkward, and I felt stupid, making one of those cliché, stereotypical gestures after hearing about someone's loss. So I gently took his hand and pulled him back down so we'd both be seated in the cool sand.

Loss is so messy, so impossible to hold or mold or shape in any way—we really can't grab on to it. I worried it was wrong of me to try in that moment. But Fitz smiled at my touch and stared out at the water and clouds. Then he cleared his throat and rested his head on his knees and looked at his feet.

He'd kicked off his flip-flops and was rolling his toes in the sand. He sighed deeply and sniffed. I could tell he was trying to hide anger and sadness and probably a whole mess of emotions behind that handsome gap, behind that mask.

"Brain damage. He was barely here. He died a month later. You know, it's funny," he said, shaking his head and looking my way.

Before he could finish the thought, I jumped in. "Don't throw something. That's how Junior always starts his rants."

Fitz smiled. "You're right. But it's true. Don't worry, I'm not planning on leaving this spot. But it *is* cosmically funny. Maybe tragic is a better word for it."

"For what?"

"Well," he said, "Remember that book about the mental hospital where they call the psych ward a cuckoo's nest? I guess it ends with the narrator breaking out, but I keep thinking about it being called a cuckoo's nest."

"What does that have to do with anything?" I said.

I sat up and kicked off my flip-flops. He was still rolling the bandana in his hands. I scooted closer to him. He was warm, and I let our bodies sink close to one another as he kept talking. I felt like being closer to Fitz might make him feel less uncomfortable. What in the world did I know about comforting someone with such a traumatic past? Hint: absolutely nothing.

"Cuckoo birds are brood parasites. They lay their eggs in the nests of other species. When the cuckoo eggs hatch, the cuckoo fledglings nudge the other eggs out of the nest, and they are raised by the mother of the other eggs, the original eggs, who is totally unaware of the switch. Or if she is aware, she does it anyway. The siblings die and the cuckoos take their place and go on as if nothing is wrong. It's awful."

I saw where he was going before he finished the thought, and

I was already working on a response. He looked calm, but like the-calm-before-the-storm type of calm. I didn't like it.

"It was an accident, Fitz," I said. "Quentin knows that."

"You didn't know Quentin," he said, clutching the bandana and wiping his eyes.

"But I know you would never hurt someone intentionally," I said. "And the fact that you care this much about what happened shows me that you didn't want it to happen. You didn't want this. Nobody wants that kind of thing to happen."

"Except cuckoo birds. It's what they do," he said.

He dug his feet deeper into the sand and looked up at the sky. His fists were tight, and he kept wiping his eyes. He wasn't crying real hard or anything, but I could tell he didn't want to let his emotions out fully because he wouldn't be able to contain all that frustration and confusion and hurt.

We didn't speak for maybe five minutes—and if you know what it's like to sit in silence that long, then you know it felt like an eternity.

"We can only see so far with our eyes. We can only hear so much with our ears. It's like we're in a room, and as soon as the lights go out, we can finally see," I said. "I think that's how it is, to die. To go on. I bet when the lights go out, we are shown some exit from the stage we never knew existed, and we walk off into some new forever where all the people we love are waiting backstage. And we do it all over again."

"That would be nice," he said. "As long as he's actually waiting for me. So I can apologize forever."

He kept his head down on his knees, drawing in the sand between his feet.

SPENCER HYDE

"I remember learning about Lincoln and his son Willie in class a couple years ago," I said.

I was hoping to break the silence with something meaningful, or at least something Fitz might be able to relate to. It's funny, I hadn't thought of that thing about Lincoln and his family for years.

"President Lincoln?"

"Yeah. His boy Willie died of typhoid fever. He was eleven years old."

"Same age as Quentin," Fitz said. "Sorry. I mean, he'd be eleven this year. Sorry. Go on."

"No, you're okay. It's just that, when Lincoln was dealing with all the big stuff—like the fate-of-the-country-type of big— he would go visit Willie's grave. I guess that's the place where love and justice met for him or something. Maybe mercy, too. Maybe he needed those visits to regain solidarity. He just needed to see him again and say sorry and ask for help. I don't know."

Fitz sat up a little in the sand and drew in a deep breath, letting it slowly out, controlling the release of air so his lips sputtered. He rested his hand on my knee.

"Thank you," he said.

Then he leaned over and hugged me close and tight, and I felt his muscles through the soft shirt he was wearing. He was still just as attractive as the first day I saw him. Trust me. But I let myself melt into that hug because it turns out I was in need of that kind of embrace as well, I just hadn't known it before it hit me, before his body rested against mine in that moment on the island.

And that's when he kissed me.

Yes, it was my first legitimate kiss. Yes, I'd tried kissing before. No, none of the kisses had ever made me feel the way Fitz's did. Yes, he was attractive. Yes, I was a mess of hormones and emotions all tied together with a giant bow of giddiness. And of course, my disorder couldn't let me take a break for even this moment of pure freedom and joy.

As we kissed, I started blinking in a numbered sequence with specific lengths for each blink. I counted them and tapped my hand on his knee. He opened his eyes and leaned back and started laughing.

"Addie Foster. Always multitasking."

"I can't help it," I said, holding my hand over my heart.

"You can count the beats this time," he said.

He kissed me again, and then he hugged me again and stared at the water over my shoulder. I listened to him breathe for a minute before he spoke again.

"I wish I could run around the island and maybe catch some trick or tear in time and space and find Quentin standing there and laughing. He deserves it more than anybody else. But I can't. Time doesn't get tricked, no matter how much we wish it might, or could, or should," said Fitz, still hugging me.

"What happened to your mom after all that?" I said, waiting a beat before jumping in.

I felt Fitz recoil, and turn his body from mine. I immediately regretted asking that question.

"My mom dealt with it the way she deals with everything. Doesn't matter. Let's just enjoy the island right now. The weather is perfect."

We both rested our hands on our knees and faced the water. We watched the clouds move through the bones and curl around the sky above the island. Then there was this noise about two hundred yards out or so, and a massive tale flapped above the water and shone super bright in the sun and then sunk back below the water.

We stood and ran out to where the water was pulling back from the shore and watched as this massive whale body rose up and opened its gigantic mouth before sliding beneath the sheets of blue.

"Wow." Then I said again, "Wow."

"You saw that, too, right? I'm not seeing things now, too? Wouldn't that be a treat—auditory and visual!" Fitz said.

I stepped closer to Fitz and took his hand. I worried about sounding too sentimental, but I still said what I was thinking.

"Maybe that was Quentin. And he heard you. From a thousand miles away."

"You really do mix your metaphors," he said. "Stages and whales? I'm not a teacher, but I'd have to give you a low score at this point."

Fitz rubbed his eyes again and then hugged me with one arm, pulling me into his side like I was being curled into a little alcove.

"All I ever wanted was forgiveness," he said.

"He heard you. A thousand miles away, maybe."

"Maybe," he said, not sounding convinced.

"We dive as deep as we can and hope somebody is listening to our call across the deep waters. All of us, at some point."

I hoped I hadn't frustrated him in some way by bringing it up like that. I was so unsure of the ground I was walking on—the shaky earth of grief, the shifting plates of loss, the tectonics of memory.

It was all pretty fascinating, seeing that whale, and I thought about the guide and how much I wanted to tell him we saw a blue whale and how it was the coolest thing ever, and all about the skeleton. But we decided it best to keep it all a secret.

"This is your spot now too," said Fitz, rubbing his eyes with the sleeves of his sweatshirt.

When I shivered in the cold wind off the water, Fitz pulled me close and hugged me tight, with both arms. I loved every second of it.

"Getting cold, Addie Foster? Sorry—I mean, losing heat?"

I nodded, and Fitz suggested we grab our shoes and head back to the boat.

"You asked about my mother," he said as we climbed back over the small hill hiding the alcove.

"Yeah, sorry. Not my place."

"No, I'm glad you asked," said Fitz. "You know she's never showed up for Parent Visit? Not one time. Not once, since she admitted me to that hospital. You know why?"

I had a good guess, but I didn't feel bold enough to say it. I was afraid it would hurt him, and I didn't want to risk it after making my way over so much history to a place where I felt comfortable hugging him and kissing him and being with him and everything.

"Because I killed her son. She can't forgive me. Should I even expect her to? It's true. I did that to Quentin. Me," he said, huffing and picking up his pace. "But I said sorry, and that's what I wanted. Thank you for helping me, Addie."

"You're welcome, Fitz."

"I mean it. Thank your."

"Your?"

He pointed at my sweatshirt, and I laughed.

"Oh. You're welcome, for."

"For what?"

"No. You're welcome, for. That's it. Just thought we should end the trip on a preposition."

Fitz laughed deep in his throat, and I smiled. Our walk to the ferry was all light as the sun swallowed up the sky and everything around us. We shed our lame sweatshirts as we boarded the boat from the dock where all the morning water had been licked back up into the sky.

Ten

I t was a surprisingly sunny day even though it was, like, near the
end of November. The sky was on fire, the clouds moving like
hundreds of small boat sails set aflame.

When the boat approached the dock back on the mainland,
I saw all these little black dots on the shore, and I worried we
might be walking into the arms of the police. I tried to get a
closer look, so I stood at the railing and squinted in the sunlight.

"Are you peering at the pier?" said Fitz.

"Nice homophone," I said. "Are those cops?"

The guide didn't hear us. Nobody heard us, thankfully. I had
to be more careful with the volume of my voice.

"Sit down, Addie. Nobody is worried about us," said Fitz.

That upset me. Not what he said, but what it made me think
about. I'd been thinking about his mother the entire ride back.
I'd been trying to concentrate on the beautiful day and lose my
thoughts in all the wonderful scenery, but once a thought was in
there, it was like being stuck in concrete, and the only way to rid
myself of those thoughts was to see them through.

Compulsive, that's right. Like clockwork. Like a Swiss watch. I never had to question my drive.

"It's only one o'clock," I said. "Let's get lunch and then go see her."

"Who?"

"Your mom," I said.

"Max?"

"What? No. Your mom."

"My mom's name is Max. Well, Maxine, but she goes by Max. And the answer is no. I don't ever want to see her again. As soon as I'm eighteen, I'm on my own. She won't notice either way."

I could tell he was lying. He said it all with too much emotion behind the words. I knew he had his mask on—the serious one, the coy one, the one that tries to hide all the worry and vulnerability. That's right, the V-word.

"You need to confront her, Fitz. She can't hold this over you forever."

"Sure she can," he said, slouching into one of the plastic chairs by the railing.

"Stop it. I won't let you live your life waiting for forgiveness. You need to act. You need to forgive yourself, too. You're holding it over yourself just as much as you think she is."

Fitz stood and turned toward the water and started talking to Toby. I know that because I heard his name. Then Fitz mentioned Lyle as well, and then I heard him scream at Willy. He totally lost it on Willy about some joke he didn't want to laugh at because it wasn't the right time.

I wanted to put my arm around him or something, but instead, I sat down and rested my head on the back of the seat and looked at the sky, hoping when Fitz returned, he would be calmer.

"Addie Foster. The comic character-turned-heroine," said Fitz with a thin-lipped smile as he walked back. "Sorry about that. Same old story, right?"

"You okay? I mean, seriously," I said, grabbing his hand.

He sat down next to me and rested his head on his chair and stared up into the thinning clouds that were starting to pass with greater frequency.

"Maybe it *is* time I paid her a visit."

"Agreed," I said.

"But only so I can get Quentin's painting." He knew I was going to ask, so he nudged his bandana back from his eyes. "He painted a Kirtland's warbler. It's kind of messy and childlike, but that's why I like it. I want it. I think he'd like me to have it."

It looked like he was stretching into the idea of getting the painting back. I wanted him to find forgiveness so bad that I didn't care how Max felt about it. And maybe I was finally starting to figure out just who I was, just how strong I was. That made me smile. But it also made me anxious.

I started tapping my knees and blinking. I thought about Dr. Morris's essay question and realized, though I'd found out more about myself, I still didn't know why the playwright would have characters sit around and talk without anything happening. It made more sense to me to get out and *do* something. Maybe that was part of the answer? That bugged me. Not the writers, but the fact that I still didn't have an answer for the essay question.

I kept thinking about the way the play ends, with the characters saying if Godot shows up they'll be saved, and if he doesn't then they won't have a life to live. They keep saying they will leave if he doesn't show. But Godot doesn't show up, and those characters just keep waiting. They don't move. Whatever.

I stared out the window at the stern of the boat. Maybe I was looking for cops with their hats and bright badges, or maybe for white jackets from the hospital. I didn't, in fact, know what I was looking for, but I knew people would be looking for *us*.

I wondered how the others were doing—Leah and Junior and Didi and Wolf and Martha. Maybe a little about Doc, but not so much. I thought about getting them souvenirs or something, but that was wishful thinking: we didn't have enough money, and even if I brought something back, it would be confiscated.

Fitz was quiet as the boat took, like, an hour to dock. When we finally got off the boat, I spoke up.

"I miss Didi. And Leah. This is weird to say, but I miss them. I didn't think I'd miss that place."

"Not the place," he said. "The people. That's how life is. People make the place, not the other way around."

The light was making all these crazy shadows on the pavement where people were getting into their cars after departing from the ferry. Other people walked along the pier or stood near the fishermen or just sat down on the benches warped from the sun and water and salt and wind.

Fitz suggested we get something to eat, so we stopped at this place near the water that was selling fish and chips. I hate vinegar, but I was starving, so we grabbed food to go and headed in the general direction of the bus stop with no ostensible plan in mind. At least, I didn't have a plan in mind.

"What would you do without your Sugar Momma to buy you lunch?" I said.

"That's really weird," said Fitz, laughing.

"True. I felt it as I said it. Sorry," I said, blushing.

I liked the salt of the chips and the deep-fried goodness of the fish. Grease was a wonderful thing.

"Where to?" I said. "This is your show."

We kept walking, and this really fine mist started to float down. Sure enough, as soon as you think you've got a sunny day, bring on the waterworks, right? In the distance, small clouds had gathered and formed this tight fist and darkened and crawled through the sky to our spot on the shoreline. It only took a matter of minutes.

Overhead, I saw this accordion of starlings shifting in the sky. I wondered how they were able to fly so close together and in unison or whatever. I loved being outside. It made me not want to return to the hospital. Like, ever.

"So what were you going to do if you didn't have any money? Wait, do you just want me for my money? I mean, seriously. Fitzgerald Whitman IV, the consummate gold digger," I said, trying out his full name. "But I guess a name like that presupposes gold digging to some degree."

"That's all I've ever wanted from you, Addie," he said. "Nice sweaters and five-star trips to the islands."

I saw these tents lined up with fishermen hawking the fish they'd wrapped up to sell in small bundles.

"Did you know that a turtle's heart goes on beating for hours after it's been butchered? Ask anyone down there. It's true. My mom's friend worked on the docks for forever, and he said he's seen one bounce on those squat wood tables where they sell their tuna and whitefish and salmon, near where the water laps at the legs of the workers. The little heart just bumps and bumps for hours," I said.

"We just ate fish, Addie. Please don't tell me that stuff."

I started blinking fast and thinking about those hearts. I placed my hand on my chest and felt the thud of that little muscle flexing behind my bones.

"Shut up!" Fitz yelled. "I don't care, Toby. Leave me alone!"

Fitz spun in circles yelling "Leave me alone!" and it made me scared. Like, legitimately scared and not just concerned or nervous, for the first time ever.

Maybe I hadn't worried about it in the hospital because there were orderlies and doctors who could help if something got out of hand. But Fitz yelling on the streets in the middle-of-no-where-Washington was not making me feel comfortable. I was worried about him, especially because he hadn't been taking his full medication doses for a couple of days—maybe longer.

"Maybe we should head back," I said. "I mean, we saw the island and you were able to say goodbye to Quentin, right? That's why you wanted to escape in the first place, yeah? I think it's best if we head back and not make the doctors or our parents worry about us anymore."

I bit my lip when I mentioned worried parents. I shouldn't have said that, or at least not in that way.

"No, Addie, you were right. I need to confront her," he said, walking with more determination.

We reached the stop just as the bus arrived. I hesitated to step aboard, but I knew that if Fitz was going to struggle, than somebody should be there who knew him and could possibly get through to him or whatever. Maybe Max would know how to handle it, though she wasn't my favorite person after hearing about Fitz's past.

Anyway, the bus ride to the southern part of Tacoma felt especially long because I kept my eyes on Fitz the whole time—between blinks, of course—and saw that he was sweating more than usual as the scenery outside passed by in little boxes of bus-window, the hair on the back of his neck curling in the wetness. He was balling up that bandana and turning it in his hands. I was amazed the fabric had lasted that long, to be honest.

"Why don't we just get off at the hospital?" I said, trying one more time.

"We're almost there," he said, standing.

He'd stood up way too soon, which was kind of awkward. It's like when people step to the elevator doors way before their floor, and because they're uncomfortable in admitting their mistake, they just stand close to the doors without stepping back. It's kind of funny to watch, really.

I stayed in my seat and waited seven more stops before we actually arrived.

When the bus's hydraulic system hissed and the one side lowered, we stepped off into overgrown grass near a sidewalk buckling from the underground tree roots. I saw a row of cookie-cutter apartment buildings, each one as boring as the next, with gray, drab colors and sagging corners where rain gutters were torn or barely holding onto the siding.

Fitz grabbed my hand as we walked through an alleyway with trash blown and bunched into the corners of the buildings' parking structures. After turning two corners and ducking beneath an oddly placed carport, we arrived at glass doors that looked like they hadn't been cleaned in years. The doors led into the artificially lit lobby of Seaside Pines. Super corny name. I know. Whatever.

Moving from natural light to artificial light made me sick because it felt so compact and condensed and grainy. Outside, dark clouds were rolling closer, starting to drip rain just as we stepped inside.

We called the elevator, and Fitz hit the button for the fourth floor. I stared at the doors and thought again about that big whale heart inching open for us, closing us in, moving us up.

We stood outside Max's apartment, and Fitz banged on the door. "Max!" he yelled.

I thought about memory and how smells can bring this incredible sense of recall. Even from the hallway, Max's apartment smelled awful, stale and sharp. A mix of rotting food, sour milk, cigarettes, sweat and mildew and wet dog. I covered my nose, and my eyes started watering.

In a softer tone, Fitz said, "Sorry, Addie. If she's not here, she'll be back soon."

He knocked again, then tried the doorknob. It turned in his hand.

"Never locks the door," Fitz muttered. "Who would want to steal from this place? It's disgusting. Max!"

He led me into the apartment.

"Please excuse the filth," Fitz said. "It always looks, and smells, like this." He looked around the room. "Max!" he yelled.

I noticed that he rarely, if ever, said "Mom" or any variation—and particularly not then, not in the apartment. The intensity of the storm outside increased, the tapping on the rain gutters now audible.

There was a stack of newspapers between an old television and a sunken, orange corduroy chair. An ashtray filled with cigarette butts sat on the table. On the wall near the television, there was a small painting of the bird Fitz had mentioned, along with a bunch of pictures of Quentin. It was like a mosaic of Quentin in different places, different positions, but always the same, large smile. I didn't see any pictures of Fitz.

Fitz took the bird picture off the wall and tucked it under his sweatshirt. "She won't miss it," he said, then, "Stop!"

Fitz shouted again, and before I could register his movements, he turned and his weight knocked me over the coffee table.

I hit my head against a stone pot holding an artificial agave plant. I started bleeding almost immediately. I touched the back of my head and felt the moisture, and my fingers came back red. My vision was blurry, but I hadn't blacked out. I moaned in pain and rolled onto my side, attempting to stand.

My face was stuck in some old housekeeping magazine, and I felt a sharp pain shooting down the back of my head and spreading into my shoulders.

"Shut up, Lyle!" said Fitz.

He started throwing things.

"I'll tell you why, Willy!" he yelled.

He knocked the television over, and I heard it shatter. He was wrestling something or someone but I couldn't make out what was going on. I used the orange chair to pull myself to my feet.

I moved as quickly as I could to the front door, walking past a mess of a kitchen with plates and take-out cartons scattered everywhere. The cupboards were open, and cracks crisscrossed the walls—it was all more than I was able to think about in that moment.

He was at a full yell at that point, knocking a mirror onto the floor and turning over the coffee table. I paused at the door and tried to get a sense of the situation. Before I could get my eyes to believe what they were seeing or my mind to understanding what was going on, a glass cup came flying at me. I dodged it and heard it break against the door.

I closed the door and started crying as I hurried down the steps and ran to the curb and tried to get the attention of the drivers zipping by. I slipped in the grass, which was slick with rain that had started to pour in earnest. I rose to my feet, totally drenched.

And nobody would stop. I kept one hand pressed against my head and tried to look stable. I saw car after car blur past in a wave of lights, and I heard the swooshing sound of the rain as it slipped from the rapidly turning tires. Water sprayed the giant gutters collecting the swelling and coursing water.

My waving finally got the attention of a taxi driver.

"Please call the police!" I said. "Call the police!"

I felt so tired and dizzy. I shouldn't have yelled because pain stabbed into my head when I raised my voice. I felt sick. My stomach hurt, and I felt like throwing up. I sat down on the curb, but I really wanted to lay down in the grass and take a nap. I was confused and hurt and angry, and I didn't know what to do. My tears washed away in the rain, one and the same.

The driver took out his cell phone and dialed. Someone must have answered on the other end of the line, because after a minute, he turned to me and said, "What's the problem?"

"Tell them two kids escaped the hospital psych ward, and one is injured and the other one is in that building right there and needs help," I said, pointing to the small window where Fitz was likely still throwing things, breaking things, and shouting back at the voices shouting at him.

There had been something animalistic in his eyes when he shouted at me, something of anger and greed and hunger, and it scared me.

I hoped it wasn't Fitz. I knew it wasn't Fitz. He wasn't that person. I didn't know him as that person. The Fitz I knew would never intentionally hurt me. He wasn't a violent person.

I don't think the driver fully believed my story, but it didn't matter because at least he was talking to the police for me. The driver stepped out of the car after putting on his hazards.

I tried to keep my eyes open in the haze of red, blinking lights. Then rested my head on my knees.

"Are you okay? Are you hurt?" he said. "Do you need a ride to the hospital?"

"I think I should wait," I said. "I think I'll be fine."

"The police are on their way. I can stay if you'd like," he said.

"I'm okay," I said.

He shrugged. "Are you sure? I'll wait just to be sure."

"No. It's okay. Thank you," I said.

He stood and reminded me the cops were on their way before getting back into his cab and driving away.

I sat on the curb debating whether I should return to the apartment or not. I was too close to the road to hear anything going on inside the apartment, but I was worried and exhausted and my limbs felt so heavy that, if I fell over, they might just pull me down through the concrete of the road and straight through to the center of the earth.

My head throbbed, but the blood seemed to be coagulating, which meant the cut wasn't all that deep. The clouds were still dark, and thick drops of rain coated the ground and slipped from the leaves of the trees and sprayed from the road as more cars passed by with an endless humming sound.

After sitting for a few more minutes, I slowly made my way back to the stairs leading up to the apartment. I was afraid of

Fitz hurting himself or someone else. I stood under an awning to gather my energy and my courage. I leaned against the wall and rested my head on my arm because the ground kept slipping beneath me in an odd slant and turn and blur.

In that moment, I heard the police sirens, and this jolt of adrenaline coursed through me. I could be in serious danger if I stepped into that room again. How well did I know Fitz off his meds? Like, not at all. Zero.

Had it really been an accident—the thing with Quentin? Yes. I believed it was, and I hated myself for even considering the alternative. But the idea had legs and it ran through my mind, sprinted through my thoughts. I hesitated before deciding it wasn't worth chasing that thread.

A short, plump cop stepped from the cruiser and adjusted his cap and his gear as he crossed the wet grass. His partner left the car lights on and walked my way. I hated those bright, red-and-blue lights. The spinning made me sick.

They talked to me for a minute before the taller, stronger-looking cop said he would take a look upstairs. He radioed something in on his shoulder unit or whatever they call it and made his way up the concrete steps.

The plump cop led me to the car and turned me around and set me in the back seat. I tried to open the door for some air, but it was locked.

"For your own safety," he said, climbing into the front seat.

"I'm not dangerous," I said.

"I know. But they all say that, sweetheart," said the cop, giving me a kind look. I think he was aware I posed no real threat, but I understood he had no way of knowing if I was lying or not. What an awful job that would be.

The spinning lights on the car's roof reflected in the windows of the cars passing by. Traffic slowed as people stared at me, like maybe slowing down would allow them to witness some massive crime scene or something. So freaking ridiculous.

I sat and blinked like crazy, and at one point the officer asked what was wrong.

"Just my OCD," I said.

He didn't seem to understand.

"I'm just nervous for my friend," I said.

I don't think he'd noticed my head, or he would have called an ambulance. Maybe it really wasn't bad or he would have spotted the blood. I was not with it, like, one hundred percent, but I was savvy enough to know when to keep my mouth shut.

I looked at the window and thought about Fitz and wondered why the other officer was taking so long. But then I saw the tall officer in his pressed uniform walking through the rain. The rain had fallen with more force and snarling persistence when I'd been ushered into the cruiser. It was totally dumping at that point, the water pooling in potholes and grassy divots. It was running straight off the rigid cap on the cop's head.

"Nobody there," said the tall cop as he slid into his seat behind the wheel, shaking the rain from his clothes and turning up the heat.

"Addie, was it?" said the plump one.

"What?" I was crying. I was worried. I was scared.

"Don't be scared. We'll find your friend. We need to know everything about him. And right now."

So I told them everything I could think of. I had to clear my throat, like, a million times so I could get to talking right. I tried not to leave any details out—height, weight, tie-dyed bandana, curly brown hair, eyes like gray stones with blue flecks, the gap in his front teeth, the broad shoulders, the synonym sweatshirt, and the way he walked, the way he smiled, the way he laughed.

Maybe it was too much information, because halfway through my description, the plump cop got back on the radio and the tall cop began driving around the block. They totally ignored me after that.

Nothing. No sign of Fitz.

And that's how our great escape ended—at least for me. Mom was at the station waiting for me, her eyes red and puffy. I felt awful when I saw that.

That was when I realized what a big mistake I'd made. I'd hurt her with this small idea of a fun escape for a brief outing to help Fitz keep a promise. I stood by that promise, but I also had never done anything beyond my OCD rituals to make Mom cry. Not a thing. At least not that I was aware of. It was a paradox that was hard to process in a cramped police station at night.

It was also when I started to cry because I realized I had someone I could call *Mom* and mean it, and I wanted to keep her in my life, like, forever.

She hugged me and brushed my hair down my back and that's when she noticed the cut. After she patched me up using the station's first-aid kit, Mom sat with me in a room that had a cheap metal table and horrific metal chairs that were about as comfortable as sitting on a stack of granite boulders. Maybe less so.

Anyway, we sat in two of those chairs, and I told Mom the whole story, from my first conversation with Fitz about the breakout until the moment I walked into the police station. She kept sniffling and getting tissues and saying things under her breath like "Should have kept you at home."

I had a real hard time telling her everything, still knowing that Fitz was lost out there. It made me feel sick. I felt like throwing up.

"So dangerous," she said.

She kept repeating that. *So dangerous. Too young. Scared to death.* The usual suspects, right? But this time those phrases actually held meaning. It's weird how phrases can have meaning in specific moments. They weren't cliché when Mom said them that evening. They were the truth. I started crying again, too.

"I'm scared they won't find him, Mom," I said. I rested my elbows on my knees and let my hands meet my face. I looked at my feet, tapping one each second while I alternated blinks. "And if they do, when they do, will he be alive?"

I think Mom noticed, for the first time, that Fitz was more than just a fellow inpatient. She lifted me from my chair and held me close.

She smelled clean, like fresh laundry, and dry. My sweatshirt was still damp, and I felt sweaty and clammy and exhausted. I was also sick to my stomach and knew that my lack of meds was the culprit. Well, partially.

"I didn't know he meant that much to you, Addie," she said, holding me as I cried.

"I didn't know it either," I said. "But I do now."

We sat in that room for at least another hour. I let Mom hold me. I let her comfort me. I didn't know how to get a grasp on my emotions. It's funny how something so big can make you feel so small, can make you want to revert back to an infant, looking for comfort in your parents, your mom.

And Fitz didn't have that.

The officers were pretty good about making sure we were

doing all right. They checked in twice and brought us both blankets and coffee. Well, Mom got coffee; they gave me hot chocolate. The drink and the blanket warmed me up, but I was still
thinking of Fitz out there somewhere, cold and alone, listening to
voices that were telling him to do who-knows-what.

"Can we go look for him?" I said.

Mom didn't respond, but just pulled my blanket closer to my
chin.

"He'll be looking for me," I said.

Mom said that someone from the hospital was coming to
pick me up, and that we could talk there after I'd had a shower
and some rest. She said she'd stay at the hospital with me and
make sure I felt safe, but I didn't want that. At least not at the
time.

"I need to look," I said. "I can't just sit here and wait."

She sighed and gave me this half-hearted parent look where
half of the smile is a grimace that says "okay" and the other half
says "but just this once," and it almost made me laugh because,
like, was I really going to break out of a psych ward a second time
and lose my friend who was going through some very specific
stuff and then get picked up by the cops *again*?

"Thanks, Mom," I said, before she could say anything.

As an only child, I tended to win those kinds of battles. And
I always knew the right ones to fight for. This was one of them.
C'mon. No question.

Mom stepped out of the room and spoke with the tall officer
for maybe ten minutes. I saw him scratch his forehead and look
in at me at least twice. He left for a moment, then returned, and
they talked a bit more.

The blinds in the room were a really nasty brown color, and

they looked stained from coffee or something darker. Dead flies lined the sill, and I saw rings of dust collecting on the reinforced glass, the small wires cutting diagonally across one another, creating this hideous patchwork of dark lines and thick, cloudy glass.

The tile floor looked hopeless—a red that had faded to a sorry orange. I was halfway through counting the chipped tiles on the floor when Mom returned with a smile.

"The officer agreed to let me take you to the hospital instead," she said. "You're lucky I'm good with men."

"Else I wouldn't be here," I said.

"Oh, Addie."

"It's true."

"Can't go a day without joking about something, can you?"

"Learned from the best," I said.

"I don't joke."

"I know. I learned from you that I should start joking," I said.

She shook her head, and we walked to the old Camry in the parking lot. Small streams of water made their way down the car lot through the path of least resistance. The water on the pavement mirrored the lamps dotting the streets and the bright lights shooting from the corners of the police station.

"I'm supposed to be taking you straight to the hospital, but I bet I can buy us an hour or two. I'll say we got lost."

It wasn't very plausible, but I didn't care. I was still in this state of belief that adults never really got into trouble. I liked that kind of naiveté.

We stepped into the car and wiped off the water from our sweaters or jackets or whatever. Some people say they don't want to live near the Sound or in the Northwest because they don't like the rain and it would make them all depressed or something, but they don't know what that word really means so it makes me laugh. I love the rain. It's a beautiful thing. Usually.

Today, though, the rain tapped on the windshield, and I felt hopeless, like, how on earth was I going to spot Fitz in this storm? Where would he go? What would he do?

I might know Fitz, but I didn't know what Lyle or Toby or Willy would tell him to do, so where did that leave us? Well, it left us searching the docks where he and I had boarded the ferry. We drove by the inn. I tried to think of what Fitz might do if he started getting cold or upset or afraid. I saw a penny by my foot and picked it up and turned it in my hands, blinking for every dark spot between the pillars on the back of the coin, then turning and blinking for the same number on the face.

Then it came to me. Lincoln. Willie. How could I have missed it?

"I'm such an idiot!" I said.

"What?"

"I might have an idea of where he is. Call the cops," I said. "No, wait. Don't call the cops yet. Let's go there."

"Where? Where is he?"

"Wherever his brother is buried. Quentin. Fitz might be wherever the grave is. There is a small graveyard near Beacon Hill—by the hospital. We can see it from the windows of the psych ward floor."

"I know the one," she said, turning the car around and speeding up.

I took deep breaths, swallowed, the knot in my throat still there. I rubbed my eyes and ignored the mild pulse at the back of my head where I'd hit it against that pot. I realized Mom was not driving me to the station like I thought she might. She was going to the graveyard.

The flutter of the wipers synced with the rapping of my heart. I put my hand against my chest and felt for that syncopated rhythm as the rain let up for just a moment and there was quiet.

Then the oddest thing happened. When we stopped near the decorated wrought-iron entrance to the graveyard, it began to snow. It was a startling shift in the weather that I didn't expect. I'm sure nobody expected it. It got really quiet. Total silence. The ground was soaked, and the temperature dropped and tiny flakes of ice-rain began to fall—a twinkling in the trees, the tapping sounding like a softer form of a rainstick turned upside down. I considered the oddity that silence could be so loud.

That's when I heard a yell, and I knew it had to be Fitz. I rushed through the soaked leaves and soggy grass. My shoes sank into the soft earth.

"Addie, wait!" Mom shouted as I took off running.

And I should have waited. And I should have walked to the scene with Mom, but I was only thinking of helping Fitz before things got any worse. And I wasn't sure what was happening, and I wanted to save him from himself, from the voices in his mind.

Really, I should have done a lot of things differently, but I was running on pure instinct and fear.

I followed his voice, and I thought I heard him yell "Quentin!" But it was muffled, and I wasn't sure if I was just shaping the noises I heard into that name so I could justify running from Mom. I sprinted, almost falling over numerous graves. I tripped on one that was embedded in the grass, the headstone a rectangle divot filled with water beginning to freeze. I knocked my knee against another stone and felt a stinging spike from my thigh to my foot, but I kept running until I reached Fitz.

It might be too generous, my saying that I found Fitz, describing that person as Fitz. He wasn't there. Sure, his body was there, and he was shouting "Quentin" and "Sorry" and "Come back" between loud sobs and angry, sharp motions as he dug a shovel into the soft earth and threw it over his shoulder, the clink of the metal against rock echoing through the trees.

The gravesite was in a grove of what looked to be red maple trees, but there were almost no leaves left on the branches, and the snow would surely wipe out the rest. The fallen leaves were under my feet, their muddy arrangement contorted in the standing water and crystalizing in the now-freezing weather.

I stood there, breathing hard. My breath plumed out in tiny clouds of white that looked like speech bubbles from a graphic novel or a cartoon just waiting to be filled. But I didn't know what to fill them with. I didn't know what to say, to think, to shout, to fear, to hope for. I fell to my knees and dropped my head and felt the blood rush to a point in my forehead and pulse there. I looked up again and felt dizzy, so I leaned against one of the maple trunks and said his name with what energy I had left—the adrenaline at least kept me present.

"Fitz."

Nothing.

"Fitz."

Nothing.

Just a string of curse words and another shovelful of dirt.

The snow was coming down in soft sheets, the flakes alighting upon my clothing and the ground and disappearing into the puddles of standing water. The trees began to collect small groups of flakes, and the whiteness started to shine in the dark night, the clouds lit by the moon in some odd outline of shifting shadows.

"Fitz!" I screamed. "You're scaring me! Stop!" I threw a rock and hit him in the shoulder.

He turned and dropped the shovel and wiped the hair from his eyes. He was four feet down, and the sides of the hole he'd dug were crumbling softly, the walls coated by new snow. It was like looking at him through the blur of an old TV screen: nothing more than white noise. He didn't say a word. He wasn't home. Nobody was in there but hatred and regret and guilt and anger and the voices fighting to tell Fitz that he'd never overcome his past.

I knew it wouldn't help—my staying there and yelling at him or hugging him or helping him dig. He wasn't there.

And then I ran. I ran so fast.

Looking back, I want to say it was because I cared about him so much, and I wanted to get him help as quickly as possible. But, if I'm being honest, and I am, I ran out of fear. He scared me, and I was afraid he might hurt me with that shovel just because he didn't recognize me. There's no way he could have known it was me, or else he would have stopped digging and joked with me about poor Yorick and the oddity of the words "exhumed" and "jester," and then he would have held me and watched the snow fall with me in a quiet moment of peace.

That's what should have happened. But it wasn't meant to be. It couldn't be helped.

He began yelling again, but I only heard faint moments of hissing and coughing and moaning. I knocked my shoulder into a tree and stopped fifty yards from the car. Mom was standing there, talking to a cop. The lights from the cop car were spinning, but there were no sirens. Just a quiet turning of color, the red reflecting off the fresh snow sticking to the ground.

In that moment, it was like the world had been encased in a thin layer of ice that coated everything like some wonderland. Only, it wasn't a wonderland—the snow was just a mask for the truth happening two hundred yards away and four feet down.

I waved to Mom and pointed in the direction of Fitz, through the trees where the flakes were accumulating, the ice-rain turning into a completely soft fall of snow.

"That way. Two hundred yards or so. Maybe three." I sucked in air, and my ribs hurt because of the pain. I hadn't run like that in months. "He has a shovel. He's four feet down near a grave marker. But he's not there—not really. And he's angry."

Mom hugged me close to her as the cops rushed past. She brushed her hands through my icy hair, the strands clumped together and my lashes starting to freeze. I fell into her embrace and let my head rest on her chest, her heart beating just as fast as mine. Little clouds of breath floated above our heads, and I wondered what the scene would look like from above: trees everywhere, cruiser lights spinning, fresh snow blanketing the landscape, small dots running through the cemetery to an empty grave like a black piano key among the white. That was Fitz. He was in that key, trying to find the sound. Flats. Sharps.

"Let's get you back to the hospital," said Mom.

Eleven

couldn't sleep. Obviously. I stared out the window as threadbare clouds gave way to a quiet night of stars reflecting off the snow. I thought of the stars and how some crazy, overwhelming gravity pulls on them all the time and how forces like jet engines inside push out on them so they can keep their shape. I wondered about the gravity pushing on me, the forces keeping me in that hospital room and shaping my fate, tying me to a life that felt at times like it had been decided for me. But I couldn't accept that narrative. That wasn't my narrative. Impossible. I wouldn't allow that.

Mom left the hospital the next morning after taking a call from the officer in charge of Fitz's case. She told me she'd be back for lunch, that I needed time with the doctors or something first. I kept asking her for more details about Fitz, upset that she would only tell me he was safe and warm and that he'd be okay. What condition was he in? What did he look like? What was he saying? She wouldn't say. Maybe she didn't know.

Nobody opened my door to get me for Group Talk. I waited, but when I heard nothing, I lay back on my bed and thought about Fitz and tried to rewrite the memory. Like, maybe I ran up to him just as he was resting his head on his brother's gravestone, asking for forgiveness, and he'd waved me to him so he could hug me.

I also thought about gravestone rubbings I'd done in elementary school, the crayon a small black stub, the rubbing a small remembrance of someone else's grief and loss.

Jenkins dropped by with my morning medication and said I'd get breakfast after a while. I guess they were giving me some time to sleep, knowing what I'd been through. I rested against the door and pulled my knees to my chest and let the sun from the window curl around my body.

I missed being out in the open, where the booming rays could really wash over me and warm me up. Then again, those rays were now hidden behind cloud cover and a deep, gray sky. An hour later, Jenkins came back to take me to breakfast. By then, I was totally consumed by my thoughts and counting the beats in my chest and the tap of my feet against the bed.

Martha hugged me when she saw me. She had this big grin on her face and jokingly covered her keycard. "Don't steal from me again, girl, or you'll see how I deal with thieves." Then she leaned closer. "I'm so happy you two are okay."

"Where is everyone?"

"The big doc didn't want you eating with the others. You're supposed to be alone until you meet with him. Don't ask me—I just do what I'm told."

"Did Leah get in trouble? Is Junior okay?"

"Everybody is fine, Addie. Junior was off suicide watch the next night. And you know I could never get mad at Leah. She just said she was teasing us and wanted to run, so we put it in an incident report, but left it at that. Told the docs ain't nothing to look into there—just a sweet girl playing a little game on Martha."

"Thanks, Martha," I said. "I wanted to leave you a note. I'm sorry. I didn't mean to make you worry."

"I'm stronger than you think. You're fine. I'm glad you're back." She smiled and hugged me. "Eat something. You're looking skinny, and I don't want any competition in here. I got the bod, and you know it." She flexed, like some bodybuilder posing for the final review. It was pretty great.

She asked me about the outing, but I kept the details vague and told her I wasn't sure where Fitz was. That much was true, at least. I'm sure she knew more than I did and was aware I was keeping things hidden.

After breakfast, she escorted me to Doc's office.

Doc was waiting for me. He nodded to the seat across from his desk and opened my folder. There was a new stress ball on the table with a crazy-big grin on it.

"A little creepy," I said, holding it up for Doc to see.

"But it works," he said, smiling. "No holes. Junior busted another one yesterday and that's all I could get last-minute."

"Can I see him?" I said.

Doc knew exactly who I was talking about.

"Not just yet, Addie. Not for a while."

"Is he okay? Nobody told me what happened after the graveyard. I've been awake all night. C'mon, Doc, you've gotta give me something."

"You found Fitz, but it wasn't Fitz," he said. "Am I right?"

"Yes," I said, dropping my chin to my chest.

"What you two did was reckless. Dangerous." Doc sighed.

"The report says he was almost to the casket. He had a picture of a bird, but the rain had nearly ruined it. He was yelling Quentin's name, but nothing else was really decipherable, according to the police. He's lucky he was found. Things could have been so much worse."

I immediately thought of Lincoln again, and it made my eyes water. In the midst of all those voices, Fitz was determined to return to Quentin's grave. Just like Lincoln and Willie. Fitz was trying to say sorry again, to find the mercy and justice and forgiveness he'd been looking for.

I didn't know quite how to reconcile that with the image of Fitz I'd seen at the cemetery. But I knew the real Fitz wasn't completely lost. The real Fitz was in there. His digging at that grave was proof. And maybe I should've shared with Doc why I found that amazing, but I was nervous about it for some reason.

"You still didn't answer the first question, Doc. Is he okay?"

"He'll be fine. He's resting. He's back on his medication, and will likely be returning to us in a week or two. Not before then."

I was angry. That was far too long. I wanted to talk to Fitz.

I wanted to tell him that every story worth its salt had some form of loss and guilt and regret. It's how the characters react to that loss that speaks to their nature as a hero. Fitz acted like a hero. Sure, maybe it wasn't conventional, but what on earth did convention have to do with meaning?

I thought about the unanswered essay question on my desk: *What are the characters waiting for, and why is it significant that it/he/she never shows up?* I thought of Morris's lesson plans and the plays I had marked up that were waiting for my return. I still didn't have an answer for the absurd playwrights, but I knew how I'd respond to the hero's journey question on the exam.

"So what am I supposed to do?" I said. "Pretend like nothing happened? Return to group meetings and behavioral therapy with Ramirez and movies on Monday night?"

"Not exactly," he said, scribbling in his folder.

"What does that mean? I mean, we all know doctors aren't known for their abundant clarity, but that was especially vague, Doc."

Doc snatched up his phone and clicked a few buttons and then said, "Have her come in," before settling back in his chair and adjusting his glasses. He folded his hands over his stomach and waited. The quiet in that moment was awkward and made me feel uneasy, so I picked up the stress ball and started gouging the eyes.

Mom walked in, smiling that awkward smile of "Hey, I knew something earlier but didn't think it was the right time to tell you." You know the one.

"Are we having a family therapy session?" I said.

I wasn't trying to be a smart aleck, though I'm sure it sounded that way.

"No. Well, sort of," said Doc.

"Wow. So clear today, Doc. It's like you've reached an entirely new level of profundity."

"Good word," said Doc.

"Thanks," I said. I wished I was wearing my new grammar sweatshirt. "So what are we doing?"

Mom sat down right as I asked Doc that question.

"I've asked your mother here so we can discuss outpatient status," said Doc.

"Outpatient?" I repeated.

"It means you get to come home, Addie," said Mom.

She was so happy that I didn't want to break the spell.

"What about the others?" I asked, even though I knew the answer.

"You're all on separate paths, Addie," said Doc. "You're welcome to come back during visiting hours. Maybe we can set aside some time on a Sunday so you can talk with them about where you are at in your treatment. I think that could be inspiring."

"That would be nice," said Mom.

I bit my lower lip and took a deep breath. I could visit, sure, but I wasn't sure if I was ready to go back to the life I had left behind just months earlier.

I stared at the stress ball and tapped my feet in unison and waited for Doc to start scribbling in his folder, but he didn't. He just stared at me over the tops of those stupid horn-rimmed glasses and waited.

"Outpatient?" I said again.

"You'll see me twice a week," he said. "We'll keep testing new medications. However, I don't believe staying in the ward is going to change the treatment path. And frankly, I think the fewer distractions, the better. In fact, I recommend you two get away from Seattle for a few days, if you can. The space could do you some good, Addie, and could provide a respite from your rituals, if even for a short time. Again, it's worth a try. And you'll also have some distance from this situation, which is hypersensitive, as you know. I'm sure your obsessions are in hyperdrive at the moment."

"A lot of 'hypers' there, Doc," I said, blinking in an alternating pattern with the shadows of the blinds hanging behind him. He was right. I was overdoing things, but I couldn't help it. Not really. Not when every thought came back to Fitz. I knew he meant Fitz when he said "distractions." He didn't have to hide behind semantics. That was my job.

I sat back and put my hand on Mom's and realized that no matter what I said, I was going home. It would be nice to be home in my comfortable surroundings, but I was also afraid. If I left the ward, would I still be as focused on figuring myself out? Would I be eager to test myself, to grow and discover and learn? Possibly, but I knew it wouldn't be in the same way. It couldn't be. It wasn't possible.

Mom helped me gather my things, and Martha made sure I left before Group Talk got out. I didn't even get to say goodbye to Tabor. I wasn't too cut up about that, but it seemed like even those people I didn't get along with held some place in my life. Like I was still trying to carve out little spaces for everybody to have a place in my heart. Maybe there wasn't enough room.

"Semester's almost over," said Mom. "But I talked with Principal Abner, and he said you can return to classes and work on the rest of your credits over the winter break, if you feel up to it."

"How many weeks until then?"

"Only a few," she said. "But like the doctor said, I don't want you sitting around and stewing in your obsessive thoughts." She put her finger on my forehead.

"Gross."

"Gross? These are motherly hands," she said, putting both her hands on my face and squeezing my cheeks, making me laugh.

The parking garage was freezing. Outside was freezing. Winter had really arrived, and I was shivering by the time we got to the car.

"No, I feel gross. I just want to shower and sleep in my own bed and not think about any of this. It's too much."

"Then just relax and go to sleep, Addie," she said as we stepped into the car and the engine turned in the quiet outside. The heater ticked in the cold, and warm air began to flow around my feet. I kicked my seat back, and we zoomed away from the hospital, from a small dot on the line of my life, a blip that maybe could grow to mean a lot more to me in the future. I wasn't sure.

We bumped our way over the freeway and dropped into the streets near Puget Sound. At a stop sign near our house, I saw this gorgeous yellow bird perched atop the thin, metal edge.

"Do you think maybe we could take a short trip before I go back to school? Just you and me? Like Doc said?" I asked.

Mom eased the car into our driveway. The old brick house looked so small and quaint set against the mansions on either side, but I liked our little alcove of peace and harmony.

"Of course, honey," she said. "I think that's a great idea."

I started tapping on my knee, careful not to overdo it. I worried that if Mom saw that my OCD was still strong, she might call off the idea of a trip in favor of staying home and visiting Doc more often.

"What did you have in mind?"

"Not sure yet," I said. "I just know I want to go see this one bird I heard about."

"A bird?"

"It's called a Kirtland's warbler. Supposed to be the prettiest bird out there."

Mom smiled and killed the ignition. The engine ticked in the garage as it cooled. I walked inside and dropped my things on the kitchen counter like I had ten thousand other times when returning from school or work. I walked through the study and ran my finger along all the spines of the books in their rows that spanned the wall. I thought of Leah and her whale book and her buzz cut and how, if she were here, she'd say it was time to enjoy the greener grass and eat it too. The thought made me smile.

I returned to the kitchen and squatted down when I heard Duck's toenails scraping against the wood floor as he tried to stay on his feet. He was so excited, and it made me smile. Duck almost knocked me over when he leapt up onto me, slobbering on me and licking my face. It was odd, really, that I had to wash for almost everything, but Duck's slobber never bothered me. Maybe because he's family.

I walked around the back of our house with Duck, throwing a small stick and bumping up against the pine trees to shake the snow from the limbs. I thought of the bristlecone pines I'd seen on Mount Washington and the way the branches turned in on themselves. In that moment, I knew how that felt. Shame wrapped its relentless fingers around my stomach and squeezed. How could I leave my friends in the ward like that and just move on with my life? How could I take Duck on a walk like my world hadn't been completely tilted?

Duck's paws left divots in the snow where shadows began to pool. After we walked through the backyard for a while, we cut through our neighbors' yards and came out two houses down. No fences—it was that kind of neighborhood. We walked back onto the street. The houses were close together, but the backyards of the cul-de-sac all lined the edge of the forest area, so we all had a lot of room behind the packed closeness up front. There were bright front doors, and Christmas lights were starting to dot the rain gutters. Everything felt so familiar.

I stopped to count the lights on three different strands on three different houses before returning home. Back inside, I built a fire in the fireplace and let Duck rest on my lap as the wood hissed and popped. Mom was baking something in the kitchen and kept yelling something about proving time and proper lamination of dough like she was on *The Great British Baking Show*.

It felt like I'd simply stepped outside of myself for a moment, only to return home filled with new ideas and hopes and eager to find out more about who I was and what I was becoming. I wanted to read and stare into that fire and forget all the memories I kept stored, the memories I revisited from the hospital, the memories and obsessions I revisited all too often when I was alone. I needed *a distraction*, as they say. They say a lot, don't they?

I fell asleep near the fire with Duck, and when I woke up, I took a long shower and then got on my computer and started researching the nesting grounds of the Kirtland's warbler. If I couldn't be in the ward with my friends—with Fitz—I'd have to find a different way to connect. I remembered Fitz mentioning Michigan, which helped. I figured Mom would be okay with something in the country. It didn't hurt to look, anyway.

The wind pushed against the tall trees outside my bedroom. Gray clouds swirled above, and a light shivering snow attempted to stick on the concrete near the street. More flakes began to amass and descend in bunches. Snow was upon us again.

I read more about the birds, and I found out where they lived and when we could see them. The birds were only in Michigan from May to July before they migrated elsewhere. So I researched where they went after that, and my heart sank. It was impossible. Mom would never go for it. Michigan was asking a lot, but a trip to the birds' winter habitat would require a bit of pathos, a bit of pathetic appeal, a bit of magic, plus a mask I rarely put on. Hint: *begging*.

I stepped outside again because I worried that if I stayed in my room I might get stuck in a whirlpool of rituals and lose the courage I needed to talk to Mom about what I wanted to do. This time I went without Duck, and I stood against the brick wall of the house and watched the snow fall and the trees sway and felt the quiet settle around me. I looked at the slush at my feet and saw separation in the water, like oil trying to mix with the snowmelt. I leaned my head back until my nose touched the fur-lined edge of my puffy jacket hood and watched my breath plume above me in rings.

I thought of Fitz and the hospital and Leah again. I wondered if she was doing all right. I hoped Didi was telling her more of his detailed, believable conquests. And Junior's presence was large enough to cast away fear at times, so I pictured him standing tall next to her.

I watched the snow stick to my jacket and blew at the flakes on my shoulder. They didn't budge. I breathed warm air into my hands and thought about how to phrase the question to Mom before walking back inside and being encircled again by warmth.

Mom was reading in the living room with the fire still going, the dry-crack of winter splitting each log. It looked cozy. I wanted to run back upstairs, grab my plays for Morris's class, and crawl under Mom's blanket with her to read by the fire. But I didn't do that. I also wanted to run to the kitchen and wash my hands, but I didn't do that either. This was more important.

"I know where I want to go," I said.

"Shoot," she said, resting her book on her lap and removing her glasses.

Maybe it was the reflection of the firelight, or because she wasn't wearing any makeup, or because I'd just put her through quite a lot, but she looked so old in that moment, like the years were sticking.

"The Bahamas," I said, smiling broadly.

She tilted her head back and laughed. "Oh, Addie," she said, resting her head against one hand, glancing my way, "Addie, Addie, Addie."

I hated when she did that, the whole repeat-my-name thing. It usually came before a "no," so I braced myself for a letdown. It was a reasonable answer, though, so I couldn't get mad at her for that.

"Yes, Mom?"

"I don't know," she said.

"Well, Doc *did* say we should leave the city and visit an island nation or a coral-based archipelago somewhere in the Atlantic Ocean with a population of around four hundred thousand and an annual gross domestic product of somewhere near nine billion dollars."

She laughed again. "Been doing a little research, dear?"

"Maybe," I said.

Mom stared into the fire for what seemed like five whole minutes. I heard Duck in the kitchen sigh before repositioning himself on his dog bed, then he started to snore.

"Well . . ."

I gave her an expectant look, both of our faces set aglow by the flames. "Yeah?"

"If you want to use your senior trip on this, I guess that's okay," she said.

"Okay?"

"Okay," she said, smiling broadly. "Maybe he did mention a coral-based archipelago and I just missed it or something."

I about lost it. I ran and hugged her and then started off to my room, but returned quickly to hug her again and then ran outside, which had worked before as a substitute for my rituals, and then hurried back to the fire again and hugged her one more time. I was breathing heavy and wet from running through the snow without a jacket, but I felt wonderful.

"I'll start looking for tickets," I said, smiling so big that I felt it in my toes. Mom wouldn't stop looking at me.

"I'll need some time, please," she said. "I'll have to work some things out." She stared at me with an unfamiliar look.

"What? Quit looking at me like that," I said.

"You're so beautiful, Addie."

"Ugh. Stop. You're beautiful too. Whatever."

Twelve

For the entire next week I lived my life in story and language. I lost myself in words, in the paths carved by language, in the abrupt turn of the *L*, the wandering track of the *S*, in the way the sounds of the sentences built bridges over my obsessions into a world where I only heard characters speaking instead of my own thoughts. Anything to keep me from thinking of my friends in the ward and the fact that I wasn't with them.

Doc was not allowing me any contact—trust me, I'd called his secretary, like, a hundred times a day until Doc and Mom had a private chat, and then Mom told me I had to leave it alone for a while.

So I went back to story, waiting for Mom to give the all-clear on our trip, and read about elephant graveyards. The legend is that older elephants wander off from a group because they know they're going to die. The truth is that when elephants die, the other elephants wait around and pick up their friend's bones and walk around with them for a while before moving on.

That made me think of the whale bones on the island, of lying with Fitz in the heart of the skeleton as we stared into the sky. I couldn't escape those memories. Nor did I want to. Just one whale rib bone was longer than my body and Fitz's body end to end.

Mom peeked her head around the doorframe of my bedroom. "I found a buyer. Come on."

I set down the play I was reading—*The Real Thing*—and stood up. "What?"

"Let's go," Mom said.

I hurried down the stairs past Duck, and as I hit the last step, I realized it was the fastest I'd descended the stairs in years. I was too caught up in the moment to celebrate, but I definitely took note. Duck was asleep at the bottom like one of those Pompeii figures frozen beneath glass in a state of suspension like, forever.

In minutes, Mom and I were circling parking spaces near Puget Sound, the sky a wash of gray.

"Did you know it takes, like, eight seconds for water to hit us after it drops from the clouds?"

"Not long enough," she said. "What about snow?"

"Jury's still out."

"So you don't know."

"Whatever. Where are we going?"

"To pay for the Bahamas," she said.

"Did you sell me to a seedy gang of Canadian traffickers? Mounties with malice?"

"It *would* make the trip to the beach a little quieter. I doubt they'd take you, though. Too smug."

"What about my passport?"

"Still good from when we went to Italy a few years ago."

Mom had taken her students on a study abroad to Florence when I was thirteen years old. I'd loved that trip because I'd gotten to see my mother in her element—animated, teaching students, soaking in the history of the place, of the people. I still remember seeing Michelangelo's *David* and wondering how he'd seen such perfection in a block of marble. How he'd chipped away the rough edges; the truth laid bare.

"What about your job?"

"I had some time off saved up. And Principal Abner understands."

It started to snow softly as we stepped out of the car and walked up a side hill right near a small inlet where a gorgeous heron sat on a rotting piling beyond some old stone crumbling into the water. The heron took off as we turned, and we watched it fly away until Mom nudged my elbow.

She held a backpack under her arm, but I didn't know what she was up to, nor did she tell me.

We stepped into an ancient antique shop. There was this really big grandfather clock painted all white, and the sign said it was from 1909 and made of spruce from Europe. Rows of books lined the walls, and a small wooden ladder leading to the second level of books lurked in the shade beyond the front desk. Mom pulled three books from her backpack and placed them on the table.

The clerk nodded. "These the ones?"

"They are," she said.

"Agatha Christie?" I said, seeing the spines of all three volumes. "Are those Dad's first editions? You can't sell those."

"Don't worry," Mom said to me. "It's only paper. And if it helps get my girl back, I'd sell them all without a second thought. These stories are written. Yours isn't."

We walked out with enough money for the entire trip, but I

felt an anchor in my stomach and counted each step thinking of Dad and his books. I wondered if he had lost himself in words like I did in order to maintain some semblance of gravity, of hope.

The snow on the grass was thin, like the ground had been spray-painted white. It crackled under my feet as I walked to the car.

"Quit thinking about the books," Mom said, noticing me staring blankly at the road as it vanished under the tires as we drove.

"I feel selfish."

"I want this for you—for us. Let it go. Dad would've loved this trip, and you know it."

"I don't like losing pieces of him."

"If it means getting pieces of you back . . ." She trailed off and let the silence fill the space between us. When she started to cry, I rested my hand on her shoulder and told her it would be all right. I wasn't sure if the tears were for the books or for my OCD or for both.

"No Christmas gifts. This is Christmas."

"I know," I said, smiling.

"And Easter."

"I know."

"And Flag Day. And your birthday. And Presidents' Day. And the Fourth of July. It's all the things," she said, pulling my head to hers and kissing me on the forehead.

"I know, Mom," I said. "Focus on the road."

I glanced at the envelope full of money that Mom had tucked between us. I couldn't quite believe it was really happening.

I mean, how was I to know that the Kirtland's warbler migrated from Michigan to the Bahamas for the winter? I had told

Mom about why the birds mattered. Well, I'd told her that they were supposed to be really cool and that I'd heard about them from Fitz and that I wanted to see them for myself. I didn't want it to sound like I was doing it for him, or she might question my motives or something. Whatever. It's not like I needed another reason to think about Fitz.

A few days later, Mom and I were flying over the Bahamas, which were just a group of small dots below the plane. After enduring so much snow, I couldn't wait for the warmth of the island sun. I rested my head against the little oval window and felt the hum of the plane and imagined the crazy-fast wind vibrating through my body.

"Talk about living right," I said.

"What do you mean?" said Mom. "This trip?"

"Well, yeah," I said, turning to look at her. "But I was thinking about the birds. They go to Michigan in the summer, then fly to the Bahamas for the winter. That's living right."

"That's a lifestyle you can't afford," she said. "Neither can I."

The guy sitting next to Mom was wearing one of those ridiculous palm-tree, neon beach shirts. Sure. Okay. It's an island for tourists and stuff, so those shirts are popular and all. I get it. But it looked absurd.

However, the more I looked at that shirt, the more I thought about Fitz and his yoga shirts. I was so excited about visiting Cat Island, where the majority of birds were supposed to live, even though I knew seeing one was nearly impossible. There were only 2,300 male warblers in the whole world, but I wasn't going to wait for things to happen to me anymore. I was going to encounter that birding world on my own and take my chances. Fast. Like, move my *asana* fast.

"Tragedy or comedy?" I said, trying to distract myself from my thoughts of Fitz and impossible birds.

"Sure," said Mom.

We liked to play this game where we gave each other scenarios, and then we had to decide if it would work better as a tragedy or a comedy. I started.

"Once upon a time a deodorant stick fell in love with BO."

"Tragedy," she said. "Once upon a time an EpiPen fell in love with a bag of peanuts."

I laughed. "Good one, Mom. Comedy."

I tried to adjust in my seat to get more legroom—something that is futile but always worth a shot, I guess. I couldn't help but think of the futile actions of the characters in Beckett's play. Never moving, never taking action, only talking and waiting. I was done waiting for these birds to speak to me, to tell me their secrets. I was going to find them and listen to their warble and go on. I had to go on.

"Once upon a time there was an owl that fell in love with a mouse."

"Comedy," said Mom.

"Really?"

"Yes," she said. "The owl doesn't have to eat the mouse. I refuse to see it that way. Okay, my turn. Once upon a time there was a stain on a shirt that fell in love with the bleach."

"Sartorial tragedy," I said. "Once upon a time there was a whale that fell in love with a compact parking space."

"Comedy."

"Once upon a time there was a group of birds who met at the top of Mont Blanc and talked about how great it would be to fly over the Alps. Then they all walked home."

"Tragedy," she said. "And you skipped my turn."

"Sorry," I said, smiling.

That afternoon we walked along the beach, the dimpled sand giving way under our feet, the water folding over itself and scrambling up the shore to scratch our ankles. I traced my steps along the parabolas of salt etched into the sand after each wave.

Mom's face was filled with a peaceful light. It was hot outside, but the water helped keep the air cool, and a gentle breeze kept the heat from totally devouring us. I picked up some curved and striated shells and collected them in a cloth bag. The clerk at the Hawk's Nest resort, where we were staying, had told us we couldn't collect shells, but I did it anyway. I don't know why. It gave me something to do, I guess, but I knew I'd have to leave them behind when we left. I wished I could save one for Leah to remind her of Dia de Leah and her family.

Later, as Mom and I were sitting on the beach, I held one of the shells and traced the wrinkles that folded over like the waves. "Did you know that some shells can grow over four feet in length?" I said, setting the shell on Mom's lap.

She lowered her book and looked out on the water, her sunglasses reflecting the swaying blue swells.

"An oyster wants to create the perfect pearl, but has a problem keeping its big mouth shut," she said, still stuck on our game from earlier that day.

"Tragedy," I said, smiling.

We watched as the waters folded, broke, folded. Gulls cried in the distance, some diving into the sea swells in search of lunch or an early dinner, no doubt.

Looking at Mom with that shell and listening to the ocean's rhythmic pulse made me think of Dad. He'd loved the beach.

He'd often take me to the coast with Duck to play near the water. The pain I thought was tamed, under control, rose again, moved in on me like some perpetual wave, the grief lapping at my soul, ebbing, flowing, rinsing. It made me feel so sad for Mom, and then it made me think about Fitz and how his pain must be so much heavier because of the way it all happened.

"Look at all those birds diving for their food," I said.

"Early bird special," said Mom.

"Oh my word," I said, laughing. "You are so corny."

"Well, you got it from somewhere, you know," she said, tossing the shell back to me.

In the evening, we ate at this place near the hotel that served some amazing coconut shrimp. I wasn't sure it was all that authentic or whatever, but it tasted fantastic. Lots of people were heading to some dance hosted by the resort, but I felt like walking.

Mom told me to be back before it got "too late," but that kind of ambivalent phrasing opened the doors for me to really take my time. Semantics.

I headed to the beach, sat in the sand, and watched the waters surge in the moonlight, the foam frothing white as each wave stretched up the sands and retreated. I spent an hour just watching the waves. I started counting them, and then I started listening to my heart, and then I got frustrated, so I ended up returning to the room earlier than I'd expected. Probably earlier than Mom expected, too.

After a cozy sleep under giant, soft comforters and lulled by quiet ocean noises, I woke up to a gorgeous land covered in greenery and sunshine. Mom decided to take another day on the beach. I snagged some food from the shop in the resort, packed a lunch, and grabbed a ride to the goat farms on the northern end of Cat Island. The taxi driver looked at me like I was crazy for visiting a goat farm, but I'd done enough research about the island to know what I wanted. I told the driver to meet me in a few hours in the same place, hoping I'd paid enough to guarantee his return.

When I stepped off the hot pavement and into the sand and rocks near the water's edge, I felt like I'd finally arrived. I mean, yes, the plane had already landed, and we'd been on the island for a day, but the whole reason I chose this place was for the birds. I stepped over numerous stalks of black torch—one of the birds' favorite foods. I also saw some wild sage and figured I was in the perfect spot for a sighting.

And that's why I was so upset when I didn't see anything.

The hush of the surf swirled behind me as I stared at the far side of the island where the sun was beginning its slow descent. It was late afternoon, and I was hot, sweaty, and hungry. For some reason, I thought of Junior and the runny applesauce in the cafeteria, and was glad the resort offered actual food.

I leaned back into a soft berm of sand and watched the clouds glide by, shape-shifting in the bright sky. I saw a cloud split into numerous rows and thought of a piano, and wondered which notes the bird might sing.

The alarm on my phone eventually buzzed in my pocket, and I hurried back to the meeting place to find the driver waiting for me. Apparently I'd given him a reasonable tip because we carried on the same routine for the next four days, with the same result. I'd hike east or west of our spot, and wait. Sometimes I'd dip down to the ocean, or I'd sit in one spot for an hour. But mostly I just waited. Always waiting.

Mom enjoyed her days on the beach, reading, and I came

home every night sunburned and frustrated. How frustrated, Mom never knew. I couldn't let her know. She needed this trip, too.

She needed to relax and not worry about her job for once in her life. She never treated herself, and she had to work hard to pay to take care of me and my issues. That always made me feel bad. Like, I often wondered if I was more of a burden than she let on, and maybe she wished that all would change or something. I had been working on it at the hospital, and I felt like I had been improving, but I wasn't sure if that was enough for her.

And I wasn't going to ask her. C'mon. She'd just tell me that I was a blessing and that nothing was better than having me around and that she'd do anything for me. Because she's amazing. Because she knows how to love. Because her heart has enough room for everybody and everything.

But I didn't want her to start thinking about all those things or worrying about me when I wanted her to enjoy the sand and the sea. It was such a gorgeous place, and I loved that she was soaking up the quiet and soft nature of the island.

On our fifth day, I was exuding hope. We only had a few days left on the island, and I felt that today would be the day for a rare-bird sighting. I took off early, leaving Mom a note. She rolled over in bed as I walked past her to the door.

The driver held the door open for me. "You know the beaches on the resort are much better than these ones. I like your business, but it seems odd to me." It was the first time he'd said anything to me other than the price and where and when we'd meet.

"Maybe I'll see one in Michigan," I said, not really listening to him.

"See what?"

"A Kirtland's warbler. They live in Michigan part of the year before returning here to Cat Island."

"Ah, yes, the Kirtland's warbler. Top of any birder's list—a beautiful bird with a striking yellow chest and a gray head with varying shades fanning over its air-light bones. Did you know that its heart beats a hundred and fifteen times a minute and over six hundred times a minute when active?" the driver said. "Birders call it a 'life bird'—as in seeing it is a once-in-a-lifetime event."

I was shocked. I knit my brow and leaned forward, gripping the passenger-seat headrest. "You know what bird I'm talking about?"

"This island is famous for more than its beaches. You are in the right spot if you hope to see one. But it's still hard to find. I've driven a birder or two, and they never seem to find it. Something tells me you won't stop, though."

"Well, maybe I'm just not that smart. I'm living the definition of insanity—doing the same thing but expecting a different result. Being 'birdbrained' must be a real thing."

"Yes. The dodo did not have a nice ending."

We talked for another half hour about the island's birding history before he stopped at our usual place.

I decided to take a longer walk and head up to the northernmost point where the rocks made the beaches nearly inaccessible—unless you scrambled over boulders and swam a bit. But I needed to move and hope. I needed to feel like I was doing something. I needed to know that, if I didn't see the bird, it wasn't for lack of effort on my part. I felt foolish waiting for one in that scrub, listening to hear that impossible little heart thumping against the tissue-paper walls of its chest, listening for the slightest chirp or fuss in the brush.

After bridging a narrow inlet of water, I sat in a gathering of small trees and drank from my water bottle. I thought of what Fitz might be doing in that moment, and I leaned my head back and pictured his handsome gapped smile. I took my shoes off and pushed my bare feet into the water and watched the sand billow around my toes. I thought of Estragon's comment to Vladimir in *Waiting for Godot*: "We always find something, eh Didi, to give us the impression we exist?"

It was more than thinking, though. It was more than an impression. It was knowing I existed. That I was meant to take action. My phone buzzed, reminding me that I had to get back to the resort. I met up with the driver and shrugged when I saw him. He knew my defeated slouch, my tired stare, my incessant blinking meant another day with no luck.

Maybe I'd have to research the birds' Michigan habitat when I got home. I certainly wasn't going to see a warbler on Cat Island.

My time was up.

It seemed kind of absurd all of a sudden. This bird just decides to migrate to northern Michigan every year to hang out near small pine trees and then come back to the Bahamas. Why would you ever want to leave the Bahamas? Sounded like those birds needed a good talking-to. A good behavioral therapist or something.

Later, after another overpriced meal of shrimp and coconut rice, I wandered off from where Mom was sitting on the beach, reading. I walked into the water and watched a group of birds in the distance written in the sky like Old English script. I felt the cold water beneath the warm surface curl around my legs. The wind pushed the scent of grass and salt into my face, and I breathed in deeply.

I thought of how little we know about what goes on beneath the surface. And I guess that's true of all of us, right? Way down, in the deep parts. Surely colossal whales were out there pushing through the waters and singing to their families. Surely. But I only saw and heard what was above the surface of the water: birds chattering to one another, high in the air; the waves; the boats in the distance, catching wind in their colorful, taut sails.

The clouds parted over the water, and I thought of Fitz's handsome gap.

On the walk back to Mom, I considered telling her about Fitz and about my stay and everything. She'd been asking me about it constantly since I'd gotten home from the hospital, but I hadn't felt ready. Maybe if I could explain about seeing the blue whale on San Juan Island, she'd understand why I needed to see a warbler here.

I sat next to her on my towel and rested in the soft sand. "A windshield wiper falls in love with a raindrop."

"Tragedy," said Mom. She kept her nose in her book.

I decided to spend our last two days with Mom. I owed her that much, even if I lied to myself and said I was being noble by giving her space all the other days.

We had a lot of fun, too. We went snorkeling, and I saw a sea turtle and all these amazing fish and anemones and sea urchins, and the reef was just bonkers. I didn't understand how so much life could hang onto those small ledges and persist. It was a cool lesson in perseverance, in going on. But it came at a cost—I couldn't stop thinking of how I'd given up spotting the warbler. The bird's wings fluttered in my mind during every activity.

The final morning came in as fast as the wind off the water. I thought of Aeolus opening up his bag of winds and how winds can take you everywhere you need to go, just like language can do great things, poetic things, but ultimately you can't tell someone how much you love them because even that won't adequately express how you feel. All the winds except the one you want or need, I guess.

I lowered my head to avoid the breeze and walked down the small rock trail from our cabin to the water. I wanted to say goodbye to this place.

It's funny, with all my research for Morris and his unanswerable essay question, I still forgot sometimes life can play out just like a drama. Truth is overlooked, ignored, searched for but never found, and only when we think the character can't possibly make it out of the innermost cave alive, we witness a resurrection.

That's how I felt when I stepped into the cool water and heard the sound of a fin slapping the surface. Well, I thought that's what I heard. I wasn't sure. I looked north but didn't see anything in the water, just a small stand of Caribbean pines ten yards away.

I should have understood there was something different about that morning. I should have noted the way the wind moved the clouds in the sky, the way the trees bowed to the rising sun. Because there it was. Just like that. From the fringes of existence. All fifty-five ounces of it, and with the most striking colors I had ever seen on a bird. Streaked flanks of bluish-gray, a stark yellow underbelly, a blue head with dark, sharp eyes.

Enter stage left: the Kirtland's warbler.

I walked slowly to the bird and got within five yards. It didn't flinch. It was as if I was watching some other version of myself approach, quietly hoping, turning over the odds in my mind, and appealing to reason through blind faith.

But there it was. And it was remarkable. The real thing.

I took a picture on my phone, and it chirped at me, turning its head.

"Quentin," I said.

I wasn't ashamed of saying his name out loud and hoping it might be true. I'd seen such hope in the faces of Leah, Junior, Didi, Wolf, and Fitz. Hope is meant to surprise us. Existence is meant to surprise. Love is meant to surprise. Love does not bow to the odds. Never has. Never will.

Swooping in along with the bird came Dr. Morris's question: *What are the characters waiting for, and why is it significant that it/he/she never shows up?* Again. Again. Again.

The bird tilted its head at me one more time, then flew away. A small speck caught between the blue of the water and the blue of the sky.

I went back inside and washed and washed, hoping to remove the stain of repetition, to rid myself of the anxiety of not having an answer to the question that I had been obsessed with for months. I even showered twice before we left for the airport to rid myself of the anxiety, but it didn't help.

What are the characters waiting for?

What am I waiting for?

On the drive to the airport, I wanted to tell Mom about the bird, but I couldn't. Look, I loved my mom, but right then I was only thinking about Fitz and the rest of the group and telling them about the warbler. Well, telling Fitz about the warbler.

Mom and I boarded the plane three hours later, both of us trying to settle in to the small seats and the nonexistent legroom. They barely hold a hint of legroom. They're not even aisles.

Then I thought of how I would make a joke with Fitz about

"aisles" and flying away from the "isles," and then mention my awesome grammar sweater and his "synonym rolls." But I wasn't with Fitz.

Yet I couldn't help but feel that having been with Fitz sort of reorganized everything in my life. Like, I had learned more about myself through him and it had reset my existence or something. I had a feeling that hanging out with my old friends at the mall and discussing boys wouldn't cut it anymore. I had outgrown that kind of thing, at least a little.

"Says here we have a one in 4,596,032 chance of crashing on our way home," I said to Mom, pointing at my phone. Sets of islands passed underneath us, numerous ellipses in the water, a geography of punctuation.

"What? That's awful."

"I don't know. If we took this flight every day, we'd last 12,591 years before going down. Pretty good odds," I said, smiling.

"How do you know that?"

"An app I just downloaded," I said.

"You kids and your apps," she said.

"Don't judge me. You love my apps," I said.

Mom shook her head and smiled at me.

"A fire hydrant falls in love with a dog," I said.

"Comedy," said Mom.

"But the hydrant is allergic to urine."

"Gross, Addie," she said.

"And the dog has bladder issues and can only relieve himself on the fire hydrant or else he'd die of pain."

"Tragicomedy?" she said.

"Maybe," I said.

As the plane landed, I felt this jolt of excitement inside. Good thing the plane didn't go down. The irony of birds migrating and me flying in a big steel bird would have been more than my soul could handle in the afterlife or whatever. I'd be immensely ticked that my death was ironic, and I'd never hear the end of it from all my literary heroes.

Thirteen

The first night after we got home, I divided my time between thinking about Dr. Morris's essay question and reading about the jack pines in Michigan. I wasn't in the mood to think after that—my brain was super tired—so over the next few days, I relaxed and binge-watched two seasons of *The Great British Baking Show* and only left the couch to satisfy my hunger. Well, it wasn't so much hunger as it was bored, mindless eating. Whatever.

Mom occasionally stepped in to see who was Star Baker or who'd been sent home and to make sure I was feeling okay. I think she was well aware of how much I wanted to go back to the hospital. Weird, right? Hate being put there, to a degree, then can't wait to get back. Isn't that how most things work?

But I loved watching the bakers complain, in the nicest way, about their dough not rising or their chocolate not being tempered properly or their custard being a little too thick and all. It was kind of nice to look at the world through the eyes of people I'd never met and see a whole new set of issues. I mean, winning that competition meant a lot to them, and it made me realize that everyone has their own struggles. It doesn't matter how big or small—they exist. It's all about perspective. That's that.

"Glad you were able to delete all your dirty shows before I got home, Mom," I said. "That shows some real foresight and maturity on your part."

"Ha ha," she said, mocking me with a fake laugh.

"No, really, I appreciate you cleaning up the place before my return. How many parties did you throw while I was at the hospital?"

"Aren't you supposed to be driving somewhere?" she said.

I was. Dr. Riddle had called Mom and told her that I could visit that afternoon if I wanted to. Of course I wanted to, and Mom knew it.

My look: I was wearing jeans and my favorite riding boots— I didn't ride, but I liked the boots, get over it—and this pretty peacoat with cool whalebone buttons or whatever. It was still pretty cold out, so I snagged a scarf and gave Mom a kiss on the cheek on the way out.

Outside, flakes of snow fell softly. It was that weird kind of snow-quiet where the world is insulated from all sound. I felt like I was ruining it just by turning over the engine in my car.

As I drove to the hospital, I began thinking about the warblers again and how they lived. Then I thought of Fitz waiting for me in the psych ward, of Leah and her soft smile and the way she always rubbed her short hair, of Didi and his outrageous escapades and triumphs in the face of reality, of Wolf and his intransigent sturdiness and undeniable stubbornness, of Junior and the kindness hiding behind the temper, of Martha and her lackadaisical attitude and her jovial comments.

I banked off the freeway and drove through a small part of town that had recently come into its own—new shops, new restaurants, new vibe, that kind of thing. The hospital towered over the houses in the area like some immense, maternal figure watching over the rooftops beneath its shadow.

I was grateful to be out of booties and into boots. The snow piled in small drifts, and the falling flakes brushed against my face as I made my way to the hospital entrance. The sliding doors breathed warm air over me and blew my unbound hair behind my shoulders. Yes, my hair was down. I was trying a new thing. Get over it.

Fitz was in the visitor's room, wearing a shirt I'd never seen. It said, *Yoga—I'm Down, Dog.*

"You been waiting for me?" I said, all smiles and anticipation.

"Only existentially," he said, flashing that handsome gap and goofy smile all at once.

I was so giddy I could hardly stand it. I almost put my hands over my stomach to calm down my insides.

"One of your better shirts," I said.

"Meaning isn't lost on you?"

"Please. Show some respect."

His eyes looked calm. He seemed content and soft in a way I couldn't quite define. His body seemed lighter—not in the weight department, but in the whole body-and-soul department. Still, I thought I could see a touch of shame beneath his mask.

"You doing okay?" I said, sitting down on a white bench across from him at a bland and disgusting-looking orange table.

I hated those tables. Leah was nearby, talking to someone I assumed was her mother, probably mentioning how a pot of watches never boils. She waved my way and gave me that quiet, sincere smile of hers. I waved back. I didn't see anybody else in the room, but I could hear Didi yelling something to Martha behind the doors.

"Better," Fitz said. "Last two weeks really put me through the ringer."

"What happened when you got back from, you know, the police station or whatever?"

I didn't want to bring up his erratic behavior at the apartment or at the gravesite. I didn't feel it was my place to mention it if he didn't want to talk about it. I also wasn't sure if he knew I had been at Quentin's grave, how I had seen him there in that moment of pure anguish, or if he would ever want to share that or talk about it.

"I'm sorry," he said, looking down at his fumbling hands. "Not now, Lyle. It's a tired joke, anyway." He didn't look in Lyle's direction, wherever Lyle may have been, and he seemed frustrated. Then he looked at me. "I'm sorry for hurting you."

"It was just a cut. Cuts heal."

"No, it wasn't just a cut. It was the entire act of leaving you totally alone while I completely lost it. I was totally gone. You had nobody. You heard where they found me, right?"

I bit my lower lip on one side and scooted around the table, feeling uneasy and awkward and unprepared to respond to his question. I sighed and played with the scarf around my neck.

"I heard. I know. I think it's beautiful, in a way. You were trying to say you were sorry. Again."

I smiled gently and put my hand in the middle of the table, reaching for him and letting him know I was there for him and comfortable with whatever emotions he was feeling in that moment.

"It wasn't beautiful after I left you. I don't actually remember much of it. Apparently I was laughing. I was crying. I seized up inside and outside, all over, catatonia took over, and I fell to the floor in the ER." He paused. "Truth is, these voices I hear—Lyle, Willy, Toby—they're not my friends, though that's the mask I put on. They are liars. Skulking in the corners. I have to keep them caged like animals, I must keep them caged, or I get lost."

Fitz sighed heavily and lowered his head to his hands before lifting his face again and faking a big smile.

I put my hand over his and mouthed that I was sorry. I was sincere, and I think he could tell.

"Like the plays you love so much, Addie—I feel like I can't escape the script sometimes. The cuckoo bird is in my mind, kicking out all the eggs of hope. I'm endangered by the very actors my mind has created. I feel like the lines of my life are being given to me, and I am destined to follow. Fated to read them, to live them. As if this life could happen to anybody, huh? Nope. Just me."

"Just *us*," I said. "We few. We crazy few. We band of nutters."

"Nice. *Henry V*?"

"Yep."

"Well. It's over now. I'm back on my horse," said Fitz.

"Are you sure it's your horse? Or is it Wolf's horse?"

Fitz laughed softly, genuinely. "My horse. But I'll tell Wolf he can have it."

"I think he'd be pretty happy with that," I said.

I sat up and rested my chin on my fists. I brushed my long hair out of my face and wrapped it around my ear. I was having trouble getting used to the hair everywhere, but I liked trying a new thing.

Fitz bunched his fingers together like he was kneading his bandana, but his hands were empty. "I'm ice on a stove, Addie. I'll drift wherever the heat takes me until I disappear. I'm not on a hero's journey. My story arc isn't going to have a happily ever after. Max won't help me. I have nothing when I get out of here. The lines are written. The ink has dried." He looked legitimately scared.

"I don't like that ice metaphor," I said.

"What, it's not mixed up enough for you? What if I said I could wait until the ducks watched me like a hawk and still not feel I could get out of here like the back of my hand?"

"Those are similes, not metaphors, but . . . better," I said with a smile.

"You're welcome," said Fitz.

"You won't believe where I've been," I said.

Fitz raised his eyebrows and leaned in a little more, waiting.

"I saw the Kirtland's warbler."

His eyes got big and he smiled. But the smile dropped as he leaned his head sideways and gave me a mocking look. "No, you didn't," he said.

"Promise."

"They're only in Michigan in the spring," said Fitz.

"I know. I didn't say I saw them here," I said. "They're in the Bahamas. Where *I was* just a few days ago."

"No way."

"Yes way."

I showed him a picture of Mom and me in front of the resort sign and then the single picture I had been able to take of the warbler. I wanted to show him the rest of the pictures, but some orderly I'd never met told me to put my phone away.

"Wow," Fitz said. "That is so freaking awesome. I wish I could have been there. What was it like?"

I felt bad offering up a description of something I knew he'd love to see himself.

"The warbler was unreal. Like, bonkers amazing. I want to go to see them when they come back to Michigan."

"You already saw them though," said Fitz.

"Yeah, but not in the jack pines. Not with you."

He looked at me in that way I loved, raising his eyebrows and leaning in and tilting his nose down. He still wore that same tie-dyed bandana, worn out and faded, but I reminded myself that he wore it as a sort of security blanket. I realized it would be weird seeing him without it. I found that encouraging in some odd way.

"The birds require the small jack pines for nesting, and the only way those jack pines grow is after a fire."

"That doesn't make sense," said Fitz. "Sounds more like a tragedy. A log falls in love with a fire."

"Yes," I said, thinking about my game with Mom. "But the cones of the jack pines need fire to open them up before they can spread their seeds. About six years after a fire, the warblers show up because that's when the trees are the perfect height. When the trees get too tall, they leave. Then they have to wait for another fire before coming back."

Fitz thought for a moment. I saw Didi step in, and I waved to him over Fitz's shoulder.

"That's pretty awesome," he said. "I wish my life was like that. Maybe it will be."

"You want to nest in burned-out trees in a forest in northern Michigan? I didn't know you were so down-to-earth," I said.

"I'm not," he said, smiling. "But our lives have been scorched in some way, right? Touched by fire? We all need new growth."

"Yeah," I said, softly, thinking of blue skies and birds.

"And once we've grown and learned and overcome, we can move on." He looked down. "But I won't know freedom or be able to fly away from here until I turn eighteen."

"*Property Brothers!*"

I looked at Didi, who was blushing because his parents were visiting.

"At least it's always something new. I like that he keeps things fresh," I said.

Fitz didn't seem to be listening. "I want to go back to school, but I don't know if it will last. When I get out, I mean. I don't know if I can ever keep the balance I need to sustain a normal life."

"Normal's boring," I said.

"Freedom isn't. Freedom of the mind—that's gold. That's independence."

"Surely not true independence, though?"

"Who will I have, Addie? I've lived most of my life in and out of these places. Nobody has any lasting relationship with me outside of these hospital walls. You saw that disgusting apartment that people call my 'home.' I need to be strong if I'm going to be on my own, to stay balanced. I don't know if I can do that, if I'm being honest. I get out of here in a year. You won't wait around—nobody's going to wait for me. People need to go on, to move forward and live. I know that. I understand that."

And it was right then that I finally understood why those absurd playwrights wrote their stories the way they did. It happens like that—in a moment. Like a whale breaching the water. Or a bird landing on a branch. I finally understood why they kept their characters waiting for something. I knew how to answer Dr. Morris's question and move on with my life.

Fitz looked upset and a little worried. The overhead fans turned on, and I heard the small whir of the motor as the churning began. I thought about Fitz and how his life was a battle of voices and ideas and emotions, like, always, and how he constantly had to fight for the right meaning to triumph. Scorched earth. New growth.

But isn't that true of everybody, on some level?

"I'll wait," I said.

He sighed and slouched. "You say that now, and I appreciate it, but c'mon, Addie. It's a *year*, and you'll be in school and then off to college. So will everyone else my age."

"You understand what waiting is, right? I do. I figured out Morris's question." I gave him a smug look and leaned in on my elbows.

He paused and looked at me for a moment. Then he grinned, back to his old self, shuffling off the pain of his recent experiences and the reality of being released from the hospital in just over ten months. "So, Addie Foster, what's the answer? Why did those characters sit around and wait with nothing to show for it?"

"Because they had everything to wait for. They had everything to show for it, as soon as that thing showed up," I said.

"*Nothing* shows up in the play. I mean, *nobody* shows. That doesn't make sense."

"Not in the play. But life is just a series of absurd rituals until some*thing* or some*one* comes along to give it all meaning, right? They were waiting for that thing. For that person."

Fitz stared at me and breathed in deeply, thinking intently.

"Sometimes it doesn't show up," I said. "We're lucky if it does. But if it does, then we have something to live for. We don't always need to wait, but when we do . . . Well, it's worth waiting your entire life for that thing, that person, to come along. It's what gives life meaning."

He took off his bandana and turned it in his hands. I took off my scarf and placed it over our hands so nobody would notice us touching.

"So what are you waiting for?" he asked quietly, hesitantly. "What's your thing?"

"*You* are my thing," I said. "Turns out I've been waiting for you, Fitzgerald Whitman IV. Even if your name is pretentious and I'm way funnier and smarter."

"Addie Foster," he said in wonder, his handsome gap standing out in his ear-to-ear grin.

"It's true. You're my person," I said. "And I'll wait as long as it takes."

"But I can't ask you to wait, Addie. That wouldn't be fair." He tried to pull his hand away, but I wouldn't let go. He stared at me with those amazing eyes. "So we're a comedy? That means you probably need to be funnier. Or are we a tragedy? Do I need to be more tragic? Do I need more flaws? I can maybe work on some flaws with Doc."

"We're in the space between," I said. " An OCD patient fell in love with a mess. It was a tragedy, if you will. And you will," I said, smiling.

"Or a comedy," he said.

"Yes. Or a comedy."

"I've heard it both ways," said Fitz.

"And that's why," I said, smiling.

"Why what?"

"Why I have to wait. We're the characters who are not just compatible because of wit, but condemned to compatibility because of it. We can't escape it. I don't want to escape it."

"So we'll write our own story," said Fitz.

"And wear whatever masks we want," I said.

"And you'll wait for me."

"And I'll wait for you."

Acknowledgments

First, I'd like to thank the doctors at Johns Hopkins for taking on an ostensibly hopeless case and their tireless dedication to my health. I'd like to thank my parents for loving me without condition amid my indefatigable tics, rituals, and consuming thoughts.

Thanks to Brittany, my wife, for continuing this wonderful journey with me and making me laugh at every turn. (And opening doors for me, so I don't have to wash my hands as much!) I threw Brittany all the complexities, all the unformed matter in my life, and she gave me a galaxy in return. Thanks also to my family and my in-laws for their continued support and constant wit.

Chris Schoebinger and Heidi Taylor are the true "Dynamic Duo." I can't ever properly thank them for their indomitable encouragement and their continued investment in my writing. Thanks to Lisa Mangum for her sharp critiques, her insightful edits, and her meticulous care. Thanks also to the entire team at Shadow Mountain.

Thank you, Julie Gwinn—the best (and happiest, kindest, and strongest) agent an author could hope for. Thanks to Samuel Beckett for his play *Waiting for Godot* and to Tom Stoppard for his plays *The Real Thing* and *Arcadia*. With these plays in mind, any reference to the ideas therein are treated fictitiously. If something doesn't fit with your experience of hopelessly waiting, of feeling damaged, of recreating memory, of finding love and keeping it, the fault rests solely with me.

ACKNOWLEDGMENTS

And thank you for reading. Each character in the psych ward really deserves their own book, their own story of love and hope, their own moment of triumph.

Finally, thanks to the ten-year-old boy, who, slouching on his bed that first day in the hospital, let me sit by his side and wonder, in tandem, what in the name of Lewis Carroll the universe had thrown our way. Because of you, I set out to find answers.

If you would like more information about mental illness or how to find help, please visit the National Alliance on Mental Illness (nami.org /Find-Support/NAMI-HelpLine).

An Interview with the Author

1. **What was the genesis for this story? When did you start writing it? Who or what was the inspiration for the characters?**

It's hard to pinpoint a genesis for this story because it feels like it has been a part of me for so long. When studying in college, I read a lot of Tom Stoppard's works and was entranced by the way he addressed weighty issues while maintaining a witty, comedic tone. I've strived to maintain that balance ever since. (Plus, I've always had a penchant for the absurd.)

I remember being totally floored after my first reading of *The Importance of Being Earnest* by Oscar Wilde. He hit a perfect note, one line after another. I also often draw inspiration from the movement of poetry. I remember the moment I first encountered the prosody of Frost and the meter of Tennyson. Look at the first lines of "The Splendor Falls" by Tennyson, and you'll see what I'm talking about. Inspired by his poetic rhythm, I wrote the line "Whitewashed walls and medical halls, and memory as told in story," and immediately I was back in the psych ward and building a world from those words.

In that sense, I started writing this book years ago, though I didn't know it at the time. I wondered at the origins of character and their background and motivation after reading Samuel Beckett's plays and Flannery O'Connor's short stories. I started thinking of how to rearrange a universe after reading *Hamlet* followed by *Rosencrantz and Guildenstern Are Dead*. I considered the importance of the first sentence after reading Gabriel Garcia Marquez's *One Hundred Years of Solitude*. My understanding of a work's final moment was forever altered when I encountered the last paragraph of Cormac McCarthy's *The Road*. My focus on dialogue was shaped by playwrights like Sarah Ruhl and novelists like Ali Smith, and I was greatly schooled in characterization by the likes of Annie Proulx.

The inspiration for the characters is a different story. I started with people in my own life and added dimensions until they rounded out into fictional characters that, I hope, carry a lot of weight. Didi (a nod to Samuel Beckett and his character Vladimir "Didi" in *Waiting for Godot*) is an amalgamation of people I've met in life. In particular, a coworker of mine from years ago that carried the name of the consummate "One Upper." He could make a stubbed toe a tragedy and a commonplace a triumph. If you ever had a story, his was better, and not just by a little. If you took on a black bear on Vancouver Island in hand-to-hand combat, this guy took on a great white shark while treading water in Drake Passage after having his hands tied behind his back and one eye bruised shut by a roundhouse from a Sasquatch. He did it all with his feet, of course, and his shark weighed at least a thousand pounds more than your bear.

All the characters, in that sense, emerged from various conglomerates. Leah came from a good friend in Texas who has a great wit and a passion for language. I combined parts of her personality with a small boy I saw on my first day in Johns Hopkins Hospital. He was sitting on his bed, head bowed in depression, looking as if his heart might fall right through his body. I couldn't handle that image, and it has never left me. In a sense, I have created Leah to deal with that quaking memory.

And I set the novel in Seattle after visiting my cousin who was attending Puget Sound University because the splendor of that place has never left me, and the landscape and feel of it seemed to lend itself to this kind of story.

2. **Why did you choose to write the story from Addie's point of view instead of Fitz's? Was it difficult, as a male author, to write from a female perspective?**

I thought about this the moment Addie's voice came to me. I was sitting in bed and had my phone next to me (ideas often hit me late at night, and I like to take notes on my phone), and I heard one line: "It's not that you need to hear it or anything—just that I need to say it." I often start stories with voice and build everything else around it, and this line gave me an ember of Addie's character. Then, I set the billows to work on that ember, and I spent the next several months chasing that personality.

When I heard her voice, I knew the only way to tell this story was through Addie Foster.

I think telling this story through Addie allowed me to navigate the OCD aspects of the narrative. A male lead with OCD would fly too close to my own experience, and I didn't want the wings to burn off before the story got going. I didn't want to spiral into my own thoughts and memories, or for Fitz to merge with my past and change the tilt of the first-person narration.

3. You have personal experience with OCD. Can you share some of your insights into the issues of mental health?

It's not talked about enough, for starters. And for finishers. And for everyone in between. It's just not discussed enough. Mental health is so idiosyncratically integrated into our personal lives, so it makes it difficult to dissect and label and distill. But that shouldn't stop us from trying.

I remember being in the car when I was five years old. The radio was burbling as the windshield wipers ticked back and forth, swiping away the slicks of water. An advertisement was playing, like one of those late-night infomercials I'm fond of joking about: "Tired of counting everything? Do you often find yourself thinking of numbers instead of people? Germs instead of friends?" It was not in those exact words, of course, but it turned out to be an ad for a local research study on OCD. I remember, in that moment, wondering why they would be researching something that was so *normal*. That's where the idiosyncratic part of the mental health world kicks in—we all take a different journey, even within the same disease. I was at a loss, wondering why anyone would want to study people who counted things and washed their hands a lot. But then I thought, *Wait—is my counting a bad thing?*

As I matured, so did my OCD, until it really became a monster. I was completely consumed by it, barely able to come up for air. I find that people often hesitate to ask me about my OCD, about my experience in the hospital psychiatric ward or my many years of therapy, but it's in that moment of hesitation that a lot of our current issues reside. Let's talk about it. Let's have all of the conversations—*all of them*—and be open about mental health. Only then can story do what it is supposed to do, and sublimate the human experience.

Fiction reminds us that we are all on our own hero's journey and that things don't always turn out like we'd expect. And that's a good thing. Perhaps if I'd encountered the right book at an earlier age, I would be able to grapple with OCD and how I felt after hearing that radio advertisement. Maybe I'd be better prepared for what came next.

Fiction allows us to practice empathy. Fiction reminds us what it is to be human. And I can say without hesitation that without fiction, without essays, without poems, without plays (and yes, a lot of other "drama"), I could not have overcome my OCD to the degree I have.

4. The symbolism of the blue whale and the Kirtland's warbler are woven throughout the story. Why did you choose these two animals?

I have always been fascinated by things I don't—or can't—understand. I think part of being human is that hunger for comprehending what we can't grasp. That's why I am so fascinated by the great blue whale. How much do we really know about whales? Surprisingly, not very much. Ditto for the warblers. Think of how many scientists each year tag birds and whales (and numerous other animals) and wait on data, or take boats out to study and dive and collect. How much information do they return with? Again, not much.

A Smithsonian researcher said whales are hard to learn about because they live too far out at sea and they dive too deep. I love that. But that doesn't stop scientists from researching or diving or writing about whalefalls; a single whale carcass on the ocean floor can provide life to other animals for more than one hundred years. Just because the topic is hard to study doesn't mean we shouldn't try.

Stoppard said all art is a projection of our own predilections, and I agree. If something fascinates me or confuses me, I chase after it. I love dealing with uncertainties and seeing what I can make of it in a narrative. I am interested in what I can observe in the natural world, and how I might connect that back to character. For example, the light particle experiment Addie brings up with Doc was something I read about in *National Geographic* years ago and it fascinated me. From that point on, I became interested in how that might work as a metaphor for the human experience.

5. Addie and Fitz share a similar sense of humor as well as a similar taste in books and movies. What are some of your favorite books and movies?

My "favorite" books and movies change every year, and if I start down that rabbit hole, I may never return. What was once Samuel Beckett's *Molloy* or Charles Dickens's *Hard Times* is now Hilary Mantel's *Wolf Hall* series. As Annie Proulx says, if you want to be a writer, you first need to be a great reader.

So I'll start with Proulx and her short stories. I have always loved the way she can animate the landscape and history of a place. I'm a big fan of Kazuo Ishiguro's immersive novels, the ideas of Jorge Luis Borges, and the intellect and voice of Marilynne Robinson. Anything by those authors leaves me wanting more.

George Saunders and Karen Russell write worlds I could never create, and use forms that surprise and delight. Alice Munro and Anthony Doerr stories have a way of staying with me for days, following me around, teaching me more and more. I've also enjoyed reading all of Jesmyn Ward's work in the last few months—she is an incredible writer.

Lately, I have been reading Tom Stoppard plays as well as essays by Eula Biss, poems by Brian Turner, and stories by William Trevor. It may seem a bit all over the place, but that is how I learn and that is how I read. I like discovering the ideas that percolate up through that process. I also enjoy Frankensteins of verse that just can't be categorized easily, like *Grief Is the Thing with Feathers* by Max Porter.

I'm not much of a movie buff, but I enjoyed *A Man Called Ove* based on the novel by Fredrik Backman. I love reading the translation while I watch foreign films. Might sound odd, but I'm odd, so it works.

6. What are some of the things you have waited for in your life?

I'm always waiting for that next thing—for that next idea or book or moment that will lead me to a greater understanding of what it means to lead a good life and appreciate the human experience. But that's now.

Years ago, when I was stuck in the throes of mental illness, it was nearly impossible—if not wholly impossible—to think clearly enough to comprehend what I might be waiting for. I was stuck, like Wolf, always striving but never fully understanding how to get to a place where I could get that "horse." My rituals were a way of repeating the phrase over and over, and they kept me stuck at the entrance of the hospital, just like Wolf. I was attempting to exist in a world that would not accommodate me because my thoughts could not allow such movement, such understanding, such light.

When I arrived at Johns Hopkins, I worked with a psychiatrist who tried everything until he found the answer that balanced my world. Once he did, it was like someone turned on the lights. Before the hospital and that specific doctor, it was like my neurons had been trying to swim through the world's most intricate and impassible gill net.

Aeolus, keeper of the winds, gave Odysseus winds in a bag, but they did not carry Odysseus home. Language can be the winds in our sailboat, but sometimes it can't take us where we need to go; some winds take us everywhere but where we really need to go.

Language may move you as it did me, but there is a next step: you need to act. For all those suffering from mental illness, never stop hoping. You are not alone. You are loved. You are needed. There is hope. Don't give up. There is a wind that will carry you home. You can find it with a doctor's help. Remember that you are more than your schizophrenia, you are more than your depression, you are more than your OCD. You may feel you can't go on, but *go on.*

Discussion Questions

1. Fitz and Addie spend a few intimate moments in the bones of a blue whale and discuss relative heart size. Has there been a time in your life where learning something fascinating about the natural world changed your outlook on religion, on culture, or on love?

2. Dr. Morris sends Addie information about Joseph Campbell's structure of the Hero's Journey. What fictional characters or "heroes" have influenced your own journey?

3. The majority of the characters in this novel suffer from some type of mental illness. What social and cultural stigmas still surround discussions about mental health? How can we change the narrative of mental illness?

4. At one point in the story, Addie is struggling to stay optimistic, yet finds hope and excitement when her request to watch the movie *Rosencrantz and Guildenstern Are Dead* is approved. What movie (or other narrative) might you choose in a similar situation? What stories bring you the most hope?

5. Didi turns his struggle with language into a game, per his therapist's request. Where he once shouted profanity, he now shouts his potentially embarrassing guilty pleasures, like *HGTV*. What TV shows or novels or movies are you afraid to mention for fear you might be wrongfully judged?

6. Addie copes with her obsessive thoughts by striving to maintain a light-hearted attitude about, well, everything. What strategies do you employ

when coping with big issues? How have you used humor to cope with difficult topics in your own life?

7. *Waiting for Fitz* is a nod to Samuel Beckett's play *Waiting for Godot*. Beckett's work asks a lot of questions about what we, the audience, are waiting for. Addie discovers what this means: life is impossible to understand, and quite absurd, until something or someone comes along and gives it meaning. The characters in the play are left waiting. Meaning is hard to grasp. Life is difficult to coordinate. Addie and Fitz find one another and begin to make sense of the absurdity. Can you think back to a time when you were waiting for that significant *something*, that significant *someone*? How long did you wait? Looking back, what does that period of waiting now mean to you?

8. Near the end of the novel, the two main characters talk about scorched earth and how the Kirtland's Warbler can only survive because the fire is integral to the life cycle of the Jack pines. What hardships in your life have led to new growth?

9. If the author wrote a sequel, what do you think would happen to the characters? How might Fitz react to his freedom?